THE HOARFROST KING

THE EYE OF TRUTH
BOOK 1

GALIT BEN-AMI

Producer & International Distributor
eBookPro Publishing
www.ebook-pro.com

THE HOARFROST KING
(The Eye of Truth, Book 1)
Copyright © 2023 Galit Ben-Ami

All rights reserved; No parts of this book may be reproduced or transmitted in any form or by any means, electronic or mechanical, including photocopying, recording, taping, or by any information retrieval system, without the permission, in writing, of the author.

ISBN 9798396822320

For Mum and Dad

Contents

The Dare 7

The Meadow 11

The Tavern 19

Annak 33

The Council of Truth 43

Beginnings 55

Consequences 63

Shaar 69

The Labyrinth of Souls 75

Darkness 83

Nomads 85

Friends and Enemies 93

Darkness continues 103

The Map 105

Artefacts 115

Realisations 121

Darkness ends 129

Lexi 131

Aftermath 135

Angel of Souls	143
Lexi again	151
Opposites	155
Omen	161
Proposal	169
Preparations	175
Choices	185
Merging	187
Backlash	193
The Balance of Life	197
Gaps	205
Farewell	215
Continuity	227
Deception	237
Hope	247
Epilogue	251
Glossary	252
Acknowledgements	255

The Dare

It all started when Tony Palermo, from the East 34th 'gang', told Lexi she didn't have the balls to visit Madam Giselle, the fortune-teller down on East Broadway street. Everyone knows Madam Giselle is a crazy old lady, living on her own above that seedy nightclub. Some swear that she is a witch, and that she can hex you just by looking at you.

Anyway, Lexi isn't the one to turn away when challenged, so off we went to see Madam Giselle. I must admit I was terrified by the idea of standing face to face with a witch, but Lexi was so confident of herself that I dared not say a thing to her. By the time we got to 52nd and 3rd it was beginning to get dark and the nightclub lights were flashing in red and yellow. Lexi came to a full stop and just stood there, staring at the flashing lights as if she was hypnotised by them.

"We don't have to do it you know. Tony Palermo is an idiot, everyone knows it..." I said, but Lexi didn't say a word, just stood there, staring. I've never seen Lexi like that and it didn't feel right. I grabbed her hand and gave it a yank.

She didn't even turn her head to me, just opened her mouth and said "NO! I'm going in!"

My heart sank, and I could feel my stomach turning over. There was absolutely no way I would let her go there on her own. As scared as I was, I looked at Lexi and said, "I'm coming with you. We're going together!" Lexi didn't say a word, she just looked at me and nodded her head.

A moment later we were making our way up the stairs to Madam Giselle's flat. It was only one flight of stairs to climb, but it felt like the steepest climb ever; my legs felt heavier and heavier with every step that we took and by the time we reached the top, I was exhausted.

The look on Lexi's face did not change. It was still very intense and focussed, like a true warrior on her mission. Flat 6A. She had just raised her hand to knock on the door when a voice from the other side said, "Enter!"

Lexi opened the door and slowly walked inside. I followed, still rather reluctantly. The room was quite dark and the only light in the place came from the hundreds of candles scattered all around. The orange-red colour of the flames bouncing off the walls, together with the nightclub's flashing lights outside the windows, made it seem as if the whole room was on fire.

There was a sweet smell of burning essence oils in the air. Lots of cushions were scattered on the floor. Decks of cards were laid out on a wooden shelf under the big window. At the far corner of the room what looked like a heavy black cast-iron cauldron was placed in the centre of a silver pentagon that had been drawn on the floor.

Once my eyes got used to the flickering lights I saw that each wall had writings in different languages on them, as well as a collection of ornaments and symbols hanging around them. The only words I could understand were North, East, South and West, each one written on a different wall.

Madam Giselle walked into the room, holding a silver tray with two glass cups of some hot drink in them. "Drink!" she said, "It's not poisoned, just Louiza herbal tea. It's good for you, you can see I left the leaves inside. Now sit yourselves down comfortably."

Lexi picked up a cup and took a sip then looked at me as if to say "Go ahead, it's safe to drink".

We each grabbed a cushion and sat down on the floor. Watching us, Madam Giselle took a small crystal ball from one of the sleeves of her gown and started rolling it between her hands. She closed her eyes and rolled her head in synchronised movement with the crystal ball.

Suddenly she dropped the ball onto the floor, opened her eyes, looked straight into Lexi's eyes, and declared:

"The road is long, the journey full of danger,
One pure of heart, one soul mate, together
Shall travel a long and dark road,
To bring the light to far away between the snowy peaks.
Beware the trickery, misleading and deceit,
For those who want to lend a hand will fool you yet again.
But don't despair, for you are strong together.
Together, not alone, you'll find your way
And allies there will be to guide you on your quest."

Then a smile lit up her face and she looked down at both of us, "Drink, your tea is getting cold."

Lexi finished her tea, put the glass back on the empty tray, turned to Madam Giselle and said, "If I wanted to listen to a poem I'd go to the library. They have poetry nights every Tuesday at eight. You should really give Tony Palermo his money back."

"I don't know this Tony Palermo you speak of, and I'm sure they read lovely poems at the library too, but this was not a poem!" Madam Giselle answered. "This was a message for YOU from the beyond and after."

"The beyond and after??!??" I said, looking at Lexi, then whispered, "She's not only old, she's really a bit crazy too."

"Look Madam Giselle, it was a nice try, really, but I don't buy it so you can tell Tony the joke's on him," said Lexi, and started to get up from the floor.

We almost reached the door when, suddenly, Madam Giselle grabbed hold of Lexi's hand.

"Wait!" she told us, "Before you go I must give you this," and she shoved a small black leather pouch into Lexi's hand.

Lexi opened the pouch and took out what looked like a silver pendant of some sort. It was in the shape of a hand, on each finger was a different symbol and in the middle of the palm an open eye had been drawn with a small aquamarine crystal embedded at its centre. Here too mysterious writings covered all around the shape of this strange looking hand.

"What is that?" Lexi asked

"This pendant will protect and guide you," Madam Giselle answered. "Please make sure to wear it at all times. Never take it off!"

"What's with the eye?" I asked.

"It is the 'Eye of Truth'. It can look into a person's soul and tell what is there. It also protects against the 'evil eye.'"

By now I just didn't think Tony Palermo was involved in this anymore, and by the look on Lexi's face neither did she.

"It belongs only to the pure of heart and will protect all of those she holds dear to her," the old fortune-teller said, looking at Lexi. Then she turned to me. "But **you** must never part from her, for the spells cannot protect **you** if you are away from her."

As we tried to take all this in Madam Giselle looked at us both and said, "Now you must go. Rest well, for once your journey begins there will be no turning back."

A moment later we were out on the street, making our way home. We didn't talk much on the way. I guess we were both trying to understand what had just happened, make sense of what we heard.

The Meadow

The following day I was woken by the constant ringing of the doorbell. I looked at my watch, it was nine-thirty on Sunday morning. My parents were already at their country-club and the maid had the day off, so I got out of bed and went to open the door.

"Okay, OKAY, I'm coming. Just STOP ringing the damn doorbell!!"

As soon as I unlocked the door it was pushed open and Lexi burst into the flat, very excited.

"Look what was shoved under my door," she said, handing me a brown envelope with her name on it, written in gold ink in beautiful calligraphy.

"What's inside? have you looked?"

"No, see, the seal is still unbroken" she said, as she grabbed the envelope back from my hands.

"Go on, open it then..."

"You think so?" she asked.

"Yes, I mean, it's got your name on it.... so it might be safer if you open it."

We went into my room, shut the door, and sat on my bed.

"Here goes...." said Lexi and gently broke the seal.

She reached into the envelope and pulled out a very creased, folded sheet of yellowish-brown paper. It smelt old and mouldy.

"Careful it doesn't crumble in your hand," I told her, laughing out loud.

She unfolded the paper and laid it carefully on the bed, an old sheet of paper with nothing on it. We looked at each other with the same puzzled look on our faces, but before any of us could say a word, lines and drawings started to appear on the paper, as if an invisible hand was writing on it. Just as the writing seemed to have been finished, a beautiful drawing of a four-pointed compass began forming at the bottom right corner of the paper.

"WOW!!!" we both said at the same time.

"This is amazing!!!" Lexi added.

"What is this, some kind of map? Is this supposed to be some special place?" I asked. "I mean there isn't any explanation on it, no writing or directions at all?!?"

Lexi gently put her finger on the four-pointed compass. As soon as she touched the drawing, the map transformed into a three dimensioned hologram rising from where the map had been. Names marking the different places on the map appeared on the hologram.

It looked so real, with flowing streams of rivers and lakes, waterfalls gushing away down the mountainside, and the treetops gently swaying in a breeze. We quickly worked out some of the marvels of the map; by touching a certain area we were able to magnify it so that new details, specific to that area, appeared. We could also 'move' within each magnified zone by gently scrolling our fingers on the streets and roads. It was as if we were walking through a model of another city, another world.

Lexi gently tapped the centre of the compass rose and the hologram collapsed on to the sheet of paper, which turned back to being a flat drawn map, before dissolving and disappearing altogether, leaving only a blank sheet of paper.

"That's incredible!" Lexi said, her eyes sparkling with excitement.

"Where did it come from? Do you know who sent it to you?"

"No idea, but I have a feeling this is the place Madam Giselle talked about," she replied.

"How are we supposed to get there? We don't even know where it is."

"I think that we should take a closer look at the map," Lexi said, "see what else we can learn from it. Let's see what's on the back side".

We turned the map over and started examining it carefully.

"Look, here, right in the middle of the sheet, can you see it?" Lexi asked.

"Oh yeah, there's some sort of symbol there, it's so faint. I think maybe it's a watermark. Gosh, if the map wasn't so creased and discoloured it would have been a lot easier to figure it out"

"I have an idea," said Lexi. "Maybe it'll be clearer if we'll hold it up to the light."

"Good idea. Let's hold it against the window," I suggested

We carefully picked the map up and held it against the glass.

"Lexi, look, it's a drawing of your 'Eye of Truth' pendant!"

"Oh yeah," she said. She took a closer look and gently ran her finger over the drawing.

"YOUR PENDANT! IT'S GLOWING!" I cried out.

Lexi looked down at her pendant; the aquamarine crystal in the middle of the eye was illuminated. I lifted my hand to touch it.

"Noooo," cried Lexi.

But it was too late, my finger was already on the crystal.

The room started to spin very fast. Lexi and I were instantly swept up by an invisible force. It felt as if we were suspended in mid-air then being forcefully pushed through a long and dark wind tunnel. A few moments later we were standing in the middle of a meadow, surrounded by thick woods.

"Listen, I want to tell you something. You won't believe me, but..."

"But WHAT Jimmy??!!" The look on Lexi's face said it all. "You're sorry? You didn't mean it? WHAT can you possibly say that will make things better?! You just HAD to touch it. You couldn't wait until we figured it all out, no, you had to touch the damn thing." She was furious.

I've never seen Lexi that angry before. I knew I should have listened to her and been more careful. But by the time I realised what I was doing, it was too late.

***

Lexi and I are best friends, we live next door to each other since.... well... ever actually. People often mistake us for being brother and sister; we do everything together, virtually inseparable, and in our neighbourhood they call us 'The dynamic duo'.

You'd think that because I'm a boy and she's a girl I protect and look after her. Well, there's nothing further from the truth. Lexi might be a girl, but she sure can hold her own. At five feet six inches, with short black hair, blue eyes, rosy cheeks and a very slim body she might look like a delicate flower, but believe me when I tell you looks can be deceiving. When it comes to punching, she's got the meanest left hook you've ever seen.

I suppose growing up in such a big city enhances your survival skills and brings out the fighter in you. Other kids tend to pick on you because you live uptown, in a nice skyscraper apartment overlooking the park, with a doorman and security and all that. But actually they don't realise that because your parents are too busy with their lives to look after you, you tend to do whatever you want, like spending most of the time outdoors exploring the city and what it has to offer. You learn very quickly how to think fast and react instinctively when you end-up in the wrong side of town.

I guess that kind of exploring is what got us into the mess we are in. Oh yeah, and me not listening to Lexi didn't help much either...

***

So there we were, standing in the middle of this meadow. We looked around trying to figure out where we were, when suddenly I remembered;

"The map, Lexi. Where's the map?"

"I don't know. I was holding it one minute and then.... I think I let go of it when we started to spin around."

"It must be here somewhere. I remember seeing it as we were pushed through the tunnel," I said.

Lexi started looking around where we stood. "Look there are some bushes over there," she said, "lets split up and check them out, it might have fallen inside them."

So we did, without any success. An hour later, as it started to get dark, we decided to look for a safe place to spend the night. We found some shelter under the trees at the edge of the forest, not too deep inside though, as we thought it would be a good idea to stay close to the meadow. Then we managed to gather some dried branches and start a small fire.

"I guess it's a good thing I always carry my grandfather's old Zippo lighter in my pocket," I said, smiling at her.

"I'm glad you're here, Jimmy, I'd hate it if I was stuck here on my own...."

"Thanks. And I am really sorry for getting us stuck here."

"I know you are. It's okay. I mean, it would have happened eventually, getting here; I'm just glad we are here together."

"Where do you think we are? Can you recognise the place from the map?"

"No, we only managed to have a quick look at it yesterday; not enough to memorise it or even see any names of places on it."

"What shall we do?"

"Well I think we should get some sleep and start looking for the map again as soon as it's bright enough," Lexi suggested.

We finally dozed off sometime in the early hours of the night, to be woken up by warm beams of sunlight flickering on our faces. We cleared the area where our fire had finally gone out the night before, and headed back to the meadow to look for the map.

"It's not here," shouted Lexi finally, "I think it's really lost".

"Yeah, I think you might be right. We've been searching for a couple of hours already, maybe we should stop," I suggested.

"Well in that case....." Lexi started to say, then suddenly bent down, picked up a stone, and threw it towards the bushes to her right.

"YOU CAN COME OUT NOW!" she shouted. "I know you're there! So unless you want me to shower you with stones, you better come out and tell us who you are and what you're doing here."

A young boy appeared from behind the bushes, still crouching, holding a small rucksack in his hand and trying to shield his head and face from any more stones.

"My name is Ari. I have some food for you," he said as he slowly lowered his hand and walked towards us, offering his rucksack to Lexi.

Lexi and I exchanged looks, then Lexi turned to the boy. "You have some food for us!? How did you know we were here?"

"It is not for me to answer," he replied. "Please eat first. Your questions will be answered later, I promise." He smiled, then opened his rucksack and started to take out some food and lay it on the ground.

We sat down and helped ourselves. We didn't realise how hungry we were until we took a bite from the loaf of bread in front of us; it wasn't too long before all that was left were the empty wrapping papers of the food we had eaten.

Feeling a bit more relaxed after eating, we began looking around us. It was a beautiful morning, the sun was shining in a lovely blue sky, with no clouds in sight. The meadow was breath-taking, bright green grass with colourful wild flowers all around. It was a carpet of Bluebells and Red Campions with white Pignuts spread all over, surrounded by tall Beech trees, their large trunks covered with Ivy.

Lexi wiped her mouth with the back of her hand, then turned to

Ari and asked "So where are we? What is this place?"

Ari smiled. "You are in the kingdom of Galya, and this is the Meadow of Peace," he replied. "And you are welcome."

He was a tall lad, maybe seventeen years old, with wavy blond hair falling down to broad shoulders, bronze-tanned skin and honey-brown eyes. He sat there, now with a calm and cool look on his face. Suddenly he got up, and held out his hand towards Lexi.

"Time to go. You are expected," he said.

Ari look Lexi's hand, and with one strong tug pulled her up from the ground.

"Where are we going?" she asked, looking straight into his eyes.

"Stormend, my village" Ari replied, then started walking off towards the woods.

"Wait!" I called. I turned to Lexi, and whispered "What's the plan? I mean, we know nothing of him or his village"

"I don't think we have much choice," she replied. "They seem to know we are here, whoever they are, so we might as well follow him and try to get some answers once we get there," then she walked towards Ari, who was waiting for us at the edge of the meadow.

The Tavern

We walked in silence, looking around to try and memorise the way we were going, just in case we should need to find our way back to the meadow. Half an hour later, as the wood started to thin out, we could see between the gaps in the trees the silhouettes of some houses. As we walked out of the woods and into the open we found ourselves standing at one end of Ari's village.

"Almost there," Ari said. "Just a few more minutes and all your questions will be answered" he added, as if he could read our minds.

"So, this is your village?" I asked "What is it called again?"

"Stormend" he replied, with a big smile on his face, "and you will not find a more friendlier or welcoming place in all of Galya."

A few moments later we stopped beside the front garden of what looked like the local tavern. It was a lovely old building, made with dark oak beams and sandy bricks, a big thatched roof, chequered glass windows, and lots of wild flowerpots hanging all around.

An unusual sign hung above the thick wooden front door:
"Friends of the realm are welcome here.
Enemies and foes DO NOT come near.
Hear this warning and go away, or else
A heavy price you'll pay!"

Lexi and I looked at each other but before we managed to say a word, the door opened and a woman greeted us.

"Welcome," she said, "Please come in, you must be tired and thirsty after your long walk".

There was something familiar about this woman, but I couldn't put my finger on it as we walked past her and entered the tavern.

Inside it was quite bright in spite of the small windows. We were standing on the ground floor of the tavern. Scattered chairs and a couple of long tables took up the middle of the room and some smaller tables were spread all around. A long oak bar-counter, covered with bottles and glasses, stood in front of one wall.

Behind the counter stood the bartender, his long black and grey hair held back off his face by a silver hairband around his forehead. A big scar ran beneath the hairband, all the way across his left eye and down his cheek until it was partially hidden by his neatly trimmed beard. He had a very sturdy build, as you would expect from a dwarf.

Opposite the bar was a grand open fireplace, a large stack of logs beside it, and nearby a few private sitting areas which could be hidden behind curtains. As it was only late morning the tavern wasn't very full, and most of the curtains were drawn to one side and tied to the wall.

Ari sat us down at one of the tables and asked the woman if she would bring us some tea.

"Louiza," said Lexi," I recognise the lemony scent of it."

"Very good" said the tavern-lady, and sat down opposite Lexi.

Lexi took a sip from her cup and looked at her; "Madam Giselle?!"

I swallowed my mouthful and quickly looked as well, "But how?"

The woman looked like an exact copy of the old fortune-teller, but she seemed much younger and more beautiful, with her long golden locks, bright blue eyes, lightly tanned and smoother skin. She looked at us both. "No, not quite Giselle," she smiled, "I'm her daughter, Mikaela. And this," she pointed at Ari, "is my son."

Lexi and I looked at each other with amazement.

"How can that be?" I asked. "I mean, Madam Giselle is from where we come from, its another world?"

Mikaela didn't answer, just stood up and, beckoning to us, said "We should go upstairs, to the living quarters, we will have more privacy there."

We walked up some stairs, which had been out of sight behind the wall of the bar, and came to a small hallway at the top. At the end of it was the door to Mikaela and Ari's quarters. We went into the sitting room and found it looking very similar to that of Madam Giselle's, with a big thick rug placed on the wooden floorboards, lots of cushions scattered all around, and a big round copper tray, standing on short wooden legs, that served as a table in the middle of the room. Dozens of candles were lit everywhere. Mikaela and Ari's personal rooms were further through. The whole place was small, but very cosy and with a real homely feel.

"You must have lots of questions. So, it is time for you to get some answers," said Mikaela.

Lexi straightened up in her seat and asked, "What is this place? I mean, what year is it? Because by the look of things and the way you are dressed it is definitely not 2023, nowhere near it! And how did you know we were here? Why are we here? How do we get back home?"

"Yeah" I added, "and where is our map?!"

Mikaela smiled softly then turned to Ari and nodded. Ari reached under his shirt and pulled out a folded piece of paper.

"That's mine!" Lexi shouted out at him. "Give it back!!" she demanded, as she tried to snatch it from him.

Ari stepped back a pace, then handed Lexi the map. "You should have taken better care of it!" he said angrily. "Many good people have died trying to protect it on its way to you."

Mikaela took his hand gently, and turned to Lexi. "It is one of a kind, you see, and there are plenty out there who would not think twice of killing you to get their hands on this map."

"But why me? What have I done? I don't even live in this world, so how did you get to me?" Lexi asked, all confused.

"Oh, but you did live here. You are The Chosen One!" Mikaela told her.

"I'm what??? Lady, you sound as crazy as your mother!" Lexi laughed.

"Let me explain and you will soon understand," replied Mikaela, in a quiet voice, and began her story.

"A millennium ago a terrible war broke between the five kingdoms of Terah, the world you find yourself in now. Galya lies in the centre of this world, connecting all four other kingdoms together - Navara in the North, Eashzar in the East, Sorden to the South and Woxion in the West. It was a long and bloody war over land and power.

"Each king hoped to be the victorious one, conquer the other kingdoms to become the supreme emperor of all the lands, with all their riches and powers at his disposal.

"Every kingdom had something else to offer. Navara has a wealth of gems and other crystals buried beneath its snowy mountains. Eashzar is known for its fertile lands, rich crops and orchards filled with fruits. Sorden holds plenty of iron, gold, silver and other precious metals. Woxion lies beside the great sea and enjoys all that comes from it. And Galya, well we have the power of the five elements of life, which we command to our will when and as needed.

"So you can see how powerful will be the one who rules them all."

"Okay, but what does this have to do with me?" Lexi asked.

"Patience, I will soon get to that" Mikaela replied, before continuing.

"As the conflict raged between the kingdoms, alliances were formed then broken, villages and whole lands were burned down and erased from the face of Terah as if they had never existed.

"Then one day a baby was born, a beautiful little girl. Zarah was her name. Her parents were overjoyed, and despite the fighting and dangers on the roads they brought her to Orra the High Sorceress, for her blessing. They placed Zarah before her and stepped back to hear her words. Orra picked up the child, lifted her high in the air and chanted:

'I present you to the four winds, North, East, South and West.'

'We ask the five elements of life to bless and protect this child.'

Orra dipped her finger in the sacred oil and began to draw five symbols on the baby's forehead. As she finished the fifth symbol a bright light engulfed Zarah and a big eye, with an aquamarine crystal in its centre, appeared floating above her.

'The all seeing eye, the 'Eye of Truth,' said Orra, as she bowed deeply before it." Then Orra gave Zarah back to her parents," Mikaela went on, "telling them 'You are blessed, you have given birth to the 'Chosen One'. You must serve and protect her for she will restore peace and balance to our world.' She placed a little pendant of the 'Eye of Truth' around Zarah's neck, kissed her gently on her brow, and sent the family on their way.

"Eighteen years later Zarah fulfilled her destiny. She brought all five kings together to sign a peace agreement between them. It took place in the meadow we now call the 'Meadow of Peace.'"

"You mean this pendant is the 'Eye of Truth'?" asked Lexi and pulled out the necklace from under her blouse.

"Yes," replied Mikaela, "The very same one. Only slightly bigger now and with powerful spells and symbols to keep you safe and protect you."

"Why? Didn't Zarah bring peace to your world?" asked Lexi.

"She did, but sadly not for long" answered Mikaela.

"What happened?" I asked.

"He betrayed them all!" Ari spit out the answer from between grinding teeth.

I looked at him and asked, "Who did?"

"Naval, the king of Navara," replied Ari, his voice full of hatred.

Mikaela looked at her son lovingly, then said, "You must forgive

Ari's anger, it is not directed at you. You see, Ari's father was killed by Naval's agents for protecting the identity and whereabouts of the 'Chosen One'. He was on his way to deliver the map to you when...." Mikaela stopped, her eyes began filling with tears.

"I'm really sorry Ari. I didn't know..." Lexi said, looking straight into his face.

"But she did get the map, so...." I asked.

Ari continued the story, "When he realised he was about to be captured, my father managed to hide the map into safe place. When he failed to reach us we knew Naval had caught him. Eventually we manager to get the map ourselves and keep it safe," Ari recounted.

"That still doesn't explain why it makes me the 'Chosen One,'" said Lexi.

"Well," said Mikaela "It is all connected to the day that we once again faced the prospect of war. Only this time everyone knew it would be more terrible and much darker than before."

"What happened?" I interrupted her.

"Naval used the peaceful period to better his knowledge of the secrets of our kingdom. He did that by getting close to an ambitious young warlock called Jonas, who was more than happy to betray his people and the sacred oath of silence for an idle promise of becoming Naval's closest adviser and confidant," Mikaela said. "Naval proved to be a fast learner, picking up all of our secrets one by one, memorising the spells and curses, and how exactly to perform them. Everything seemed to come to him so naturally and with hardly any effort. Then almost at the very end of his learning, the final piece needed to gain absolute power was revealed by the traitor."

Lexi bowed her head and looked down. "Zarah, it was Zarah, she was the final piece," she whispered.

"Yes, you are right, it was her. Your instincts are correct, they serve you well," said Mikaela.

"But how? Wasn't she the 'Chosen One', protected and safe from harms' way?" I asked.

"She was," replied Mikaela. "And the only way for Naval to get close to her was by making her his wife. You see, the last thing Jonas revealed to Naval, before being killed by him, was how to get absolute power. To do that he needed to take the life of the 'Chosen One'. So, on the night of their wedding, he tricked Zarah and got her to remove her pendant, killed her cruelly and fled back to his ice fortress in Navara. But he was so intoxicated with his new-found powers, that he rushed away and left the 'Eye of Truth' behind."

"And Zarah was dead?" I asked, looking at Lexi with fear filling my heart.

"Her lady-in-waiting found her on the bed, she was barely alive," said Mikaela. "With her final breaths, Zarah passed on her last prophecy:

"Do not despair. All is not lost, good shall still prevail.

A thousand years from this sad day a saviour will be born,

A little girl, the source of life, that peace once more will bring."

The lady-in-waiting kissed her mistress on the forehead, picked up the 'Eye of Truth' and swore to Zarah that she would find and protect the child she had foretold. Being a Galyan, she mastered the Span of Time and learned how to slow down her ageing process so that she could fulfil her promise to Zarah. On the day the prophesied 'Chosen One' was born she took the baby and her parents to a safe place, far away from Naval and his agents. She took them to your world," said Mikaela, looking up at Lexi.

"What became of the lady-in-waiting?" asked Lexi

"She was to remain in your world for the rest of her life, looking after you from afar. That is until your eighteenth birthday. Then she was to reveal herself, tell you who you are, and prepare you for your destiny… but then you found her, earlier than expected," smiled Mikaela.

It took Lexi a couple of seconds and then, "Madam Giselle, she's your mother; she was the lady in waiting, my guardian."

"Yes," replied Mikaela.

"Look, I appreciate what you are saying here, but this is a mistake. I'm not the 'Chosen One'. I mean, the only reason I went to see Madam Giselle was because of Tony Palermo and his 'dare' thing, so..." said Lexi, shrugging her shoulders apologetically.

"I knew it!" yelled Ari, "I knew she would turn her back on us, and why wouldn't she? She wasn't raised here, she never felt real fear, real loss. Look at her, she is still only a child! How old are you anyway?"

Lexi turned so red you could just about see the steam coming out from her ears, she was so angry. "Who the hell do you think you are, talking about me like that?! You know nothing about me!! And yes, I might look young to you, but I'm fifteen and know more than you do, FOR SURE!"

"Enough!" said Mikaela sharply. "Yes, she is young and knows nothing about us and our world, but it is not her fault. She was taken away for her own good, for her own protection, so that we will have a chance to defeat Naval once and for all." Then Mikaela turned to Lexi and said, "Faith brought you to my mother and we must trust her to know that this is your time. I understand your reluctance to help, but you are our only hope. Please think about it, as you are here now."

Lexi looked at me, "Jimmy.... What..."

"Hey, we're in this together. Whatever you decide, I will always be with you. After all, you are the 'Chosen One.'" I winked at her and smiled.

Lexi waited a moment, then stood up abruptly, turned to Mikaela, and said, "Well then, I guess we're in!"

" So, it is settled! That is good," declared Mikaela.

"What's next then?" asked Lexi.

"You will start your training. We must prepare you for your journey," said Mikaela. "But first you must eat and rest," she added, before getting up and going to the kitchen. Soon she called us to join her.

Later in the afternoon, Lexi, Ari and I were back in the living room. Mikaela came in with a newly-brewed pot of Louiza tea. We sat down once again around the table to drink, not sure what would come next.

"The 'Eye of Truth', did my mother explain about it?" Mikaela asked Lexi.

"Not really. Not much," Lexi replied.

"Right," said Mikaela. "In that case, can you please place the pendant on the table?"

Lexi reached her hands behind her neck and undid the pendant's necklace. She held it in her hand, remembering Madam Giselle's warning, paused for a moment and looked at me.

"It is all right child, you are quite safe here." Mikaela smiled at Lexi. "You need to learn how to use it so your connection with it will be complete."

Lexi placed the pendant gently on the table. "What do you mean by my 'connection' with it?"

"This pendant was designed and made for the protection and use of the 'Chosen One'. The 'Eye of Truth', which rests in the centre of the pendant, is the original Eye which appeared at the blessing ceremony of baby Zarah. It is spiritually linked to you, as it had been to her. After she was killed, the elders realised that as it was, on its own the pendant was not enough to protect the 'Chosen One', so they re-designed it. By adding powerful spells and symbols, they hoped that the 'Eye of Truth' would be better able to protect and serve the 'Chosen One' in her battle to defeat Naval," explained Mikaela.

"Okay, can we please drop the 'Chosen One' references?!" said Lexi.

"It is who you are child, you cannot escape that. But as you wish." Mikaela gently nodded her head at Lexi. "Shall we continue then?"

"First of all, as you can see, the pendant is shaped like a hand; this is the 'Hand of Peace'. Now look at the fingers, on the tip of each one is a symbol of one of the five elements of life; Air, Fire, Water, Earth and Aether. They represent your connection to life, the universe, to all that was, is, and yet to come.

"The 'Eye of Truth' lies in the centre with its aquamarine crystal. Above the 'Eye', and to its right is the symbol for 'Shield' and opposite it, the symbol for 'Peace'. Around the pendant are eight powerful words: Justice, Blessing, Happiness, Wisdom, Safeguard, Strength, Life, and Love. Alone they represent the essence of life, but when combined together as they are on this pendant, they form an all-powerful guidance and protection spell."

"And the eye in the middle?" asked Lexi.

"The eye translates and relates the appropriate message from the symbols. As well as helping to see the inner truth of those you will meet," replied Mikaela.

"How?!" Lexi asked in amazement.

"Well" replied Mikaela, "Let me ask you this; What did you feel when you first saw Ari?"

"What kind of question is that?!" I jumped up off my seat.

Ari looked at me then stared at Lexi.

She turned bright red "What do you mean?"

"I can ask you the same question regarding myself. When you met me, was there some sort of physical sensation you felt?" asked Mikaela.

Lexi closed her eyes; she seemed to be concentrating and the look on her face became more and more intense.

"Yes! I felt warmth, on the skin, where the pendent was resting." said Lexi, with some surprise.

"Was there anything else you felt?" Mikaela continued.

Lexi thought for a minute then answered, "Yes, I felt safe."

"And was it the same sensation that you felt when you met both Ari and I?" Mikaela went on

"No... well, yes, but differently," Lexi replied, a bit confused.

"Different how?" Mikaela asked again, trying to lead Lexi to some conclusion.

"When I first saw Ari, as he was coming out from behind the bushes, I didn't feel a thing. But as he drew closer and we started to talk I could sense some warmth spreading on my skin. I thought it was because of the sun maybe heating the pendant's silver surface. Then as we sat down to eat, and talked a bit more, it felt warmer. The longer we were together the stronger it became, like when you feel good about something, feel safe. And then it was gone." Lexi looked surprised at what she was saying, then continued, "It was kind of the same with you. Only it happened almost as soon as you opened the tavern door. And when I saw your face, I felt a mix of emotions, warmth and kindness, welcoming and safe."

"Good," smiled Mikaela, "you are becoming one with the 'Eye.'"

"Are you telling me that it's talking to me? How is it possible?" asked Lexi.

"It is possible because the 'Eye of Truth' was created out of your life force, to protect and be used by the 'Chosen One' alone," explained Mikaela.

"I thought it was created a millennium ago for Zarah, so I still don't understand how it makes me the 'Chosen One,'" said Lexi

Mikaela held Lexi's hands in hers, looked straight into her eyes and said, "It is possible my dear because Zarah and you are one and the same. You were born on the casting day when the sign of Pisces ends and that of Aries begins. At midnight, the twenty first of March, the same day as Zarah; and just like her you too have black hair and blue eyes - aquamarine blue to be precise - like that on the 'Eye of Truth.'"

Lexi let go of Mikaela's hands and sat back in her seat. It was all too much to take in. She just sat there quietly, with her eyes shut. Mikaela refilled our glasses with more warm tea.

Lexi straightened up again and took a few sips of her tea. "I think I'm ready to continue now," she said.

Mikaela nodded her head, and continued with her explanation of the pendant. "By using the different symbols on the pendant, the 'Eye of Truth' can communicate with you, just as it did when you met us."

"Will it always be a physical sensation that I will feel?" asked Lexi

"Yes," replied Mikaela, "but you must also pay attention to the strength and intensity of the sensation, for it will serve you well when you will meet strangers on your journey. You see, a warm feeling might suggest you can trust that person, but the intensity of the heat will tell you how much. A cold sensation will serve you by warning you that you should mistrust a person."

"What else?" asked Lexi, "what about the other symbols? How do they translate into physical sensations?" You could tell she was intrigued.

"I'm afraid this is all I know." Mikaela said quietly. "You see, the elders re-designed the pendant a long time ago, and in the years that have passed since then, some of the knowledge we had about it was lost. You must now discover things for yourself."

"Even so, this is incredible!" I said, then jokingly added "Is there anything it can't do?"

Mikaela turned her head towards me, and spoke in a severe tone of voice. "As powerful as it is, it may also fail at times." She looked back at Lexi again, "There are evil powers working against you, wanting to kill you, and they will stop at nothing until you are dead! They are masters of deception, shape-shifters, vicious, wicked and malicious. They will try to trick you any way they can. So most of all, trust your instincts, your feelings, and true friends, for we all want to help you."

It was dark outside by the time we finished.

Mikaela went into the kitchen and brought us out some supper. "You have learned enough for today" she said, "but before we retire for the night, there is one last thing you need to do in order for your connection with the 'Eye of Truth' to be complete."

Lexi looked at Mikaela, not sure what to say or do.

"Give me your right hand," Mikaela commanded.

She held Lexi's hand above the aquamarine crystal on the 'Eye', then took out a small dagger from under her dress. She pricked Lexi's index finger so that it started bleeding, then held the finger and let the blood drip directly onto the crystal. The drops fell, but instead of running all over the pendant, they were absorbed into the crystal, turning it red, before disappearing and leaving it a clear aquamarine blue once again.

"It is done! You are now ONE!" said Mikaela, and handed the pendant back to Lexi.

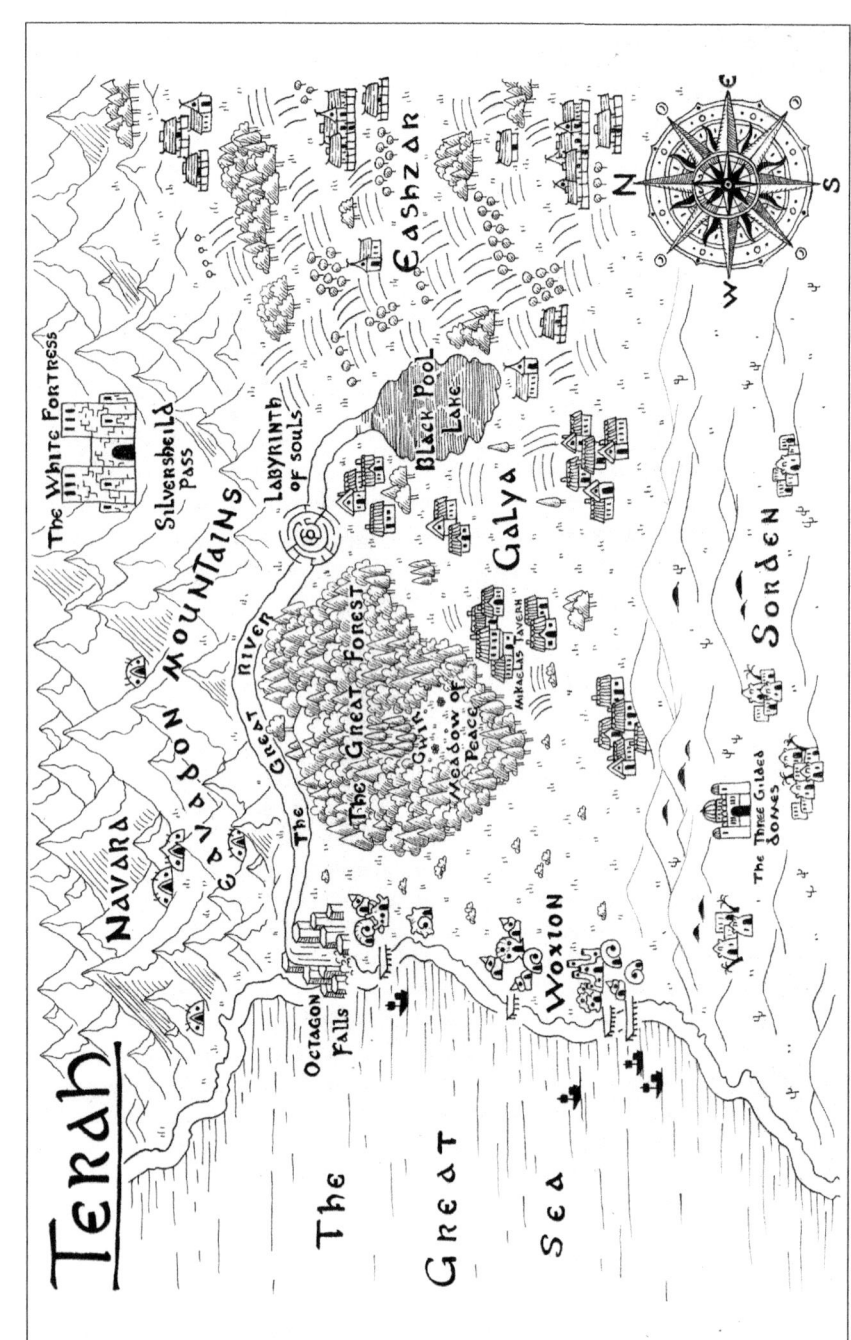

Annak

The sounds of the early morning birds outside the window woke me up. I straightened up on the bed and looked around the room. It was still quite dark. Ari was asleep in his bed. I peeked outside the window. Behind the thick curtains, the sky was changing from deep dark blue to a lighter shade of pale blue, full of pink and purple streaks all over. The sun was just beginning to rise. Getting out of bed, I quickly put on my clothes, left the room, and walked into the living room only to find Lexi sitting by the window, staring outside.

"Morning. You're up early," I said.

Lexi turned her head to me "I've been awake for a while. Just couldn't sleep."

"Don't blame you, it was an intense day for you yesterday. Lots to think about."

"I still can't believe it," said Lexi. "The strange thing is, as tired as I am, I also feel rejuvenated, full of energy. I can feel the blood run through my veins, my heart beating in an orderly way, as if it has its own rhythm linked to the beat of the world around us. As if my senses are intensified and my thoughts are now clear to me. I know who I am."

"Do you think it's to do with the pendant? With what Mikaela did to you last night?"

"Maybe. Probably."

I looked at Lexi as the sun was rising behind her through the big window. She was quite literally beaming. The impression on her face was full of calm and self-confidence. In all our years of friendship, I've never seen her so whole, so beautiful.

"Good morning." I heard Mikaela's voice behind me.

She was standing at the kitchen door. "I trust you slept well?" she smiled.

"Yes, thank you," I replied.

"Good. Now please sit down and have some tea, while I bring out some breakfast."

Ari came out from his room and joined us at the table.

"So, are you ready for today?" he asked, with a hint of a sneer in his voice.

"Bring it on!" I replied, looking straight into his eyes, not daring to blink.

"Relax," Ari said, "I'm only teasing you." He smiled and poured me a cup of tea.

"What's your problem?!" I asked, my eyes locked with his.

"You better drink your tea before it gets cold." Ari ignored my question.

Mikaela walked into the room, carrying a big silver tray full of small dishes, and what smelt like freshly baked bread. We raised our cups off the small round table in the middle, as she placed the big tray on top of it. It looked marvellous; there were freshly-cut salads; a variety of meats and cheese; brown hard-boiled eggs sliced on a plate, with crushed black pepper and finely chopped parsley sprinkled on top. There was a bowl of fresh fruit, with some yoghourt in a smaller bowl placed in the middle. And a big loaf of freshly-baked wholegrain bread, still warm from the oven.

"Please help yourselves," Mikaela said. "There is much for you to learn today. But first, you must eat."

"What do you mean? What's the plan?" asked Lexi.

"Well, first you eat. Then you will need a fresh set of clothes, as you can't run around in what you are wearing now," Mikaela said.

"What's wrong with my jeans and T?" Lexi asked, looking down at her clothes

"Ahrrm, they smell," replied Ari, "and second, 'jeans and T's' are out of fashion here.... if you get my hint."

"What Ari is trying to say is that you don't see your kind of clothes here. It will be quite obvious that the two of you are not from here. You need to be able to blend in as easily as possible and not draw too much attention to yourselves," said Mikaela.

"Fair enough. But there is no way I'm wearing a dress," Lexi said, pointing at Mikaela, who had on a long flowing dress which covered her from neck to toe.

"I'm sure we can find something that will suit you just fine," Mikaela smiled back.

We finished our breakfast and Mikaela gave us new clothes to wear. I went back into Ari's room to change. Narrow brown leather trousers, with a pair of laces where a zip would usually be; a large beige cotton shirt with wooden buttons, with a matching waistcoat; some cotton socks, and a pair of leather boots. It was a lot more comfortable than I expected. I came out of the room curious to see Lexi.

She walked into the living room and stood in front of the window.

"Well?" she asked.

She looked amazing! Black leather trousers tucked into knee-high black boots. A long-sleeved white hooded tunic, with long slits on its sides, and a black leather corset with some delicate gold embroidery covering the upper part of her body.

"Nice," I said.

"You too," she replied.

But the look on Ari's face said it all.

Lexi turned bright red, "Yeah, it'll do, I guess," she said and looked down.

"I'm glad you like it" Mikaela said, "Shall we go downstairs?"

"What's happening there?" Lexi asked.

"Your next lesson," answered Mikaela.

"Isn't the tavern down there? I asked jokingly, "are we learning how to pour and serve drinks next?"

"Maybe later," smiled Mikaela, "But there are a few other things you need to learn first" she added, then turned and started walking towards the door.

We followed her out and down the stairs into the tavern.

As it was still very early in the morning, the tavern was closed for business. Behind the bar was the dwarf, sorting out bottles and filling up the shelves with clean beer mugs and other cups and glasses. He nodded at us, then stood down from behind the counter and walked towards us.

"Lexi, Jimmy, this is Annak" introduced Mikaela.

Lexi stretched her hand out to him but he did not move. He just stood there with a harsh expression on his face. Lexi lowered her hand and looked at Mikaela.

"Please forgive Annak, he is not very good with his manners, or words for that matter," she said, looking at him.

"Hmmm!" he grunted back.

"But you will never find a better or more skilled swordsman than him," Mikaela said.

"He is the master of all iron weapons, as well as of archery," added Ari.

"I bet I can guess what our next lesson is going to be...." I looked at Lexi.

"So can I..." Lexi replied.

"Well, as you both correctly guessed, Annak will be teaching and training you everything you will need to know in the arts of weaponry," said Mikaela.

"Follow me!" We heard a deep hoarse voice coming from where Annak was standing.

Lexi was the first to take a step forward and follow the dwarf. He took us through the tavern kitchen and into a storage room at the back. There, Annak stopped in front of some wooden crates. He moved them aside to reveal a trapdoor on the floor. He turned the round metal hatch in the centre and pulled the door up. We followed him down steep stairs, leading into a large spacious cellar, where Annak lit some oil lamps. He had an impressive display of weapons hanging on the walls. It was a complete armoury and all located underneath the tavern. At the far corner of the cellar, behind a folded wooden screen, was what looked like his living area. It was very simple and basic; a bed, a closet, chest of drawers, a table and chair, and a washing-up corner with a small metal bath and basin.

"Where did you get all of these from?" I asked, as my eyes were inspecting the different swords, daggers, long spears, short spears, bows and other weapons around.

"I made them," came a short and snappy answer from Annak.

"You what?! All of them?" I continued.

"Yes!" he replied sharply.

"Wow, you really are a man of few words." I teased, but no reply came.

Lexi gave me one of her 'quit it!' looks, then turned to Annak.

"You made them all yourself, that's amazing. Are you some sort of a blacksmith then?" she asked.

"I'm a dwarf. That is what we do," Annak gave her another short answer.

"But don't you work in the tavern?" she continued.

"Yes" he said.

"So are you also the blacksmith of this village?" she kept on asking

"No. Just the bartender," he answered.

You could see he was feeling uneasy with the questions. There was clearly more to him than met the eye and, if I knew Lexi, she would find out what it was.

"Are you not from here then?" she pressed on.

"No, I come from the kingdom to the south. Sorden," he replied.

"I'm guessing you are a long way away from home. So what brought you here?" Lexi continued.

He looked up and straight into her eyes. "Fate," he almost whispered at her.

"Fate?" she asked.

It was quite obvious he was not happy with Lexi trying to unravel his private life. But she was not about to give up. She stared back into his eyes, hoping to break that tough wall surrounding him. Her pendant was getting warmer and warmer against her skin. It was a deadlock. No one was moving. No one spoke. No one dared to break the tension building between them.

"Okay. I will tell you my story providing you stop your interrogation," Annak announced, then quietly added, as if to himself, "Wretched girl!"

Lexi nodded her head silently and relaxed her body.

"We better go back upstairs then," he said.

We climbed back up to the tavern. Mikaela was just finishing cleaning the floor. We sat down in one of the private booths and Mikaela brought us some drinks. Annak looked a bit tense and nervous. It was obvious he did not want to talk about himself, let alone share his story with us.

"It has been almost more than a century since I left my homeland and fled to the unknown. Dark times force you to make decisions that you otherwise wouldn't; make you choose a different path then the one intended for you. And most of all, you do anything you can in order to survive another day, even at the expense of leaving all of those you hold dear to your heart behind." He looked aside trying to stop his eyes from watering. "You have nothing left to call your own, except for the clothes on your back," he continued.

Annak directed his look at Lexi, as if it was only the two of them there.

"However down and low you feel, one thing keeps you going.

One thing you must believe in." Annak paused, then said "Hope!"

He took a deep breath before going on: "I once lived a life of luxury, surrounded by all the wealth and goodness that Sorden could provide. After my mother died giving life to me, there was only my father, brother and I. We were very close. No one loved us or indulged us more than my father. We lived in the palace of the 'Three Gilded Domes', the royal palace of Sorden. As the eldest, Kattan was first in line to the throne and I was trained to become the high commander of the army, as well as Kattan's first adviser and confidant.

"They were happy days. When I turned two hundred I married my 'life mate', T'mirah. I truly was blessed."

"When you were two hundred?! How old are you now?" I asked in amazement.

He turned and grunted at me "Four hundred and thirty."

"But..... You look forty three!" I said.

Ari was sitting opposite me with a 'know it all' smile on his face. He was really starting to get on my nerves. But before I managed to say something to wipe that smile off his face, Lexi kicked me under the table. She turned her head slightly towards Ari and gave him one of her looks. The smile was instantly gone.

"So how" I started to say.

"My kind can live to be a thousand. You see, a hundred years in a dwarf's life equals that of a decade for other people. So I suppose if I was like you I would be forty three."

"What happened next?" asked Lexi.

"Years later the darkness of Naval's reign took over our world. It was Sorden he coveted first. He knew that with our precious metals, knowledge and expertise in weaponry he would be unstoppable. He came with his army, and when my father refused to give in to his demands, Naval killed him. Thinking to save the kingdom from war, my brother Kattan agreed to cooperate with Naval and offered to provide him with all the weapons he needed but nothing else.

"Naval does not appreciate his requests being refused, so he turned his army loose and enslaved my people. He forced them to work the deep, dark mines, day and night; to forge the weapons for his ever-growing army. He left Kattan as king, but he is a puppet king. He may still live a life in a palace, but he is being kept there to do as Naval commands. When I tried to talk to my brother, to remind him who he was, what his responsibilities to our people were, he said that was exactly what he was doing. He really believed that. But he told me that I should keep quiet if I value my life, and when I kept urging him to fight back against Naval he sent me and T'mirah to work in the deepest mines.

"Witnessing first-hand what my people were going through, and seeing our beloved kingdom turning into one big black smithy, I realised there was only one thing to do. There were a dozen ex-soldiers working the mine alongside me. I knew them well as they used to be under my direct command, and I knew I could trust them with my life. We decided to raise an underground army, create an arsenal full of weapons, train those who were willing to take the risk, and fight for our freedom.

"But Kattan learned of our plan. Afraid of what Naval would do to him if he found out, he killed everyone, all of those that were with me. I was his brother, so he banished me from the kingdom and kept T'mirah as hostage. There was nothing I could do. I was helpless, broken and betrayed by my own brother. Sorden was no longer my home. I wandered alone as the days turned to weeks, the weeks to months and the months to long, long years. I was lost, didn't know where to go, what to do or who to trust.

"Then one day, as I was passing through yet another village, I heard a whisper about some prophecy. An ancient prophecy about the 'Chosen One.'" Annak looked straight into Lexi's eyes.

Lexi squeezed my hand under the table. Once again their eyes locked in an intense and long moment.

"I knew what I needed to do. If there was any truth to the prophecy then I had to try and find the 'Chosen One', to protect the 'Chosen One' and to take part in the ultimate fight between good and bad, pure and evil.! It is the only way if I am to save my wife and free my people!"

Annak had what looked like a very awkward smile on his face as he said, "You see, hope really is a powerful thing. It can bring you back to life, give it a new purpose."

Lexi let go of my hand.

The Council of Truth

If Lexi and I were still a bit confused and overwhelmed after our previous night with Mikaela, Annak's story was a harsh wake-up. We suddenly realised the dangers of the reality we now found ourselves in. Until that moment, neither of us had really understood what was at stake. These were no 'war games' like between the local street gangs back home. This was real, lives were jeopardised; houses burned to the ground; places erased from the surface of this world, Terah. People were dying, innocent people.

Lexi was wiping tears off her cheeks. In all the years I've known her, this was maybe the third time I had ever seen her cry. I forgot how sensitive she really was, under that tough exterior of hers.

"Thank you," she said softly to Annak, "thank you for being here, for helping us. But most of all, especially in light of all that you have been through, I wish to thank you for believing in me."

Annak didn't say a thing, he just nodded his head and let-out some sort of a quiet grunt, as if to say, "you are welcome."

"So what now?" I asked.

"Now we go back to the cellar, and you begin your fighting training," replied Ari.

We followed Annak back down to the cellar. The thought of learning how to use those magnificent weapons, which Annak had forged himself, was both intimidating and exciting at the same time. He gently took an axe off the wall, and held it in front of us.

"This is a 'Short Hand Axe'. You can use it on its own, shifting it from one hand to the other. Or, with a matching axe, to hold one in each hand in a 'Double Axe' face to face combat," he explained, as he handed it over to Lexi.

"Wow. It's very light!" she said, surprised, then added "And so beautifully decorated too."

"We have mastered the technique of weapon-forging. The special blend of metals used, as well as the way we fold the melted blend on itself and shape it, is what gives our weapons the extra edge in battle," Annak explained. "As for the decorations, they symbolise your rank and the family you come from. The more intricate and delicate the design, so the higher is your rank in life. In addition to your family markings, you also add your name, so that your enemy will know the name of the one who took their life."

"No wonder Naval wanted to get his hands on your kingdom first. That would certainly give him the edge he needed to take over all other kingdoms," I said.

"Yes." Annak replied curtly, and continued "When using an axe in combat, your aim is to cause as much damage as possible to your opponent, before landing him with your final and deadly stroke. When fighting with a single axe, you will also use a round body-shield, to help stop and counter-attack your opponent. Another advantage of having an axe on you, if necessary, is that you can always throw it to kill your opponent from a distance."

Annak then went on to demonstrate, as he threw his axe and hit the middle of the bulls-eye hanging on the wall, at the far end of the cellar.

He then turned back to the display of weapons on the wall and picked another axe. It was longer than the Hand Axe, about a meter long, and its head was double-bladed. Annak held the shaft with both hands, one just a bit above the middle, towards its blade, and the other close to the bottom end.

"This is a 'Long Double-Bladed Battle Axe'; you hold it with both your hands. Its double-bladed head allows you to strike opponents attacking from opposite directions. Using the long haft to hook the blade around various parts of your opponent's body, then pulling, will force him to move in the direction you wish him to. You can find another advantage by hooking the blade around your opponent's ankle, then pulling it towards you and dropping him to the ground. Another use for the long haft is to deflect incoming strikes and push your opponent away from you." As Annak finished explaining about the Long Double Bladed Battle Axe, he once again demonstrated the various moves and ways in which you can handle the axe.

Then he handed the Long Double-Bladed Battle Axe to me, grabbed a broomstick, and shouted "Attack!"

Before I realised what was happening I was on the floor, with the long axe lying beside me.

"Again!" shouted Annak

I just about managed to get on my feet, when I felt my head hit the hard floorboards. Annak was standing directly above me. He swung me up on my feet with one swift movement and handed me the axe again. I was out of breath already and feeling pretty stupid. I held my hand out, signalling him to stop so that I could catch my breath.

"Aaah!" he grunted, "I know dwarf babies who fight better than you."

"Well forgive me for growing-up in a world where axes are used to chop wood!" I answered back, still breathing heavily.

"That was the world you left behind. If you wish to survive in this world, you must let go of your previous notions. Learn to look at things and experience life as if it was for the first time. Terah is your home now, your world. This is a new beginning," Annak said, looking at both Lexi and me.

Suddenly understanding the full meaning of Annak's words, I took a deep breath and said, "I'm ready. Show me what to do."

Annak nodded his head once as if to confirm my feelings, then continued with his lesson.

"Balance is the most important thing a warrior must have. Balanced state of mind; balanced body; balanced posture and, most of all, balance of your soul, your spirit. Lose your balance, and you lose your life. It's as simple as that!"

"You should always be prepared for what might come, both good or bad," he continued. "Focus on your mission. Never forget or let go of the important things in your life, big and small. Always remember who you are, where you came from. Don't be afraid to make mistakes; learn from them, for everything we do makes us stronger. Balance your feelings and your thoughts, and you will be able to stand strong against your enemies. Learn to balance your mind and the rest will follow."

Lexi ran to the far end of the cellar. She pulled out the Short Hand Axe from the bulls-eye hanging on the wall, then joined us again. We started by practicing balancing our posture, while holding our axes high above our heads in a 'Top Strike' position. After a few long hours of striking, attacking, blocking as well as working on balancing our minds, bodies and souls, we finally collapsed on the floor with exhaustion. Every part of my body was aching, every breath I took felt as if a herd of elephants were sitting on my chest. I probably would have cried from the pain, if I wasn't afraid it would hurt too.

"Enough," I heard Annak say, "you have done well. Now rest, let your bodies heal".

"Good timing! I don't think I could keep on going," I said.

"I don't think I can climb back up the stairs," said Lexi, "Just the thought of it hurts."

"Same here," I replied.

We just lay there, trying to relax our bodies, as Annak made his way back up to the tavern.

"Here, drink some of that, it will help cool you down." said Ari, who had come back down to the cellar with a tray of drinks.

"What is it?" I asked. I was so tired I couldn't open my eyes.

"It's Louiza tea with honey, it will refresh you and replenish your energy levels." he replied.

I opened my eyes and reached my hand out to him, he pulled it and helped me sit up. Lexi was still lying on the floor: she was fast asleep. She appeared so calm and relaxed, and yet her eyes were rapidly moving around in a frantic way.

"She's amazing," I heard Ari say, "I've never met someone who fights with such grace and force at the same time before."

"Yes, it did look like it comes naturally to her. As if the weapon she was handling was some sort of extension of her arms."

"And you are not too bad either," said Ari, "But you still need to work on your balance; maybe your next lesson will help with that." He smiled at me.

"What next lesson!?" I asked in horror. "I can hardly move after the last one."

"There is much more you need to learn, and time is running out." Ari replied.

"Time is running out?! What's that supposed to mean!?" I snapped at him.

"It means that things are happening behind the scenes which you, and Lexi in particular, will have a major role in how they unfold." Ari shot his answer back at me.

"What THINGS??!! Stop talking in riddles and give me a straight answer," I demanded.

"Are you two bickering again?" Lexi said. "Honestly, you two sound like grumpy old men."

She slowly sat up, then turned to Ari and said, "You are so full of yourself, aren't you?! You think you know it all, just because you are from Terah. Well, let me tell you something, I don't care how hot my pendant gets when you're around, I don't like the way you act! You're just like the other guys back home, thinking they are smarter, or better, than the rest of us, just because they're a bit older. Well they soon learned, as you will too, that I'm not a little girl and that I give just as much as I get, and let me warn you, when I hit back, no one is left standing!"

"And YOU!" she looked at me, "I expect more from you. Can't you see he is teasing you?! Really, just ignore him."

"But he's hiding something from us, information." I was trying to defend myself.

She didn't say a thing, just turned her look back at Ari, staring straight into his eyes.

He lowered his head. "I can't. I'm not supposed to tell you anything, yet. Not until you are ready to face what's coming," he said.

"That's rubbish! How am I supposed to help save Terah if you don't include me in your little plans?!" Lexi's face was turning red with anger again.

"Look, it's for your own good," Ari said. "At least for now it is better that you don't know. You need to concentrate on your training; there is no need to distract your focus from that."

"But.." Lexi started to say.

"But nothing. Why worry about things that are, for now, out of your control? It is better this way, trust me." He looked into her eyes. "Even your pendant agrees with me, you said so yourself," Ari added with a smile.

"This is not over," Lexi replied, "Not by a long shot."

She got up and walked towards the stairs leading back into the tavern.

When we had walked back into the tavern we were greeted by a chilling silence; it looked like a stand-off between the people in the tavern and a small group of heavily armed men. They were wearing some sort of dark, deep-crimson coloured leather armour. Woven top to bottom around their bodies, it actually looked as if it was wearing them, rather than the other way around; like a second, tougher, protective layer of skin. You could just about see the handles of the flat daggers stuffed into their hilts, embedded along both sides of the body armour. Behind their shoulders peeked the handles of two crossed long-swords which were resting on their backs. A leathered whip was tightly wrapped around each man's waist. Beneath their helmets a mask covered their entire face, hiding any kind of facial expression apart from the one moulded in their mask. All you could see were their eyes, peering through the dark mask, and even they were cold and empty. They looked very much like clones of each other, moving together in synchronised movements, as if they were extensions of one living organism.

"Naval's elite guards," whispered Ari.

"Elite guards?" I asked

"Yes. They volunteer to give Naval their 'life force' and become one with his consciousness. He can command them from afar, and through them remain informed of things when he cannot be there in person. But what are they doing here now? They are too early," Ari said.

"Too early?! You knew they were coming?! And you didn't think it was worth mentioning?!" I felt my face burning up with anger.

Ari didn't reply, he swiftly positioned himself in front of Lexi, who was frozen at her spot.

One of the guards must have caught glimpse of Ari moving, and at once all the guards turned their heads towards him.

"MOVE!" an eerie sound came from the guard.

Ari stepped aside, keeping his eyes on the guard.

"You. Girl." Came the eerie sound again, "Step forward."

I looked at Lexi. She was pale white, as if all the blood was drained out of her body. Her lips were blue and her skin was covered with goose bumps.

"She is of no interest to you," said a familiar voice behind us, "That is, unless you wish to order a drink from my waitress, of course." Mikaela walked towards the guard, with a smile on her face. All at once their attention was directed at Mikaela.

"This is a tavern after all; people come here to relax, eat, have a drink or two and be merry. So as personal guests in my fine establishment, what can I get you? Or is it my lovely waitress who caught your eye?" She went on teasingly, trying to keep their focus on her.

Suddenly their heads gave a subtle twitch, as if they had just finished processing some piece of information. Collectively they started moving towards the tavern door. As the last guard reached the door, they all turned around, towards the room, looked at Lexi again and said, in their eerie voice, "He'll be back."

Then they walked out of the door, though it looked more like they were gliding, as if they were walking on an invisible cloud, but in slow motion.

As soon as the door shut, I grabbed hold of Lexi. She took a deep-breath, and at once the colour returned to her face and her body felt warm again.

"What the hell happened to you?!" I asked

"I'm not sure," she said "But as soon as we got back up from the cellar, I felt a cold wave going through my body. I thought it was my body cooling down after our training session earlier, but the closer we got to the main room of the tavern, the colder I became."

Suddenly it hit me. "The 'Eye'! Do you think it was some sort of warning?"

"Must be. I mean, till now I only felt warmth from it, and even then it was nowhere near the strength and intensity of what I just felt."

"That's because you never came face-to-face with pure evil until now," said Ari.

"YOU!" I shouted at him, "You KNEW about it! You knew they were coming, and didn't say a word!" I shot my right fist towards his face, but he was too quick and managed to duck.

"Back in the cellar... Is that what you were hiding from us? from

ME?" Lexi looked into his eyes with a betrayed look on her face.

"Lexi, I'm so sorry..... I...." Ari began to say as Mikaela came towards us.

"Please forgive Ari, it is not his fault. He wanted to tell you, warn you about it, but we forbade him."

"We?!" Lexi looked puzzled as she turned towards Mikaela.

"Yes, We. 'The Council of Truth,'" replied Mikaela.

Lexi and I looked at each other, It was obvious we were thinking the same thing. Being such good friends for so many years, we could almost read each-others minds.

"Wow! Aren't we full of secrets!" said Lexi sarcastically.

Mikaela gave her one of her soft, motherly smiles, then said "Now, there is no need for that. I know you feel confused at the moment, but please believe me when I tell you, it was for your own good, keeping that information from you. We did not think you were ready to deal with that yet, and we were clearly right."

"Who do you think you are, playing with my life like that?!" Lexi said in a quiet, yet firm, tone of voice.

"I am truly sorry for what has happened here today. But as your guardians, we must put your safety above all. Protect you even from yourself if needs be," replied Mikaela

"My guardians? Why did you not mention this before?" asked Lexi

"For your protection, as well as ours." Mikaela stopped talking and gestured to us to follow her back up to the living quarters.

A few moments later we were sitting down on the soft cushions on the living room floor.

"'The Council of Truth' was formed fifteen years ago, on the day you were born," Mikaela said. "Our sole purpose was to prepare in every way possible for the day you returned, so we could guide and help you fulfil your destiny. All members are sworn to secrecy and, for our own protection, as well as yours, none of us know the true identity of all guardians apart from the 'High Protector', and she is well hidden in your world."

"Madam Giselle!" Lexi and I said together.

Mikaela got up, turned and stood with her back towards us. She then gently swooped her long golden hair up, and pulled the top of her blouse down to reveal, at the top of her back, a small silver tattoo of Lexi's pendent. She quickly covered it again, then sat back down on the cushions.

She continued, "This is the only way we can recognise and verify the Guardians. In order to prevent the revealing of anyone's identity to any of Naval's men, you can, by pinching the centre of the eye very hard, erase the tattoo from your skin. However, by doing that you immediately, and permanently, sever your one and only connection to the council as well as any memory of ever being a Guardian.

"As head of the local council, it was up to me to decide when and how to reveal the information regarding Naval's elite guards. The day you arrived to our world we got word from one of our allies that Naval's elite guards were seen north-east from here. They were stopping in every village they came to, looking for something. Our friends did not know what it was, except that it must be something of great importance for Naval to unleash his elite guards. Unfortunately, we misjudged the time we had to fully train and prepare you for what lies ahead. I truly hoped you would be more prepared and better informed as to what you might expect to meet on your quest to fulfil your destiny."

Mikaela looked straight at Lexi. "I am sorry to say my dear, but our time is up. You must start your journey sooner than expected and leave us today, now in fact. I have prepared a small backpack for each of you with a change of clothes, some first aid, medicine, food for the next few days, and a small bag with a few gold coins."

Someone knocked on the front door. It was Annak.

"I couldn't let you go without a goodbye," he said in his husky voice. "And I brought you these."

He pulled two Short Hand Axes from behind his back, as well

as a Long Double Bladed Battle Axe. "I thought they might come in handy" he said.

Lexi picked-up the two Short Hand Axes and strapped them to her back, then turned to Annak and stretched her arm out to him. "Thank you, Annak. For everything."

Annak grabbed her hand then gently pulled her towards him and gave her a great big hug.

I grabbed the other axe and put it across my back. "You're not planning on giving me a hug? Are you?" I said jokingly.

"Arrrrh...." grunted Annak, before grabbing hold of me and firmly hugging me too.

We went back downstairs and walked towards the back door of the kitchen. I was feeling scared but full of excitement at the same time. The idea of facing the unknown with Lexi by my side felt good, felt right. Soon we were standing outside, in the tavern's vegetable garden.

Mikaela reached her arms out to me and gave me a hug, a motherly hug, loving and warm. I surrendered completely.

Then she hugged Lexi. "Let the 'Eye of Truth' guide you safely on your way. Trust your instincts, your feelings," she said softly. "Remember, you have many friends and allies waiting to give their hand to you and fight on your side." She let go of Lexi and gently wiped the tears from her face. "You will always have a home here."

"No goodbyes for me?" I heard Ari's voice from behind Mikaela.

"That's ok," he went on, "because I'm joining you." Ari had a big smile on his face.

"You're what?!" I asked.

"Coming with you. After all, someone needs to show you where to go and to keep you out of trouble." Ari winked.

"He's right. We need him with us," Lexi concluded.

And just like that 'The Dynamic Duo' became a trio.

Beginnings

We left the Tavern behind and decided to backtrack Naval's elite guards by heading north-west. Our hope was that they would continue going in the opposite direction. Ari explained this would allow us to move more freely towards our final destination, Navara and Naval. As we reached the edge of the woods we stopped and turned around, for one last look. The sun was just beginning to set and the sky above the village of Stormend was lit in gold and orange. Not sure when, or if, we would see it again, we looked at each other, then walked into the 'Great Forest'.

"I thought we could camp close to the 'Meadow of Peace' tonight, then head towards 'Gwir'" said Ari.

"What's Gwir?" Lexi asked.

"It's a circle of trees in the middle of the 'Great Forest'. We believe that the principle of life, the Eather of all Creations, originates there. It is a place of peace, truth and harmony. That is where we hold our most sacred ceremonies and celebrations. It is customary to go there before embarking on any new journey in life, for good luck," Ari explained.

"Sounds good to me," I said, "we'll need all the luck we can get where we're going."

Ari looked at Lexi, as if waiting for her approval.

"Yeah, okay, might as well." She didn't sound very convinced.

We silently walked into the forest. It was very still and calm. Every so often we heard the call of some animal or bird nearby. By the time we reached the camp-sight, it was already pitch black. We gathered some wood for a fire, intending to sit down beside it and eat some of the food that Mikaela had prepared.

I opened my bag and looked inside for some matches, "Hey, does anyone have the matches to light the fire?" I asked.

"No need," replied Ari.

He knelt down by the pile of wood, leaned a little forward, then slowly started rubbing the palm of his hands together. Every so often he lifted his hands closer to his mouth, opened them slightly and gently blew air into them. Lexi and I exchanged looks, not sure what to make of it. Ari increased the pace then, suddenly, he opened his hands and blew a long gush of air through them and onto the wood. In less than a second a flame rose from between the logs and the fire was lit.

"How did you do THAT?!" I asked, not quite believing what I had seen.

"You just started a fire! From thin air!" Lexi added in amazement.

Ari smiled, "That comes from learning how to control and channel the elements of life."

"You mean, you can manipulate all five elements as you wish?!" I asked.

"Manipulate, no. Use them when and as needed, yes," he replied.

"But how is it possible?" Lexi asked.

"I am a Galyan," Ari said, "That is our gift. It is a sacred bond between us and the elements. A special connection to the source of life."

"That is some powerful bond," I said.

"Indeed." Ari replied, "but it is not as simple as that. We must never take advantage of our bond or we will lose our privileged powers forever."

"But isn't that what Naval is doing?" I asked again.

"Yes, but he has learned how to enlist the dark powers, and that is why we are all in so much danger," Ari said.

I looked at Lexi, "So what's the plan?"

"I'm not sure," said Lexi, "I know what I 'need' to do, what is expected of me, but I don't know how to do it. This is all too much to ask of me. I mean, just for starters, in order for me to find Naval we need to get to Navara, but how do we get there? This is all happening too fast, and I'm just not sure any more.

"Look at us, what difference can the three of us make? Honestly, I don't know what I was thinking, going against this Titan king on my own." Lexi gazed at the fire, tears were running down her face, shimmering in the flames.

"You are right," said Ari. "It's crazy, trying to go against such a powerful man as Naval. It's stupid and irresponsible thinking that a young girl can come face to face with such evil and defeat it."

Ari's tone had been sarcastic. Now he got up, clearly angry, and walked across towards Lexi. "There are plenty of good people waiting to help in any way possible. Just say the word and they will happily fight and even die for you, as so many others before, all in the belief and hope that one day you would come and fulfil your destiny." He looked into her eyes and said, "But if you cannot do this, then stop right now. Don't let them go on believing in false hope!"

Lexi blushed at Ari's words, but said nothing. He threw another log onto the fire then silently sat back down in his place.

We finally fell asleep as the last log of wood burned out.

The early morning light woke me up. Ari was already awake and cooking us some breakfast.

"Good morning you two. I trust you had a good night's sleep? Breakfast is just about ready and there is fresh coffee brewing over there." He pointed at the small metal coffee pot placed over a couple of burning logs.

"Looks like you've been busy," said Lexi.

"Well, there's nothing like a good breakfast to start your day," Ari replied, looking straight at Lexi. "Besides, it could be a long journey ahead of us."

I grabbed a cup of coffee and sat down opposite Lexi, "So, boss, what are we doing?" I winked at her.

"I think that first we need to plan our route up north. It's crucial that we know beforehand, where are the places we can safely travel through, and which ones we should keep away from." She looked at Ari with a smile, then continued, "And that is where you come into play. I rely on you to help plan our route and guide us through." Her eyes firmly locked into his.

Ari nodded his head at her. "I'm glad to see you are back on top of things…and ready to take charge," he said sarcastically. "Now, can I see that map of yours please?"

Lexi opened her backpack and carefully took out the map. She gently unfolded it and placed it on the ground in front of her. A few moments later, just as it did the first time, we saw lines and drawings start to appear until the map was visible. When it finished drawing the four-pointed compass at the bottom right corner of the sheet, Lexi ran her finger over it and the map instantly transformed into a three-dimensional hologram, hovering above the page. As we looked closer, we realised it already showed our present location inside the Great Forest.

"As you can see, we are here, in the Meadow of Peace," Ari said, pointing to the hologram.

It was amazing. Not only did it show our exact location to the last blade of grass, but it was also environment sensitive. As the sun was rising higher and brighter, so did the brightness and lighting of the hologram adjust itself. It was an accurate reflection of the 'real' world.

"Our next stop will be here, the Gwir," said Ari, and as soon as he touched the small, round cluster of trees in the hologram, they were magnified and we could clearly see a circle of trees in the centre of a clearing in the forest. The trees in the circle were so close to each other that the light could barely shine through them and heavy mist lingered around their trunks, creating a sort of barrier between them and the rest of the forest.

"What is that place?" Lexi asked, pointing at something that looked like the sun.

"That is the 'Labyrinth of Souls,'" Ari replied. "It is situated on the 'Great River', a gateway between Navara and Galya."

"Wait, do you mean we can cross straight over to Navara through it?" Lexi asked.

"Well, technically, yes. But...."

Lexi cut him off, "Then we should go there. We can be in Navara in no time."

"It is not that simple. There is a reason why even Naval did not dare cross into Galya through the labyrinth. You see, only the truly pure at heart can safely cross it. You cannot have a bad or cruel bone in your body. Your thoughts must remain clean and your reasons for crossing pure. If the labyrinth detects darkness in your soul, it will draw you downstream towards Black Lake where your soul will be absorbed in its tar-like waters for eternity."

"And what is the other alternative?" asked Lexi

"If you are pure of heart, you will go through and out of the labyrinth safely. You will flow upriver towards Navara," replied Ari.

"That sounds good to me," said Lexi.

"Good enough to risk your life, your soul? You must be very sure of yourself to risk yourself and all of our lives." Ari looked at her, "Many have tried to cross the labyrinth, none survived."

"The way I see it is simple. I mean, it wasn't too long ago that we were little kids, so how un-pure can we be? Besides, can you think of a more worthy or purer cause than ours, to cross through the labyrinth?" replied Lexi

Ari looked at me, "What do you think?"

"If Lexi said so, then I trust her with my life," I replied. "I've known her all my life, she is very level headed and calculated. She will never do something on a whim or take a risk that will put herself or others in real danger."

"Well…" Ari started to say, "I suppose there is logic in what you say," He sounded hesitant.

"Good. Then we all agree. We are heading to the Labyrinth of Souls as soon as we are done at the Gwir," Lexi concluded. She tapped the centre of the compass to hide the map, then carefully folded the blank sheet of paper and returned it into her backpack.

We started walking, heading towards the Gwir. Lexi and I didn't know quite what to expect once we got there. As we walked silently through the woods, I couldn't stop thinking about how we came to be here. Running through my mind, over and over again, all we had learned in just a few days about this world called Terah; it's past, it's possible future, and our, or rather Lexi's, part in it. Looking around us at this magnificent forest, I suddenly realised how the 'urban forest' we were so used to, with its tall, crowded skyscrapers and crazy traffic zooming all over the place, had now been replaced with real trees and live animals. The smell of the forest, the sound of the birds, as well as catching sudden glimpses of a deer speeding through the trees, was truly amazing.

"Hey Lexi," I said "can you imagine Tony Palermo's face if he knew where we are or what we're doing?"

"I know!" Lexi replied, with a big smile on her face.

We had another short break for lunch before starting the last leg of our journey for the day. As we got closer to our destination, Lexi suddenly stopped.

"I can feel it!" she said. "It's all around us, warm and welcoming, calm and revitalising. And look," she held her pendant out, "Look how it glows."

"We are very close to the Gwir, your 'Eye' must be sensing that and reacting to it." Ari said.

A few moments later we were walking into a cleared part of the forest, staring straight at a very dense circle of trees at its centre. The lower branches and trunks were hidden behind a thick layer of white mist and we could just make out the dark-green leaves at the top of the trees. It looked exactly like it's smaller replica on the map.

Ari stepped forward, holding the palms of his hands upwards, so that they gently touched the mist, and began to whisper to it:

"Peace and harmony, joy and love bring us here to fill our hearts. We seek the blessing of this sacred place, to help us in our quest."

Then he closed his eyes and blew some air at the mist. Almost immediately the mist in front of him started dissolving, creating a clear opening between the trees for us to go through. We followed Ari between the big, thick, tree-trunks and further into the 'Circle of Trees'. As soon as we were standing in the middle of the circle, the mist returned to close the gap we had passed through. I looked at Lexi and she was quite literally shining. It was the reflection of a light, bright, white contour line beaming around her body. Because of the height and thickness of the trees around us, not much sunlight managed to come through, which made Lexi look like a bright star in the dimness of the circle. It was then that I suddenly realised that the aquamarine crystal, in the middle of her pendant, was pulsing along with her heart, combined together and transforming into one unified empowered organ.

"What is happening to me?" Lexi shouted at Ari.

"It is the Gwir, " he replied, "It is sensing the essence of life in 'The Eye of Truth', recognising the bond between you. Just relax, let it embrace you."

Lexi closed her eyes, letting her head fall gently backwards. A moment later, she was slowly lifted above the ground until she was suspended in mid-air. She was shining so bright that Ari and I had to shield our eyes and look away. Then, just as suddenly, she was once again on the ground and back to her old self.

"That was AWESOME!!!" I cried as I ran towards Lexi.

"Indeed, a very good sign" said Ari. "Now let us get some rest."

Consequences

It was early dawn when we started making our way out of the Gwir and on towards the Labyrinth of Souls. The Great Forest was still quite dark and very misty. Despite the previous day's events in the Gwir, there was an eerie feeling in the air. I glanced back at Lexi. She looked a bit tense, pre occupied with her thoughts. Ari, on the other hand, was focused on getting us safely to the Labyrinth as soon as possible. He was in such a good mood since we reached the Gwir, that he seemed to be completely oblivious to how Lexi and I were feeling.

"Is it me, or is there something out there?" I asked Ari.

"This is a big forest we are crossing and we are sure to come across some wildlife, it's only natural." Ari replied.

"No, Jimmy is right. I've been sensing something… well the 'Eye of Truth' did…almost from the moment we left the Gwir," said Lexi hesitantly.

I stopped in place and turned to her, "What kind of sensation?"

"I'm not sure. It's not as clear as the other times. It's kind of like when you have a really high fever, and you're hot but still have the chills at the same time. I just don't know what to make of it."

"Why didn't you say anything?" I asked.

"Because I was trying to figure it out. Understand what it is that the 'Eye' is trying to tell me," she said.

"And??" I went on.

Lexi had a puzzled look on her face, "And I have NO idea. Whatever it means, it's going to happen soon, because the sensation is becoming stronger."

"That is not good." Ari said, in a very serious tone of voice. "We must be more vigilant from now on. At least until we figure out what it is that the 'Eye' is telling you."

"Agreed!" Lexi and I said together.

We walked through the forest cautiously, fully alert and ready for anything. Anything but the events that followed. We were about to stop for some lunch, when Lexi suddenly stood still. She signalled us not to make a sound.

"Look up," she whispered, pointing to the top of one of the trees above us. Something moved so fast, we only managed to get short, snap glimpses of it.

"What is it?" I whispered.

"I don't know, it's too fast to focus on." Lexi replied, then turned to Ari, "Any suggestions as to what it might be?"

"No. I do not believe I have seen anything like it before," he answered.

"We need to lure it out to the open." Lexi said very decisively.

"We are quite close to the edge of the forest. Another couple of hours and we will be out in the open again." Ari said. "There will be nowhere for it to hide".

"Good," I said, "then we should eat something and quickly get out of here."

The knowledge that something was out there, hovering above us, didn't help much in trying to calm my nerves. Once again the reality of where we were hit me.

"You know," Lexi suddenly said, "I was thinking about what the 'Eye' might be trying to tell me, the way it makes me feel and the connection to whatever is out there."

"Go on," I said, hoping to hear something positive and reassuring.

"Well, I don't think that whatever's out there is out to get us. Otherwise I wouldn't be feeling heat, radiating from the pendant." She paused for a minute, then concluded, "So it must be a good sign."

"Not to spoil everyone's optimism" I said cautiously, "but what about the cold chills you're feeling at the same time?"

Her face dropped and those worrying lines between her eyebrows scrunched tightly together. "That's what I'm still trying to figure-out." She relaxed her eyebrows, and trying to keep a positive tone of voice, she said, "Whatever it is, my gut feeling is that it will not harm us. We'll be fine."

"It is not that I do not trust your feelings," Ari turned to her, "but I will feel a lot better once we know exactly what it is that we are dealing with."

I was becoming more and more frustrated and blurted out at him "How do you propose we do that then, when we're down here and whatever it maybe, it is up there, hovering above us in super speed?"

He gave me one of his 'I know it all' smiles and said "Just help me get it out in the open and leave the rest to me."

"We know it's up there, following us.... but I don't think that it's aware that we know" Lexi quickly said, "so that should give us an advantage over it."

"My thoughts exactly," agreed Ari.

"Then what do you suggest?" asked Lexi.

"Just before we reach the end of the forest, the trees will start to thin-out, creating a small clearing at the top. Once we get there, you will need to do whatever you can in order to get it to fly above us long enough for me to trap it," he replied.

"I might have an idea." I smiled at them, "Once we get there, before we cross through, we split. Lexi and I will hide in the trees, opposite each other. Ari, you will position yourself between us, but much closer to the edge of the clearing. That should allow you to jump out into the open and trap it as it passes over. As soon as you are ready, give us a loud call. We will keep running, criss-crossing and switching our positions between the trees, through the clearing in the middle. That should, hopefully, keep it flying above us and in the clear, long enough for you to do your thing."

I could feel the adrenalin pumping through my veins as we got closer and closer to the forest clearing. Every so often we looked up to make sure it was still up there, following us. Eventually we reached the edge of the clearing. The excitement of what we were about to do was quite obvious on our faces. I could almost hear Lexi and Ari's hearts beating in perfect synchronisation with mine. We took our positions and waited for Ari to call.

"NOW!!!!" cried Ari, "Lexi go right. Jimmy, cross straight. Lexi cross and cross again. Jimmy now you. Faster this time. FASTER!! Again. Cross. STOPPPP!!!"

Ari jumped into the centre of the clearing. His hands were stretched high above his head. He was waving and turning them as if he was trying to fold a giant sheet of paper. His movements were so fast, it was mesmerising to watch.

"Lexi can you see what it is yet?" I called to her.

"No, the trees over here are still in the way. Can you?"

"No. Not very clearly."

"What about Ari? Can you see him?"

"Yes. Looks like he's weaving something with his hand. He's moving so fast, it's incredible. Hold on a minute, I'm going to try and get a better look."

"Stay where you are. Do not come closer." Ari commanded me, "You must wait until I am finished building the cage around it. I have to make sure the air is bent tight enough to hold it."

Lexi was getting impatient, "I can't see a damn thing from here. What's happening now?"

"I'm not sure but I think...... GOT IT! Ari is lowering it down to the ground."

"I'm coming out!!" Lexi shouted.

We both ran out from behind the trees. "That was fantastic!!!" I shouted at him, "How did you do it?"

"What is it?" Lexi was calling from behind me.

We stopped short of Ari's catch.

"It's..." Lexi paused, getting a closer look at it, "It's beautiful!"

"Look at its size. Its huge." I said.

Lexi was mesmerised by it. "That coat, soft and white, covered with all those silver spots everywhere. So graceful!"

"Indeed it is." Ari replied, "But what is it doing out here?!"

"What do you mean?" I asked.

"This is a white silver spotted Gyrfalcon. His kind are not indigenous to this place. It comes from the snowy peaks of Navara," Ari replied. "They are known to be very good hunters, and excellent trackers," he added.

"A SPY!! One of Naval's people!" I jumped back, pointing at it.

Lexi looked into its beady, brown eyes. "You might be right Jimmy. It might explain the mixed sensations I am feeling from the....." she suddenly stopped.

The falcon's head was moving, slightly twitching from side to side, as if to tune in better to our conversation.

"You can understand what we're saying....." Lexi said very slowly, looking directly into his eyes.

The falcon moved its head forward, "Indeed I can. 'Chosen One."

Lexi kept her composure, "Not sure what you mean."

"Come, come, my dear, let's not play that game. We all know what I meant, so please, do not insult me," it said.

"Well, well, aren't you feisty," she said before looking at Ari. "Is he quite secure there?"

"Most definitely. Although you cannot see the strings of air tightly woven and folded around him, I can assure you we are safe. He cannot fly away unless I release the knots around him," Ari reassured Lexi.

"What are you doing here? Why are you following us? Who sent you?" Lexi went on, trying to get some answers from it.

"I am Tercel, a sentinel in the falconry guard. I am not following your companions, I am following YOU, and I think it is obvious why, 'Chosen One.'" Its brown, beady eyes were glowing.

"Go on," Lexi said.

"I was doing my regular patrol across the border..." Tercel started explaining when Ari suddenly interrupted him. "What do you mean 'regular patrol across the border'?! Since when do you leave your snowy peaks and venture south into my kingdom?!"

"Your kingdom," Tercel sneered at Ari. "My master will find that most amusing indeed. Anyway, there I was flying over the 'Great River' and across into 'your kingdom' when I saw a flash of bright light from somewhere in the distance. I immediately made my way towards it, to investigate the matter. It was gone by the time I arrived, but, as I thought it to be of some interest to my master, I decided to stay for a while in case it should happen again. Imagine my surprise when out of the emptiness of the mist, the three of you emerged. I followed you from above, keeping a close watch and a sharp ear, listening in on your conversations."

Ari, Lexi and I exchanged horrified looks between us. The consequences of our decision to go to the Gwir, our naive assumption that it was safe enough to discuss the 'Eye of Truth' out loud, while sheltered by the Great Forest were, it seemed, reckless actions that had put us, and Lexi most of all, in grave danger.

"What do we do now?" I asked.

It was Ari who spoke first. "We will make a short detour before we continue onward to the Labyrinth of Souls. We will take the Gyrfalcon with us to my uncle, in the village of 'Shaar', he will know what to do with it." Ari answered in a very cold tone of voice.

Shaar

We walked silently on through the last part of the Great Forest. Ari was in the lead. Tercel was hovering beside him, in his invisible cage, while Lexi and I walked next to each other, close behind them. It was dark by the time we came into the open and on to a road again. The night sky was full of shining, glittering stars, like a big blanket wrapped around our shoulders. After spending days in the deep Great Forest, it was reassuring to know that soon we would be back amongst people again.

"What can you tell me about this village we are going to?" Lexi asked.

"Plenty. I've known it all my life. My father's family is from there." Ari smiled.

"That's handy" I said, "so what's their story?"

"Story?" Ari looked at me, puzzled.

"Drop it, Jimmy!" Lexi scolded me, then turned back to Ari, "don't mind him, he's just messing with you. So, what can you tell us about Shaar?"

"As the northernmost village in Galya, the people here are the keepers of the 'Northern Gate' into our kingdom. And they are also masters of the third element of life."

"What do you mean by 'masters of the third element of life'?"

asked Lexi

"Well," said Ari "because their village is very close to the Great River, they have mastered the third element of life - water. They can, very easily, do as they wish with water. They can bend it and re-shape it as if it was a solid substance."

Lexi's eyes lit-up with excitement, but she kept any thoughts to herself.

We continued walking, in silence, when I noticed Lexi was starring aimlessly down at the ground. "How are you feeling?" I quietly asked her.

"Confused, annoyed, tired. What about you?"

"Same, I guess. At least we stopped Naval's the spy from telling anyone about us." I tried to cheer her up.

"Yes... but why didn't Tercel fly off and inform his master when he could? Unless...."

"Unless there is something else." I finished her thought out loud.

"Exactly!"

"Over there," called Ari suddenly, and pointed. "Those lights in the distance. It is 'Shaar'."

"That's the best thing I heard all day," I said.

"Not much longer to go, another half an hour or so," Ari added.

"In that case," Lexi said, "Lets pick-up the pace and get going."

It was as though we were injected with an overdose of energy. We doubled our speed and walked faster than ever before. The closer the lights of 'Shaar' got, the faster we walked until, finally, we were running.

"STOP!!!!" Lexi shouted at us.

"Why?" Ari asked. "We are almost in the village."

"Something is wrong! Here touch my hands." She stretched her arms towards us.

"They are cold as ice!" Ari said.

"My whole body is cold. I thought you said this place is safe?!"

"But it is. I can assure you.... The pendant must be wrong...." Ari sounded confused.

"I'm sorry Ari, but I can't ignore what I'm feeling. All that happened earlier today has shown that we must be more vigilant. We have no other choice but to keep a careful watch for any possible danger, from both friends as well as strangers. We'll go in if you say so, but tell no-one what has been happening to us."

"What about the falcon?" I asked.

"As far as anyone is concerned, it's Ari's pet. Remember, 'need to know' basis only. Do not volunteer any information." Lexi instructions were firm. "As for you," she turned to the falcon, "If you cherish your life you will keep silent."

We were like thieves in the dark, silently sneaking through the main street of the village. Walking in the shadows, between the closed shops. Trying to avoid the pale light that a few street-lamps cast around them. As we passed the first houses of 'Shaar', we saw that some of them were wide-open and empty. The rest were so tightly shut that it seemed as if whoever was inside was trying to keep whatever may be outside, firmly out. Finally we reached a small cottage. At first glance it didn't look any different than the other houses we had passed.

"This is my uncle's home," said Ari.

As we walked through the front garden gate, a faint light was flickering from between cracks in the wooden shutters over the windows.

"I'm sure everything is fine with your family." Lexi tried to reassure Ari.

"It is kind of you to say so, and I might believe you, if I didn't see you shivering so much. Shall we go in?" Ari hesitantly raised his hand and softly knocked on the door. When no reply came, he knocked again.

"Maybe we should try and peek through the shutters, we might be able to see what's going on in there," suggested Lexi.

"Good idea," Ari agreed.

We started towards the window beside the garden, when we heard a sound coming from the front door.

"Someone's unlocking the door." I said.

The door opened slightly, barely enough to let a small grain of sand in. Lexi stretched her hands to her back reaching for her battle-axes. "We better be ready, just in-case," she whispered to us, as she was about to pull them out.

"ARI!!!" the voice behind the door said, then "Come in, quickly" as the door swung open to let us in.

Lexi relaxed her hands and followed Ari inside.

"Aunt Lily!" He hugged the woman who was closing the door behind us. "What is going on?" Ari let go of her and looked around the room. " Where is Uncle Josh?"

She looked away, trying to hold back her tears. "Oh Ari, he is gone. They took him away."

"Who took him? When?" Ari asked

"Naval's elite guards came here three days ago, looking for something, for someone. It was horrible." She wiped the tears off her cheeks. "They went through each and every building in the village, be it a house or a shop. Ripping up floorboards, tearing down walls. They didn't ask any questions, did not say what it was they wanted." She stopped, then hugged Ari again. "Not finding what they were looking for made them angry. They rounded up every able-looking man, thanked them for volunteering to join His elite guard, and took them away. After they had left, some of the families decided to leave the village and go to their relatives elsewhere."

"Why did you not come to us? Does Mother know of this?"

"The rest of us decided to stay, keep watch in case our men will come back. You know your uncle, he will not give-in so easily. I must hope that somehow he will find his way back home."

"Aunt Lily, I am so sorry. What can I do to help?" Ari looked devastated. The news about his uncle, seeing his aunt weeping and looking so fragile, must have brought back the memories of what had happened to his father.

"Just seeing you here, now, is plenty," his aunt said. "But where are my manners?" looking at Lexi and me. "Please forgive the state of the place. Come in, feel as though it is your home, and I will go and make us all some warm tea."

"Let me first introduce my friends, Lexi and Jimmy," Ari said. "And that is my falcon, Tercel. I hope you don't mind him being in the house. He is very good, won't make a sound," sending a warning look at the falcon.

"It is very nice to meet you all," Lily replied, staring at the falcon, then made her way into the kitchen. A few minutes later she came back holding a tray with some tea and cookies on it.

"Oatmeal and chocolate, your favourite." Lily smiled, then asked, "but what brought you here? How long will you be staying?"

Ari looked at Lexi and me as we sat down around the small wooden dining table beside the kitchen door. "We can only stay for the night. I am taking my falcon back to his natural home. It is long past the time I should have set him free, and we must continue on our way as soon as possible."

"I understand," Lily said, clearly disappointed.

"Thank you for the tea." Lexi smiled at her. "I'm very sorry for what has happened to you. To all the village."

"Thank you, dear. But no need to apologise, it was hardly your fault," she replied. "But perhaps it might be very cold where you are heading. You should have much warmer clothes than the ones you are wearing now," Lily said, as if she knew where we were going. "Not to worry." She smiled and got up from the table. "I have some warm clothes in the back that you may borrow."

Lily looked like a pile of clothes with legs, when she returned. "These should do the trick," she said, as she spread-out a bundle of clothes, as well as thick leather and sheepskin coats to go over them.

"Thank you, very much," we answered together.

"And will you be stopping over on your way back?" she asked.

"I hope so," Ari answered, trying to avoid looking her in the eye.

We hardly slept that night. As soon as the sun started rising, we packed our bags, making sure everything was ready to go.

"Please take care and keep safe," she told us as we made our way towards the front gate. "I shall send word to your mother. Tell her you were here."

By the time we reached the gate she was already back inside the house. We could hear the sounds of the locks being put back in place behind us. Another reminder of the consequences of our actions. There was no going back, only onwards, to the 'Labyrinth of Souls'.

The Labyrinth of Souls

It was a bright and bitterly cold start for the morning. You could see the snowy mountaintops of Navara in the far distance. The sound of the water gushing through the 'Great River' was clear and became louder and louder as we got closer to the Labyrinth.

"I do not suppose you will free me, before losing your souls in the Labyrinth?" Tercel's question broke the silence.

"We intend to lose nothing, except maybe you." Lexi said, "So I would keep quiet 'til we are across the other side. Or would you rather we left you to your fate?"

"Did it ever occur to you that I might be of use to you?"

"I doubt that very much" Lexi replied, "We know where your loyalty lies."

"Know, or assume?" Tercel asked.. "My dear, that brave and clever facade you put on does not fool me, I know all about you. You see, I was here to witness the downfall of your predecessor and she was just as naive as you are!"

I looked at Lexi and Ari. "What are you smiling at?!" I asked Ari.

"I just happen to think that there is some truth in what he said" Ari replied.

"So, what, now you're on his side?" I lunged at him, "I knew we couldn't trust you. You're just jealous of Lexi, of who she is, of what she means to your world!"

"Jealous? No. It is because I know what she means to my world that I joined you. I have never hidden my feelings or my doubts about the two of you, but rather than stay behind and leave you to fail, I chose to join you and help in any way I can," Ari snapped back. "Did you really think I would sit aside and leave the fate of my home to the two of you? Two little children who know nothing about my home, my world? It is my family which suffered first-hand the consequences of fighting for our freedom. So do not for a minute think that I will keep quiet when there is something important to say."

"Enough!" shouted Lexi. "Can't you see what's happening? All this bickering is just weakening us and pulling us apart." She turned to Ari, "So you might not like us, okay you have made that clear before. But we have a mission, a common mission which we will only succeed in doing if we work together. You might think that we, that I, need to prove myself to you. Well, the fact that we are here, doing this together, should be good enough proof for you. We might not always see eye-to-eye, that is fine, but we must not let outside forces undermine our mission."

Tercel was watching it all, trapped and unable to move inside his invisible cage. "Clever girl. While it does not change what I've said, it does present you with an opportunity. You need me, so I propose that you set me free and I, in return, will help you."

"You have 'helped' enough, falcon," said Lexi. "So let me make it clear to you, since we can't risk you flying off to your master, you will remain confined where you are until we cross the river into Navara. Or you can try and make your own way through the labyrinth from within your cage. It is your choice."

"Well, since you put it that way, how can I refuse such a gracious invitation to join you all across the river," Tercel answered sarcastically. "But mark my words, you will set me free."

Lexi turned to Tercel. The furious look on her face said it all: "I have had enough of your poor attempts to undermine our mission.

You are right, it's time you contributed something positive to the conversation."

"Positive you say. Well, let me think. Hmmm, set me free and better your chances to live. Now how is that for positive?!" He had an odd look on his face, as if his beady eyes were smiling.

"So you like playing games," Lexi said, then she turned and looked at Ari. "Tighten the cage grip around him!"

Ari looked surprised "You do realise this will restrict his oxygen significantly!"

"Do it!" Lexi ordered.

Ari's hands started weaving the air around the falcon. He pulled them back towards himself tightening the invisible straps surrounding Tercel. The more he pulled the tighter the vacuum.

"Lexi," I shouted at her, "Stop!" But she ignored me.

Fixated on the falcon she yelled at Ari, "Tighter!"

Unable to move and with so little air to breath, we could see the spark in the falcon's eyes getting dimmer and dimmer.

"Enough!" she called, "Give him air."

"What were you doing? This is not like you!" I was furious with her.

"I will do whatever is necessary to get any information we need," she answered coldly.

"Necessary? You nearly killed him! Is that what you're turning into now, judge, jury and executioner?"

"This is war! In case you haven't realised it yet, Jimmy, we are about to cross the river into enemy territory. An enemy much more powerful than us." She turned and pointed at Tercel, "And he is withholding important information; he's playing games with us, taunting us!"

"But torture? Killing? I know you Lexi and you are better than that. You're smart, you'll find another way." Strangely, I felt as though I was pleading for her life, her soul.

"This is MY responsibility, my destiny." All of a sudden Lexi wasn't talking like Lexi.

"And you need our help to fulfil it. Don't forget Madam Giselle's words to us," I said. "'One pure of heart one soul mate together in the dark... But don't despair for you are strong, together not alone.' and you are not alone, we are here to help." I looked into her blue eyes and could see the cold frozen look there was starting to fade away, as if a cool mist was lifting from them.

Lexi lowered her head and spoke, almost in a whisper. "I don't know what happened, as if someone or something else took hold of me. I could feel the 'Eye' pressing harder and harder against my skin, sending freezing cold pulses throughout my body. The more vicious I became, the stronger the pulses. I wanted to stop but I couldn't. I could feel evil running through my veins."

"But how is it possible?" I asked, "I thought the 'Eye' was supposed to protect you."

"It must have reacted to something," Ari suddenly said, "like a trigger."

"Him!" I pointed at Tercel, "It must be him!"

"No, as much as I would love to blame it on him, I don't think it is." Lexi said, looking at the falcon, "I think Ari's right, it's reacting to where we are. A place. How far away are we from the Labyrinth?" she asked Ari.

"I am not sure. I have never been there before," he replied.

Lexi took off her backpack and got the map out, "Right, let's have a look and see. If my instincts are correct than we should be very near to the Labyrinth. I have a feeling that is what the 'Eye' reacted to and if that's the case, then it might get worse once we're there."

We gathered round the map, waiting for it to reveal our present location.

"Impossible!" I shouted.

But the map was clear, we were standing only a few meters away from the Labyrinth.

"How can it be? I mean, if we're that close to it, we should be able to see it from here."

"Jimmy's right," Lexi said "how come we can't see it?" She looked around for some glimpse of the Labyrinth.

"Do you think it's kind of like the Gwir, that you need to whisper something or do something to it?" I asked.

"I don't know, I never heard anything to suggest that, but I do think we should keep on going." Ari replied, "and we should also keep the map open, to guide us."

We doubled our pace, keeping one eye on the map while looking out for the Labyrinth. All this time the falcon remained very quiet, floating in his invisible cage next to Ari. I guess he was still shaken-up by what had happened to him earlier and he didn't want to draw any unnecessary attention to himself.

"We are here!" Lexi announced.

"Are you sure?" I asked, "because I still can't see anything."

"Well, unless the map is wrong, this is the place. The 'Labyrinth of Souls' is here." She pointed to our marked location on the map.

"We're practically on top of it, so why can't we see the Labyrinth?" I was confused.

Lexi slowly walked towards the riverbank and carefully looked into the gushing water of the Great River, then slowly turned around. "Ask Him!" she ordered, with an intense look directed at Tercel. Her eyes were completely black and her face was a pale white with dark blue veins drawn all over them.

I rushed towards her. "Stay!" she yelled at me, and I froze in my spot. I tried to move but I was pinned to the ground, all I could feel were cold waves going through my body.

"Lexi, No!" I shouted at her, "don't do it. You're better than that." She paid no attention to my words, or to me. I tried to move, but the coldness surrounding me started to freeze my body. First I lost the feeling in my toes, then my feet. Slowly, slowly, it crept up my body, turning it into ice.

"I'll help you!" I heard Ari's voice from behind me.

Lexi turned her head toward him, "Good!"

Ari started walking towards her. As he passed me he turned his head and softly blew some hot air in my direction. As soon as I felt the warm air on my face, the cold sensation drifted away, allowing the heat to take over and de-freeze my body.

Ari stood in front of Lexi, blocking her view of me. Being able to move again, I ran towards them as fast as I could and moved to grab Lexi from behind. She began twisting and turning, trying to break free. She was very strong; I felt my hold of her slipping away.

"She's getting free! Do it now!" I shouted at Ari.

He tore the pendant off her neck and threw it onto the ground.

A high-pitched shriek came out of Lexi's mouth, then darkness. The next thing I knew, Lexi was gone.

"LEXI!!!!" I shouted, looking around me. "What happened?"

"That shriek of hers was so loud, it must have knocked us both out for a few seconds" Ari replied.

"And Lexi, where is she?" I asked.

"I would suggest looking in the Labyrinth," said Tercel. "That is, if she's still alive."

Ari and I rushed towards the riverbank. "Lexi!! Lexi!" I shouted.

"I can't see a thing. Not Lexi or the Labyrinth!" said Ari.

"Hey, what's going on," I turned to Tercel, "where is it?!"

Tercel's eyes were glowing. "You can't see it from where you stand, you need to have a bird's-eye view for that! Set me free and I'll help you" he said.

"You must be joking," I told him.

"Do you really want to take that chance?" Tercel answered, "she doesn't have much time, if it's not too late already" he continued.

"Okay, but I swear, if you betray her..."

"You have my word" Tercel said.

Ari elevated Tercel's' invisible cage until it was floating just above his head. He closed his eyes, held both palms of his hands open under his chin, pointing slightly towards the Falcon, and blew into them. Then he closed them as if he was holding a small ball between them and tossed it at the cage. Tercel spread his wings, took to the air and vanished.

There was no time to try and catch him again if we wanted to save Lexi. Without thinking twice, Ari and I jumped into the gushing freezing water of the Great River. We were pulled under and towards some sort of a whirlpool. Trying to turn away from it, and following our air bubbles to the surface, we finally managed to get out and float on top. Once we could breathe fresh air again, we felt some movement from beneath us; something was happening under the water.

"You must hurry" Tercel called from above us, "The Labyrinth walls are starting to rise!"

Ari grabbed my arm and pulled me towards him, just before a great wall of water started to rise before us from within the river.

"Tercel, can you see Lexi?" I shouted at the Falcon.

"She's being pulled towards 'Black Pool Lake'" Tercel called again. "Quick, swim to your right. Stop! Now carry straight on for about fifty meters, then turn right again. Lexi is submerged under the water there. Hurry! Once the walls are fully erected you will be trapped between the dividing walls of the Labyrinth, the fate of your souls to be decided by the currents within the Labyrinth."

I was never a strong swimmer; growing up in a big city you don't get to spend much time at the beach. But that day I swam as I've never swum before. I was struggling to keep above the freezing cold water as the currents grew stronger, pulling me away from my course. I could see Ari's head somewhere in the far distance. I sure was glad one of us was a good swimmer and hoped he would get to Lexi before it was too late. Finally I reached the spot Tercel directed us to, but Ari wasn't there.

"Ari! Ari!" I called looking around me, but there was no sign of him or Lexi. "Tercel, can you see them?"

"The water is too wild there, the current too strong and my vision cannot penetrate under it" Tercel replied.

"No! no! this can't be it! LEXI! ARI!" I shouted, struggling to keep myself above the water.

"Jimmy, over here!" I suddenly heard Ari's voice. "I have her! Help me to pull her out."

As I reached him, Ari dived underwater and pushed Lexi up, out of the water. I grabbed hold of Lexi and pulled her closer to me. A moment later Ari joined us. He crossed his left arm over Lexi's upper-body and started swimming with her towards the riverbank. The Labyrinth walls were closing in on us as we began to swim out and away from them as fast as we could. I could just about make-out the contours of the riverbank, but my arms failed to pull me forward. I looked up to the sky but Tercel was gone again; he probably took off as soon as we found Lexi and by now was likely well on his way towards the 'White Fortress' to tell Naval of where we were. By now I could now feel my body slipping under the water, and had lost sight of Ari and Lexi.

Darkness

"JIMMY!!! ARI!!! Are you there? Can you hear me? I can't see a thing. It's so cold! Where am I? JIMMY....?! ARI.....?!"

Nomads

"Foolish kids. What were you thinking!"

I slowly opened my eyes, but even though my vision was still a bit blurry, I could recognise that grumpy voice anywhere. I wiped my eyes and smiled, "Am I glad to see you, Annak!"

He grabbed my hand and pulled me up on my feet. "Lexi and Ari?" I asked him.

"By the fire" he replied, keeping it short as usual.

I looked to my left and saw Ari and Lexi, wrapped in thick sheepskins, sitting in front of a big bonfire. I started running towards them when suddenly I realised, we were not alone. There was a large hog being roasted, close to where Lexi and Ari sat, and about twenty or so people scattered around three other bonfires. Some were engaged in conversations, others just warming up by the fire with a drink in their hand. Nine large, beautifully decorated, wooden wagons stood only a few meters away from us, creating a sort of protective border around the camp.

"Jimmy!" I heard Lexi calling me. She dropped the sheepskin wrapped around her and ran towards me. "I'm so happy you're okay." She hugged me; "You really had me worried there for a moment."

"Me? What about you? One minute you turned into this scary thing and the next you're in the water, pulled by the Labyrinth toward Black Lake." I answered her, then turned to Ari to ask, "What triggered the 'Labyrinth'? How did Annak get here? And who are all these people?" I badly needed to know what had happened while I was unconscious.

We sat down in front of the fire, huddling together so that no one would overhear us.

"I can only answer a few of your questions" said Ari, "as for the rest, we can only speculate."

"Go on," I said.

"This is what I think happened: The Labyrinth of Souls must have triggered something in the 'Eye of Truth'. It, in return, brought out the dark side in Lexi's soul, which explains her strange behaviour as we got closer and closer to the Labyrinth." Ari paused, looking at Lexi.

"We assumed that as we are young our souls are pure, therefore, we will be safe to cross the Great River without triggering the Labyrinth of Souls," I continued his train of thought.

"Exactly," he went on, "only we did not know two very important factors. One, that there must be a very dark side to Lexi's soul for it to take over her in such force and viciousness. Something even she was not aware of. The second thing is that the 'Eye of Truth' must have realised that, and as a result brought it out to the surface, trying to warn us before we got into the river."

"I don't think so," I cut him off. "Whatever it was, its hold over Lexi was so strong that the only thing that managed to cut the connection between 'Dark' Lexi and the pendant was to physically tear it from her neck."

"Hmmm, good point," Ari said.

"And how did she end up in the water? After all we were unconscious when it happened," I added.

Ari and I turned to Lexi, hoping she could fill-in the blanks.

"I'm really sorry," she said, "But I don't remember what happened. By the time I came back, I was in the freezing water of the Great

River, struggling to keep above water. I could feel my soul being dragged out and away from me, as my body was sinking deeper and deeper. And then, out of nowhere, someone grabbed me and pulled me back up. The closer we got to the surface, the stronger I felt my soul returning. I could feel it coming back, settling slowly inside me. And then I saw Ari. He was dragging me up with him while he tried to swim in that freezing gushing water and reach the riverbank. By the time I was fully conscious and reunited with my soul, we had reached the riverbank and I was pulled out by a group of men led by Annak."

"We still don't know what exactly triggered the 'Labyrinth.'" Ari said.

"On the other hand," I said, "we do know it lies underwater, is made of pure water, and that it rises slowly from beneath you while trying to trap you in."

Lexi was very quiet, staring at the ground, as if she hoped it would open up and swallow her in.

"We were very lucky this time." Ari said quietly, as if he was making a remark to himself.

Ari was right of course; he did warn us about it, but I chose to back Lexi up when she suggested we cross the river. I should have been more open and listened to his advice, paid attention to my own gut feeling, rather than blindly follow Lexi. As close as we are, she does tend to be overwhelming with her self-confidence, so it is very easy to believe she is always right and has all the answers.

Suddenly and quite unexpectedly a voice behind us called out, "Well, I see the final face of the triangle has finally joined us at last."

We all turned to see who was speaking. Two dark figures were making their way towards us. One of them was Annak, he was easily recognisable, but the other figure was harder to make out as they were still walking in the shadows. At first glance, and from a distance, he appeared to be a very impressive man. But it wasn't until the two of them stood close to the bonfire that we saw him clearly.

He was quite tall, with broad shoulders and an athletic body build. His hair was long, straight, and dark blue, his eyes were pale blue-grey, and as he stretched his arm out to shake hands with us, I could see a thick leather band, with colourful tassels running along its side, covering his right arm.

"Jeseppe Manuel Azzurro Palermo El Nómada," he declared with a smile, "but please, call me Azzurro."

Lexi was the first to stand up and shake his hand. "Very pleased to meet you, I'm Lexi."

"Nice firm handshake you have there," replied Azzurro, looking straight into Lexi's eyes.

"I'm Jimmy." I hurried to follow Lexi's lead.

"And you must be Ari, Mikaela's son." Azzurro turned to face Ari, "You look just like your father."

Ari just stood there, not moving a muscle, starring at Azzurro.

"Don't look so surprised, my lad, I've known your parents for a long time. Your father was as close to me as kin. He was a good, honourable man, as brave as they come, and when I got word of his fate I cried over him as if he was my own brother," said Azzurro, stepping forward to grab hold of Ari and hug him tightly to his chest, before gently letting go of him. "It is good to finally meet you all: we've been looking forward to this day for a very long time."

"Azzurro," Ari finally spoke, "I have heard of you; you are Chief of the Nomads, the head of the Travellers Resistance. My mother told me about your people. They are artists and performers, travelling between the five kingdoms. You gain access to all places, meet lords and commoners with no restrictions or limitations, and because you can travel more freely than others all over the different kingdoms, you are the perfect 'eyes and ears' for the resistance. But how did you know where to find us? We didn't come across any Nomads on our way."

"We have many allies in many places, ready to help us. In fact, we have been keeping a watchful eye on you for a very long time." Azzurro was looking directly at Lexi as he said that.

"Wait, did you say Palermo?!" I asked

"Yes, Palermo was my mothers' maiden name," he replied.

I looked at Lexi, full of excitement, then turned back to Azzurro: "Do you know a Tony Palermo?"

"I know many men by this name, it is a very common name amongst my people."

"Yes, but I'm asking about a BOY called Tony Palermo. He's about my age and he lives..." I paused for a second, "in my world."

"But surely that would be impossible," Azzurro replied. "How could I possibly know someone from your world?" He smiled at Lexi and his blue eyes sparkled.

"But you said you have allies everywhere, didn't you?" I looked at Lexi. The expression on her face was one of shock and surprise. "That's it! It's the only explanation," I continued "Tony knew the truth about Lexi and that's why he dared her to go and see Madam Giselle. They were all in on it from the beginning. It was all meant to happen, planned from.... well from the day you were born!" I grabbed Lexi's hand and shook it, trying to snap her out the state of shock she clearly was in. "It must have been them that informed you of our arrival here, that is the only way Ari and his mom could have known we were coming."

"Is that true?" Lexi finally said. "Do you have Nomads in my world? Spying on me? Am I just a pawn for you to move about however you want?!" Lexi looked at Azzurro, then Annak, and lastly at Ari. The disillusion and disappointment on her face, in her eyes, was unbearable to see, and all three men turned away from her look.

"I'm sorry you feel that way," Annak broke the silence, "but you were not meant to discover it. What we did, and all that we do, is in order to save and protect you. You must believe me when I tell you that you are the single most important reason we are all here. We swore to protect and serve you as best we can; our lives, our world, everything is in your hands. When you are willing to give up your life for the greater good, for the chance of living a peaceful, loving life in the light, rather than be afraid and oppressed in the dark, you will do anything to protect that flame of hope, even if it sometimes means not disclosing the whole truth." He placed his hand on her shoulder and looked into her eyes, "Trust me, it's for your own protection that you do not know everything."

After a moment of silence, Azzurro spoke; "We've always kept a watchful eye on you, but only that. We made it clear to everyone not to intervene, or interfere in your other life, except when instructed otherwise or if you were facing grave danger. You have also been under our surveillance and protection here since your arrival to our world, and even more closely since the three of you left the Tavern. That is, until we somehow lost sight of you when you vanished shortly after leaving the Gwir." Suddenly Azzurro stretched his long arm out and whistled. A moment later we heard a great wing-clap as a white silver spotted Gyrfalcon came flying down towards Azzurro's outstretched arm, and landed there softly.

"So we meet again!" said the falcon.

" YOU!!!" I shouted.

"Indeed" replied Tercel.

"But how is it possible? You answer to Naval, your master!" Lexi accused him.

"If my memory serves me right, what I said when you caught me was that my master will be very happy to know what I have found; but I never told you who he was. You assumed it was Naval because I'm a sentinel in his falconry guard. But we are not all as loyal to him as he would think: some of us would like nothing more than to be free of his rule, just be free again to fly and soar as we wish, free as we were intended to be." said Tercel.

"Yes, but..." Lexi began to say.

"But why didn't I tell you all that when you caught me? My dear, you hardly expect me to give up my cover story, now do you? Just trust that you are never alone in your quest and that help is always at hand." He lowered his head as if to bow to Lexi, then flew from

Azzurro's arm and up towards the star-studded sky.

"Please forgive my winged friend, despite his appearance he prefers soaring in the skies than engaging in conversation, unless he absolutely needs to" said Azzurro.

"I feel so bad for the way we treated him, but how could we have known?" I said. "As far as we were concerned he was spying for Naval and we had to do all that we could to protect ourselves."

"Yes," said Lexi, "That was wrong of us, but it had to be done."

"She's right," agreed Ari, "There was nothing else we could do at the time. We did what we had to do."

"No need to apologise, you did the right thing and Tercel knows it." Azzurro added.

"Come to think of it," I remembered suddenly, and turned to Lexi, "there was something you said when we first saw Tercel that could have helped us."

"What do you mean, Jimmy?" Lexi looked at me.

"Remember what you felt through the 'Eye'? You said it was a mix of hot and cold sensations."

"So…?" she asked.

"Well, since you first felt the warmth on your skin and the cold chills were weaker in sensation than the heat, I think that the 'Eye' was indicating to you that there is a good force near you. The cold chills could be linked to the fact that Tercel was, initially, under Naval's command." I felt excited at perhaps being able to decipher one of the enigmas surrounding the 'Eye of Truth'.

"That's very interesting" Lexi replied. "The 'Eye' is a lot more complex than I first thought. The sooner we understand how it fully works, the better our chances at beating Naval." She smiled.

Friends and Enemies

It was getting very late at night, but the excitement over the revelation of another way by which the 'Eye of Truth' could communicate with us all, through Lexi, filled us with new-found energy. We wanted nothing more than to try and understand what else the 'Eye' may have tried to convey to us. It seemed that Lexi was no longer interested in Tony Palermo, the Nomads being in our world, or how it all came about that we had ended up here. She was now most eager to decipher all the mystery of the 'Eye of Truth' and there was no stopping her until that was done.

"Please follow me," commanded Azzurro, as he started walking towards one of the wagons.

We followed him inside. It was much bigger and spacious than it looked from the outside. The interior of the wagon was covered in mahogany, delicately carved and decorated with golden drawings. A pair of closed cut-glass doors were at the far end of the wagon, directly opposite the entrance, hiding Azzurro's sleeping compartment. Two small windows, partially covered with heavy velvet curtains, were on the wall to the right of us. Below them stood a leather seater with some storage compartments underneath it and a small coffee table standing in front of it. On the opposite wall, in a small niche, stood a copper stove and oven, framed by a shelving unit full of old leather-bound books. A beautiful stained-glass lamp hung from the ceiling, lighting up the place with a warm inviting glow.

"Welcome to my home," Azzurro smiled as he turned to the small coffee table, lifted its top surface and took three folded stools out of it. "Please sit down, I'll have some hot tea for us in no time," he continued, as he put the kettle on the stove.

We sat down quietly, watching Azzurro brewing some Louiza tea. Once the tea was ready, he bent down in front of the cupboards under the leather seater and took out beautifully decorated glass cups for all of us. He swiftly raised and lowered the teapot while pouring the light-green liquid into our cups. It was mesmerising to watch.

"Now, I believe you have some questions for me, for us" Azzurro said.

Ari was the first to ask, turning to Annak, "From what Azzurro told us outside, it was Tercel who alerted him to our whereabouts. But exactly how did you find us?"

"Your Aunt," Annak grunted quietly under his dark beard. "She had sent word to your mother, and mentioned you stopped by on your way north, to release your falcon."

"I should have known my mother would figure it out." Ari smiled in embarrassment.

"Yes, you should!" Annak agreed.

Azzurro laughed out loud. "Good old Mikaela, she is definitely a force to reckon with. There isn't much that gets by her unnoticed. She is as sharp as they come."

"And how did you two meet up together?" Lexi asked.

"As soon as Mikaela realised which way you were heading, she sent word to Azzurro," Annak answered. "By the time I caught up with the Nomads, they'd already been alerted by Tercel as to your whereabouts."

"And a good thing Tercel got to us on time. If we hadn't arrived to pull you out from the Labyrinth, when we did, you probably would have frozen to death in the icy water," Azzurro continued.

The three of us exchanged looks, not saying a word. Our guilty conscience was showing itself all over our faces.

"So what now?" Lexi asked, before taking a sip from her tea. As soon as her lips touched the green liquid she made a hissing noise as she inhaled some air, and her head twisted slightly, then she dropped the cup on the floor, spilling the tea everywhere.

"Are you okay?" I turned and looked at her

"Yes, fine, the tea was a bit too hot that's all. I'm sorry I made such a mess," she replied.

"Not to worry," said Azzurro. "I'm sure it was," he added, and smiled at her.

After we cleaned the spilt tea we once again sat down around the small coffee table. Annak picked up the conversation, "There is a good reason why no one tries to cross the Great River through the Labyrinth of Souls, not even Naval himself. Your reckless actions may have cost us all the element of surprise. There are unknown forces at work there, beneath the water, no one has ever come out alive. They all ended up in Black Pool Lake, forever condemned to repeat their mistakes, only to feel the sorrow and hurt in their lives and to have their hopes and dreams crushed over and over again. Seeing the light but never to touch it, never cross it, never purify their souls in it."

"But we did. We survived it." I said.

"Barely survived." Annak raised his voice, "You were very lucky. Lucky to have Tercel get to the Nomads on time; lucky Mikaela got your aunt's note; and most of all, lucky you all stayed together." He was so angry at us, so upset, that the scar on his face was pulsing. "That is why…"

"That is why, my young friends," Azzurro cut in, "it has been decided that we will join you. Just to make sure you are not tempted to do something rash again." He winked at us.

"Decided by who?!" Lexi snapped.

"By the Council of Truth" Azzurro said, in a very sharp tone of voice. "We were directed by them quite soon after we found you."

"No! I'm not a little child you can order around" Ari protested.

"Oh, but you are" Annak said. "It was a mistake to let you go, just the three of you, on your own, and that is why we shall accompany you now."

"Ari's right" I said, "it's not his fault; the reason we got into this mess is because we didn't listen to him. Ari tried to talk us out of it, explain about the danger of crossing the Labyrinth, but we disregarded his warnings. We thought we knew better, and if Ari hadn't joined us we probably would have died."

"What's done is done," said Annak. "You have been given a second chance and we will help make sure you do not waste it."

The three of us exchanged looks, then turned to Annak and silently, without any words, we nodded our heads as if to say, "Okay, we agree."

"That settles it then." Azzurro clapped his hands together as if to seal the agreement. "Let's continue from where we left off before. Is there anything else you wish to ask?"

"Why now?" Lexi asked.

"Yes. Why is all this happening now?" I repeated her question. "I mean, Mikaela told us that you were waiting for Lexi to turn eighteen before telling her the truth about herself, so what changed it?"

Both Lexi and I looked straight at Azzurro, hoping to finally get the whole story.

"We simply ran out of time" Azzurro replied.

"What do you mean?" Lexi asked.

"We discovered that Naval..." Azzurro stopped and turned to Annak.

"Tell them" said Annak.

Azzurro's look was very intense and serious now; "Naval discovered that we could move between our world and yours. We think he doesn't know yet how to do it himself, but he is very well aware of it being possible."

Lexi was horrified, "But how do you know that?"

"Your father told us," said Azzurro, looking at Ari, "he was tracking a small company of Naval's elite guard when he overheard them talking about 'The Rift.'"

"My Father? When?" Ari's astonishment was clear in his voice.

"It was shortly before he was captured," replied Azzurro. "Once we knew from him what Naval was after, it was quite obvious time was working against us. It was no longer just about the future of Terah that was at stake; the implications of Naval knowing the whereabouts of 'The Rift' would be disastrous to both our worlds. We could no longer wait for you to turn eighteen before telling you the truth. You had to come back to Terah."

"And the map my father had, how did it end-up with Lexi and Jimmy?" Ari asked.

"Ahh, the map," Azzurro paused, then poured some more tea into our cups, "at that time the map was with the Nomads."

"The Nomads?" I asked.

"Yes, the Nomads." Azzurro smiled at me, "As its creators, we are also the guardians of the map."

"You're what?!" Lexi nearly jumped off her seat.

"Let's just say that some of our artistic abilities have more to them than simply being hung on a wall to be admired. But we shall get back to that later on." He left it at that, and continued to explain how Lexi and I ended-up with the map. "So your father informed the Council about his discovery and they all agreed it was time to bring Lexi back to Terah. They sent your father to fetch the map from us and take it to Lexi, but as we know, he was intercepted by Naval's elite guard. Luckily for us he managed to hide it before being captured. It was Tercel who informed us of his capture and the whereabouts of the map."

"Tercel?" Ari asked.

"Yes" replied Azzurro, "you didn't think we would entrust such a powerful artefact in someone's hands without making sure it is protected? Tercel watched over your father from above, and a fortunate thing it was as Tercel was the one who warned him about the guards. Unfortunately, due to the density of the trees in the forest, by the time Tercel spotted them closing in on your father, all that your father could do was to hide the map before getting captured."

Ari's eyes were tearing up and his face went red with rage, "He was there?! He saw it all?! Why didn't he follow them, see where they took my father? He could have saved him!!!"

Azzurro stretched his long arm across the small coffee table and placed it gently on Ari's shoulder. "Your father was a brave man, he knew the high risks involved in what he did and yet he volunteered to do it. He believed in our cause, in a better future for us, for Terah, and most of all for you, his beloved son whom he loved more than anything. He was willing to give his own life for you, so that one day you would be free. As for Tercel, he did the right thing, he did what was expected of him and your father would have been pleased to know he fulfilled his mission."

Ari silently nodded his head then turned and looked at Lexi, "Yes he did, he brought you here." His voice was full of pride.

"What happened next?" Lexi asked Azzurro.

"The news about Ari's father was devastating, but we could not give up. We had the map, and one of my people was entrusted with the responsibility of getting it to you. He was told where to find my sister, who was amongst the nomads in your world and give her the map, together with the Council's instructions. She had to make sure that you would pay a visit to Giselle before receiving the map, and used her son Tony as a way to get you there. Once you had spoken to Giselle and she placed the 'Eye of Truth' safely in your hands, my sister could then pass the map on to you. It was very important for you to believe that it all this happened by chance. That is, until you arrived here on Terah, where you would learn the truth about yourself," Azzurro explained.

"You took a big chance on us. How could you be sure we would come here?" Lexi raised a valid point.

"After all," I added, "when we got the map it came without any instructions as to how it works. I mean, it was only because I touched Lexi's pendant that we ended-up here, in the middle of the meadow."

"We couldn't risk putting any instructions together with the map, in case it fell into the wrong hands. In any case you didn't need any, because you already possessed the important two main elements that would bring you to Terah." Azzurro's eyes had a mischievous sparkle in them.

Lexi and I exchanged quick looks between us, "The 'Eye of Truth' and the map!!" We said together full of excitement.

"Bravo!" Azzurro clapped his hands.

"But how do they work?" asked Lexi.

"Very simple," Azzurro explained, "the map is the gateway, the pendant with the Aquamarine in the middle of the 'Eye of Truth' is the key. You need both artefacts to open the gateway back to Terah. That is why we never kept them together, and that is why none of those who were sent to your world could ever come back."

"So as long as I have both I can move between our worlds?" Lexi said. Her voice sounded almost as if she was talking in some sort of a trance, her eyes fixed on something invisible in the air.

"We," I corrected her, while still trying to figure out the strange look on her face.

"We, yes, of course I meant we." she said in her normal voice, smiling at me.

"I am sorry to shatter your plans, but it seems that we have lost the map," said Ari.

"We've what?!" I couldn't believe it. "How?"

"My guess is that we lost it sometime between losing our consciousness and following Lexi into the 'Great River,'" he answered.

"Not lost," said Azzurro, in a mysterious tone of voice, which immediately changed the mood around the small coffee table, "just misplaced." He stood up and walked towards the bookcase above the stove. He then pulled out a very old, thin book, and came back to the table.

He opened the book and inside, safely beneath the cover, was the map. We couldn't believe our eyes. Lexi couldn't contain herself, she immediately stood up and stretched her arm forward, trying to get hold of it.

"Just one minute there," Azzurro said, "I'm not sure we can trust you with it again," he added, then folded the map carefully back into its cover.

" GIVE IT TO ME!" Lexi practically jumped off her chair as she tried to grab it from his hands.

"LEXI!" I pulled her back into her seat, "What's got into you? Can't you see he's only joking?"

Lexi calmed down and relaxed back into her chair, then looked at the four of us. "Sorry" she said, "I guess I'm still a bit stressed after all that happened today." She closed her eyes and added, "It's getting late; I'm tired."

"Apology accepted." Azzurro looked closely into her eyes, "I believe you are right, it is getting late and you three have had a long day."

Just then the caravan door opened and the most beautiful creature I had ever seen stepped inside. She was tall and slim, wearing a long traditional dress, all hand embroidered. She had green eyes with long lashes, dark skin and red cherry lips. Her magnificent flowing hair, full of striking red and deep amber locks, all twisted and curled together, made me feel as if I were staring into a live flame. My heart was leaping in my chest. I couldn't breathe.

"My friends," Azzurro said, "allow me to introduce to you my niece, Soulange."

Ari immediately stood up, and by the look on his face I could tell he felt the same as I did.

"Really Azzurro," she said in the sweetest voice I had ever heard, "why so formal? Just call me Soul," and she beamed as she smiled at us.

"Right then, if you don't mind Lexi, you will share Soul's caravan on our journey, and you two boys will share Annak's. And now, I suggest we should retire for the night and start fresh in the morning." Azzurro politely pointed to the door.

"What about my map?" Lexi asked.

"It will remain with me, for now," replied Azzurro. "We can talk about it in the morning."

Lexi didn't seem very happy about it, but I guess like us she was too tired to argue. We left Azzurro's caravan and each of us made our way to our own. As I lay down on my narrow bed, exhausted after a long day and all that had happened, I couldn't stop thinking of Soul. For the first time since we arrived on this strange world called Terah, I finally fell asleep with a smile on my face.

Darkness continues

"Help me, please! I can't move....! I can't see....! It's so cold and wet. What is this place? Where am I? Jimmy!! Ari!! Can you hear me? Please....!!! Anyone.....help me!

The Map

I woke up to the smell of freshly brewed coffee. Ari, wrapped up in his quilted blanket, was still fast asleep in his bunk, and Annak was standing over the small stove cooking breakfast. The top half of the caravan door was wide open and the cool, crisp air coming in from outside felt rejuvenating and cleansing. I was full of energy and felt a lot more confidant in the task at hand, knowing we no longer had to go it alone. I got up from my bed and put on my clothes. Outside were the voices of people greeting each other at the start of a new day; then I heard it, that sweet, soft voice, singing in such grace, welcoming the morning. It was as if Soul's voice alone was entrusted with the delicate task of summoning the sun to rise. And what a beautiful sunrise it was. As the sun slowly ascended against the deep blue backdrop of the morning sky, it looked as if it was crowning the new day with its magnetic golden beams, breaking through the feathery white clouds. I was completely and utterly mesmerised by it all. My heart was about to leap out of my chest as my legs followed Soul's singing across the small caravan, towards the open door and outside. I couldn't control myself. I was drawn to her. I felt my day could not start unless I saw her, talked to her.

"Breakfast?" Annak's deep husky voice drew the curtains down on my beautiful morning outside.

I was instantly pulled back into the caravan, back to my place by the door. "Yes please," I answered Annak, my tummy confirming my hunger as it rumbled loudly.

"Good. Sit." He gestured at the small table in the middle of the caravan.

"Thanks" I said. "Shouldn't we wake him up as well?" I added, looking at Ari, all snuggled up in his cosy bunk.

"Huh" grunted Annak, then in one quick movement pulled the blanket off Ari and dropped it on the floor beside his bunk.

"What?! Where?! Who?!" Ari muttered, half asleep, as he struggled to find his warm blanket.

"Morning!" I said.

"Is that fresh coffee I smell?" Ari asked as he quickly got up from his bunk, threw on his shirt and pulled up his trousers.

"Yep! And fried eggs to go with it" I answered.

The three of us sat around the small table enjoying Annak's breakfast, when a voice greeted us from outside.

"Morning, are you all decent in there?" Lexi joked.

"Sure," I replied "and we have breakfast: you are welcome to join us."

Lexi swung open the bottom half of the caravan's door and stepped inside. "Wow!" she said, looking around, "that is some display of weaponry you have here."

It wasn't until then that I noticed the interior walls of Annak's caravan were covered with weapons.

"You brought them all with you?" I asked Annak.

"No" he replied, "only the ones I thought will come in handy."

"How many more do you have?" Lexi asked, amazed.

"At least twice the amount you see here on the walls," I quickly answered, looking at her a bit puzzled, "don't you remember his cellar at the tavern?!"

"Um… sure I do." She hesitated a moment then added, "I only meant, how many are there altogether, just out of curiosity."

"Enough for you to train with." Annak abruptly ended the questioning, taking a long, loud sip from his steaming coffee.

"Do you mind if I pour myself a cup of coffee? It smells delicious," Lexi asked, as she took a mug from the small kitchen cabinet above the stove.

"But you never drink coffee!" I exclaimed in surprise.

"Only when it's freshly brewed. I mean, how can anyone resist the taste of strong, sweet, black coffee in the morning? It's just what the body needs to get going." She looked at me with the same strange look on her face from last night.

I was about to get up and walk towards her when, "Good, you are all awake."

Azzurro's voice came from the opened door, "Why don't you all join me at my caravan after you have finished your breakfast?"

"Very well" answered Lexi, and she poured herself some coffee.

"Here, you can have my seat" I offered Lexi, "I've finished my breakfast."

As she came closer to me, I felt a chill coming from her direction. I got up from my seat and grabbed Lexi's hand, "You're freezing! You feeling okay?"

She paused in her spot; "Another cup of hot coffee and I'll have this body ready to go."

"Another cup of Annak's coffee?!? I wouldn't do that, his coffee can wake-up the dead." Ari joked, but something about what he said stuck in my head.

We finished our breakfast and made our way to Azzurro's caravan. On the small coffee table lay a few antique-looking books, stacked one on top of each other. I turned to look at Lexi, her eyes were wide open and fixated on a small book at the top of the pile. As we sat down around the table I realised what it was she was looking at. The book with our map inside beneath its beautiful leather-bound cover. Lexi could barely stop herself from grabbing it. She had to sit on her hands in order to contain her excitement. Her legs were tapping fast against the floorboards, sending gentle vibration throughout the caravan.

"I warned you not to have another cup of coffee." Ari's voice broke my concentration. "You'll be shaking all day now," he laughed.

"Not to worry, a nice warm cup of Louiza tea will soon fix that" Azzurro said, and smiled at Lexi as he got up from his chair.

"No! no tea for me. I'll soon be fine. I'm sure." She held his hand, stopping him from leaving the table.

"In that case," he sat back down, "let us begin," and he opened the map, laying it gently on the coffee table in front of us.

"After the death of Zarah, Terah plunged into darkness. Naval forbade any moving or crossing between the five kingdoms. People are allowed to travel freely within the borders of their own native lands, but risk crossing to a neighbouring kingdom and face a gruesome death, for yourself and your kin. You see, reducing the movement between places makes it harder for people to meet and conspire against Naval. And to be sure that no one will try and disobey his orders at night, Naval created the 'Night Snatchers'"

"Who are they?" I asked.

"Not who, but what," Ari replied.

"Vicious creatures." Azzurro said. "The 'Night Snatchers' are a hybrid of creatures. They are very fast, four-legged beasts with thick black, impenetrable wrinkled-skin; their claws are so sharp, they can tear through anything in minutes and once they have stuck their claws deep into your flesh, they will never let go. The end of their long tail is a razor-sharp tip, that can slash open anyone or anything trying to get near. Their jaws can stretch open as much as they need in order to wrap them around their victims, and inside their mouth there are double rows of needle-sharp teeth. They use the external row of teeth to hold and chew through their victims, while the inner row is used to inject venom that will paralyse the victim, and later on help smash their smaller bones, before grinding them into dust. As for their eyes," Azzurro paused for a second, a look of horror appearing in his eyes, "if you see two bright luminous lights, glowing in the darkness of night, then it is too late. They will snatch you long before you are able to exhale your last breath."

"Charming." I said, "I guess we're lucky we never came across them."

"As night creatures, you will never see them in daylight," said Ari, "and as long as you have some source of light with you at night, they will not dare come near you."

"Why?" I asked.

"Because of their eyes. They are very sensitive to light," he answered. "Also, they only go where Naval sends them, so you can never be sure where to find them. They are impossible to track down at night and they sometimes hide between the thick, lower, branches of trees. During the day they dig underground tunnels which allows them to move around unseen." Azzurro took lead of the conversation again, "So as you see, no one would dare leave the safety of their homes and venture outside into the darkness."

"What about the Nomads? I mean you seem to move around freely," I asked him.

"As Nomads we have no land to call our own. In addition, we provide a variety of services that are unique to us and cannot be obtained any other way. There is also another reason, one that created a contradiction to Naval's decree, the Nomads bloodline."

"Your bloodline?" I wondered.

Azzurro explained, "You see, over the generations the inevitable happened. 'Everlasting Bonds' were celebrated between Nomad and 'Permanent' folk across the five kingdoms. As it is not in our nature to stay put in one place for too long, the newlywed spouse would join the Nomads. Once the bloodlines were joined, it was hard for Naval to keep track of the offspring of those unions, as they have direct connection with both Nomads as well as 'Permanents'. That is why Naval granted free passage to the Nomads."

"How is all that connected to the map?" I was confused.

"Well, with blood relations spread across the five kingdoms, as well as our being the only ones able to travel freely between them, we were able to gather important information about Naval's activities from our relations. However, in order to establish a strong underground resistance, we needed something to help us travel safely. In order to do that, our elders came up with a simple yet brilliant solution; using our unique artistic abilities, they created a map that can show you, at any given time, a true and accurate visual representation of Terah."

Lexi's look was fixated on the map, "Such a powerful weapon and right under the watchful eye of Naval."

"As I said, we needed a device that will ensure our safety while travelling around. By viewing a place in advance on the map, we were able to achieve that. We managed to avoid or better prepare for harsh weather conditions, make quick diversions on route to avoid unexpected problems and learn about the type of villages and the people there as we moved around." Azzurro was running his fingers quickly across the hologram, zooming in and out of places, demonstrating some of the abilities of the map we already had discovered on our own. "But most importantly," he now looked up at Lexi, "we could guide the 'Chosen One' to safety, in if one day she was to return to Terah." Azzurro then held out the palm of his hand open above the map, "Now, may I please have the 'Eye of Truth.'"

Lexi open her eyes in total surprise. "It's here!!" she said and frantically looked around.

"We don't have it," Ari said "We lost it."

"LOST IT?!" Lexi yelled at him, "How could you! What good is the map now, without the pendant?"

"Wait, when?" I couldn't believe it. "I remember Ari tearing it off Lexi's neck and tossing it to the ground before we lost consciousness, back at the Labyrinth of Souls. It must still be there somewhere, we just need to go back and look for it."

Ari silently shook his head, confirming his news about the loss of the 'Eye'.

"The pendant please," Azzurro asked again.

Did he not understand what Ari just said? What wasn't clear enough, with 'it is lost'?

Annak stood up, slowly let a thin silver chain drop into Azzurro's open palm, then sat back down in his chair. Bewildered Ari, Lexi and I stared at the silver pendant now resting in his hand.

"The 'Eye of Truth'!" Lexi could barely contain her excitement.

"But how...?" Ari's look moved rapidly between the pendant, Azzurro and Annak.

"Actually it was Tercel who spotted it," Azzurro said. "From his vantage spot above us, and with his sharp vision, he saw the blue sparkle of the aquamarine crystal in the middle of the 'Eye' and directed us to it. It was lying in the deep grass, on the riverbank close to where we had found the three of you. Luckily, it was us that found them both, the 'Eye' and the Map. The consequences of what will happen if Naval gets his hands on both artefacts, knowing that he is looking for 'The Rift'..." Azzurro closed his hand and sat back down. "Lucky," he added quietly, as if he had just had a glimpse of the alternative outcome if indeed Naval would have found the 'Eye of Truth' and the Map.

Azzurro gently placed the pendant on top of the four-point compass at the bottom of the Map. The hologram of Terah floated above the map and between them eight new symbols appeared, floating above the pendant. The strongest shape was of four arrows in a cross-like formation ⤰ .

An additional four triangles, floated nearby. Two of them, had a short line across the tip of the triangle, but one pointed up △ and the other pointed down ▽ in opposite directions of each other. The other two triangles were pointing towards the same directions as the first ones, only they did not have any markings on them △▽.

"Now, point and touch a place on the map," Azzurro said.

Ari zoomed into the hologram, then pointed at 'Stronghold', his home village. The four arrows started rotating left and right in their spot until finally they stopped. One of the arrows, now slightly bigger than the rest pointed southwest, towards 'Stronghold'.

"Compass. It's a compass!" I said, full of excitement

"Indeed it is" confirmed Azzurro. "All you need to do is point to any place on the Map and the arrows on the 'Eye' will show you the way there. He then touched the White Fortress of Navara, Naval's stronghold in the north. Once again the four arrows started rotating in their spot, trying to get their new bearings until they stopped and the North arrow pointed towards Navara.

"What about those things?" I pointed at the other four symbols floating above the 'Eye'.

"I believe they symbolise four of the five elements of life." Ari said and continued, "The triangle pointing up, with the short line going through it near its point is the symbol of Earth. The one opposite it, pointing down, with the short line going through it near its point is the symbol of Air. The next one below it pointing up but without the line in the symbol of Fire and the last one, pointing down without a line, opposite 'Fire' and below 'Earth' symbolises the element of Water." Here Ari stopped his explanation, saying "What I do not understand is how this is connected to the map?"

Azzurro tightly zoomed in on the Meadow of Peace, which was hiding behind thick clouds. Using his index finger he traced the symbol of Air ▽ above the Meadow of Peace. Instantly a light breeze came through the top branches of the forest trees and gently cleared away the clouds. A few minutes later the Meadow of Peace was visible to view. Next Azzurro zoomed in on the Great Sea of Woxion, the fourth kingdom in the west. The turquoise and emerald waters were so still we could clearly see hundreds of colourful fish in different shapes and sizes, swimming around, oblivious to what was about to happen. Once again Azzurro traced a symbol above the calm sea, this time it was the symbol for Earth △.

Almost at once, small ripples appeared on top of the still surface of the sea; they soon grew bigger and wider as the ground beneath the water started to shake. The beautiful blue-green water was now changing into brown as suddenly, from beneath the gushing waves, a plot of land surfaced. He created land in the middle of the Great Sea of Woxion, an island.

"Impossible!!" Lexi stared at the newly-created land.

"You cannot do this!" Ari protested, "you are meddling with things beyond your control. You are abusing our sacred bond with the gentle fabric of life itself! You have no idea of the repercussions of doing that. If the Galyan's elders were to know of this….." Ari was furious.

Azzurro calmly removed the pendant from the Map and placed it gently inside a small velvet pouch. He then turned to Ari and said, "Spoken as a true Galyan. Please rest assured that we will never do anything to compromise the sacred bond with the 'Eather of Life'. What I have just shown you, what we have created, I would not have been able to do without the help and guidance of the Galyan elders."

"They are a part of this?" Ari asked. He couldn't believe what he had just heard.

Azzurro went on to explain, "When Lexi was born, the newly formed Council of Truth realised that in order to give Lexi some advantage over Naval and his evil powers, they would need to create more than just a powerful pendant to protect her. So the Council, with the help of the Galyan elders, added new symbols to the original 'Eye of Truth' and linked some of them to the Nomads' Map."

"What about the other two symbols? Which elements do they belong to, and what can you do with them?" Lexi seemed very anxious to learn more about it.

"Well, as you saw, the Earth symbol △ can create solid ground or dry patches of land over water; the symbol of Air ▽ can create winds in various speeds and strength; as for the other two, with the

Fire symbol △ you can create diversions such as smoke to cloak your arrival somewhere, you can melt snow and ice or even get the sun to come out and warm up or dry out your destination; and lastly with Water ▽, well, tracing this symbol over an area where you are planning to go to will allow you to create rain, control the tide, even lead you to clean drinking water if needed. Just trace the symbol you require over the place you intend to go to, then visualise in your mind what it is that you wish to create." Azzurro explained. "However, in order to keep the balance between the elements, the Galyan elders made sure to add a safety restriction. Any changes that you create using the Map and symbols will only last a short while."

"How long?" asked Lexi, her eyes never leaving the small pouch containing the 'Eye of Truth'.

"No longer than half an hour. Just enough time to allow you to do what you need to do and leave," replied Azzurro.

Completely overwhelmed by all that we saw and learned, I turned and looked at Lexi, thinking to myself how much is resting on her shoulders; how many lives, how many events has she completely altered without even knowing she had done so. I was staring into her blue eyes when suddenly a piercing pain shot through my head.

"Hold on," Ari's voice broke through my pain, making me turn to look at him. "You said that the Council of Truth needed to create more than just a powerful pendant to help protect Lexi."

"Yes," Azzurro said.

"So…" Ari started to say, but Annak cut in before he could finish his sentence.

"Tell them!" he ordered Azzurro, "it is time they are told about the other Artefacts."

"Other Artefacts?" Lexi, Ari and I said together.

"Yes," replied Azzurro, "The extraordinary 'Artefacts of Terah.'"

Artefacts

"Extraordinary 'Artefacts of Terah'?" Ari found it hard to keep calm and cool. "How is it that I never heard of them?"

"That is because no one outside the Council of Truth knows of their existence," Azzurro replied calmly.

"Why extraordinary? How many are there?" Lexi's leg was now rapidly shaking against the floorboards; her eyes squinted tightly as she concentrated on every word coming out of Azzurro's mouth.

"Please, there is no need to get upset," Azzurro said, "I will tell you everything you need to know about the 'Artefacts.'" He paused then continued quietly, "there are five 'Artefacts' in total, representing Eashzar, Woxion, Sorden and Galya, four out of the five kingdoms of Terah, whilst the fifth 'Artefact', the 'Map', represents the Nomads. There should have been another, sixth, artefact but unfortunately, the only contact the Council of Truth had with the people of Navara, a very senior person, was captured and killed by Naval's elite guards before the Council was able to finalise the arrangements with him.

"The Artefacts themselves are unique to each Kingdom. They are ordinary, everyday devices capturing and representing the essence of each Kingdom; but what makes them extraordinary are their unique attributes bestowed upon them by the Galyan Elders."

Azzurro pulled a small book out of the pile on the table in front of us. He opened its first page and turned it, so that it faced us. On the page was a drawing of a map, the Nomads 'Map'. "The first Artefact of Terah", Azzurro said and then turned the next page.

"'The Eye of Truth,'" Ari said, "created in Galya."

"Correct," Azzurro nodded his head, "no explanation needed." He turned another page. There was a drawing of an odd-looking pair of glasses. They were round in shape, with four layers of lenses, in four different sizes, attached to them.

"These were the 'Spectacles of Vision', created in Eashzar. The Eashzarian's Council Guardian implemented some of their special glass manufacturing techniques in their Artefact. You see, each lens, each layer, will allow you see beyond your normal vision. The first lens is simply a magnifying glass, allowing you to magnify anything so that you will be able to easier touch its image to better examine it; using the second set of lenses will allow you to see clearly in darkness; the third set grants the person using them the ability to see everything that the last person wearing the 'Spectacles' ever saw, and the last set of lenses will give you the ability to see anything or anyone that is invisible." Azzurro then turned over to the next page of the book.

The drawing on that page was what looked like a plain fishing net, which Azzurro said was called 'The Confining Net' of Woxion. He went on to explain, "The people of Woxion are highly skilled fisherman, and their Council Guardian used their knowledge to create an impenetrable silver net; very thin and lightweight that can expand or shrink to the size you need it to be. Much like fishing nets, whatever is caught in it will not be able to get out unless released by whoever casts the net, and is compelled to only speak the truth when asked any question."

The next drawing showed a suit of armour. "The 'Reflective Armour' of Sorden" said Azzurro before turning to say to Annak, "I think it is best if you tell them about it, since you were its creator."

"You're a 'Council Guardian', you created that?" Lexi and Ari shouted out at the same time.

Annak didn't say a word.

"Is Azzurro right? I thought the identity of the Council Guardians was a secret, known only to the High Protector of the Council?" I asked.

Annak ignored my question and began talking. "After my banishment from Sorden I finally found my way to Mikaela's tavern, where I learned that she was the daughter of the High Protector. However, as a Council Guardian I had sworn an oath of secrecy which, for everyone's safety, prohibited me from revealing my identity." Annak turned towards Ari, "When Mikaela received the devastating news about your father I could hear her heart stop beating as it silently shattered in her chest, and the spark of life was extinguished in her eyes. I knew her pain. I felt it the day my own flesh and blood forced me to leave my home, my love, never to return there. I could not keep silent any more, I revealed my identity to her and swore to help avenge your father's death."

"I assume you know about my mother," Ari said'

"Yes. When she, in return, told me that she too was a Council Guardian I was not surprised. As the daughter of the High Protector, I expected Mikaela to step into her mother's place in leading the Council to fulfil its purpose. It was then that I told her about the Reflective Armour."

"When did you create it? What does it do?" I asked.

"It was long after I left Sorden. One day, as I was preparing to hide for the night inside a huge, hollow tree trunk, a small illuminated ball appeared hovering before me. It was so bright I had to shield my eyes. I stretched my other arm forward, gently moving it aside. As soon as my fingers touched it, the ball transformed into a hologram of a lady. She introduced herself as Giselle, the 'Grand Protector' of the 'Council of Truth.'"

Ari barged in, asking "But how is it possible? I mean, shortly after the forming of the Council, my grandmother left Terah together with Lexi and her family."

"Before she left, Giselle created five holograms," Annak explained. "Concealed in a small ball of light, they were sent to the five kingdoms of Terah, where they will seek out the true Guardian of each kingdom. In her message, Giselle asked the Guardians to create a unique Artefact to best represent the nature of their kingdom. Once it was created, they were to bring it before the Galyan Elders, to have all five blessed together at the Gwir as the extraordinary 'Artefacts of Terah'. Once that had been done, each back one was to be taken back to its own kingdom to be carefully hidden for safe keeping. And so," Annak continued, "I designed and created the Reflective Armour of Sorden; a unique armour that reflects the area around the wearer, rendering him invisible. But I could not have done it without the help of the Nomads. They were able to smuggle the precious metals out of Sorden that I needed in order to make the armour."

Lexi leaned forward towards Annak, "It's here, with you!"

"No!" Annak answered her sharply.

"Liar!!" she shouted back at him, "you lie! You're an exile, banished from your kingdom, so you couldn't possibly take it back to Sorden."

"Lexi, that's enough," I scolded her, "Annak wouldn't lie to us… to you."

Annak didn't say a word; he just sat there quietly, looking at Lexi. Then, after what felt like forever, he told her quietly, "Breath in, calm down. You need to focus, balance yourself."

"The 'Armour' is well hidden in Sorden," Azzurro said suddenly. "We took it back there for safe keeping."

"Safe keeping? Sorden?" Ari asked

"Yes" said Azzurro, "hide something in plain sight and no one will see it."

"Making it the safest place… Of course," Ari smiled.

"So what now?" I wondered.

"Now. Now we go to get them. All of them," replied Azzurro. "It is time to unite the 'Artefacts of Terah.'"

"You know where they are?" Lexi asked, clearly trying to control herself and talk calmly.

"No," Azzurro winked at Lexi, "but we have what we need to find them."

Lexi's eyes lit up. "The pendant, the 'Eye of Truth,' will lead me to them!"

Before we realised what was going on, Lexi lunged forward and tried to grab the small velvet pouch containing the 'Eye of Truth.' She was too slow. I snatched it from under her outstretched hand.

"Is this what you want?" I took the silver pendant out of its pouch and held it in the air in front of her. Ari had already grabbed Lexi, who was wriggling in his arms, trying to slide out of his strong grip. Annak jumped over the table, drawing his sword and holding its blade against her neck.

"Azzurro, quick, bring me some Louiza leaves," I shouted, stretching my other hand out to him, but not losing my eye contact with Lexi.

Azzurro got up quickly and pulled out a small wooden box from the cupboard above the stove. He took a handful of leaves and placed them in my open hand. As soon as I felt the prickly dried leaves in my hand I thrust them towards her body, holding them tight against her heart.

Lexi screamed in agony, trying to fight it off, get free. I looked deep into what had become her black eyes. "Where is Lexi?! What did you do to her?" I demanded, looking at what had become a dark shell of the real Lexi.

Realisations

"Where is she?!" I shouted, as I twisted the Louiza leaves hard against the imposter's chest. It was screeching in agony. The dried leaves pierced through its clothes and white smoke was coming from the exposed, scorched skin. "Answer me or I swear I will burn every bit of this body, inch by inch, over and over again until you tell me what I want to know!" My eyes were fixated on It, staring directly at Its' black eyes.

"Jimmy," Azzurro's voice broke in, "let me take over, you are too emotional and it will get us nowhere." He gently moved my hand from the thing's chest. "Now, let us try again," he said calmly, as Annak tightened the blade of his sword against Its' neck.

"Where is Lexi?"

It stopped wriggling and looked straight at Azzurro. "She is gone!" It hissed quietly.

"NO!" I shouted at it, "you're lying!"

"I am all that you have." It grinned at me.

I took a step back and fell into one of the chairs. My heart was pounding so fast I could hardly breathe, my shirt was soaking with cold sweat, my head was spinning. All I could think was, "She's gone! Lexi is gone. My best friend! My only friend on this strange, cursed world, and now I am stuck here, alone, forever!"

Through the haziness which surrounded me I suddenly heard my name, "Jimmy! Jimmy!" Annak's husky voice brought me back into reality, "This is not the time to despair, all is not lost. We are still here with you. You are not alone!"

It was as if he could read my thoughts. I looked at Annak, then grabbed another handful of Louiza leaves. This time I placed them directly on Its' cheek. The smell of burning flesh was nauseating, but I didn't let go. "Who-are-you!!" I demanded, through gritted teeth.

It was shaking its head ferociously, trying to get my hand off its face, screaming in pain the whole time.

Slowly I removed my hand and quietly asked again, "Who are you and what did you do to Lexi?" I kept my handful of leaves near enough to Its' face to remind it what would happen if I didn't get answers.

"I did nothing! It was she who summoned me. She is gone and now I am she. I am all that you have," It said again.

"She summoned you? Lexi? But how is that possible?" I looked at the thing in front of me.

"She is me just as much as I am her; we are one and the same, only apart," It hissed.

"Impossible!" Azzurro said. "I have heard of your kind, but never thought I would ever come across one of you in my life." He was staring at the thing, examining it from top to bottom. Then he pulled out a dagger from within his right boot. Ari tightened his grip around It as Azzurro grabbed a hand and cut across Its' open palm. There was no blood. In fact, there was nothing. The open wound healed itself almost as soon as Azzurro drew the blade away from the cut skin.

"What the....?!" I couldn't believe my eyes, "what is this thing?"

"It is a 'Doppelganger'" Azzurro replied, "Lexi's doppelganger to be exact."

"Doppelganger?" I kept staring at It.

"The 'Doppelganger' or a 'Double-Walker' is an exact duplicate of any living creature. They are empty soulless ringers. Created in the shadows. They are the essence of one's evil and darkness. As empty shells they cannot cast a shadow nor do they have a reflection. Doppelgangers are malicious, devious creatures and if they are strong enough, they can take over their double's souls. They are drawn to darkness and serve it through eternity." Azzurro looked into the Doppelgangers black eyes and added, "They cannot exist without a double counterpart, so something very powerful must have brought it to life, as most Double-Walkers are dormant."

"Hold on," I said, as hope began to fill me, "that means Lexi is still alive! We just need to find her." It was hard to contain my excitement at the prospect of getting my best friend back, and once again perhaps being able to return home.

"Well yes." said Azzurro, "but we don't know where she is or how she is."

"What does that mean?" I asked.

"If what It said is true, then there is a good chance that, during the awakening of the Doppelganger, Lexi's consciousness was fused together with that of her Doppelganger, which means that Lexi as we know her is gone."

"But she is still alive!" I shouted, "we must try to save her; she would have done the same for any of us!" They can't just betray her like that, I thought to myself. "I'm sure there is only one place that this awakening could have happened," I insisted, "and that is the Labyrinth of Souls, which means that Lexi must still be there, somewhere, swept away by the stream."

"We nearly lost the three of you there once before, we are not going there again," Annak declared.

"Annak is right," Azzurro added. "If the fusion did happen when Lexi was in the Labyrinth, then all that is left of her is her body, an empty shell. Lexi's soul is somewhere inside her Doppelganger now."

"So that's it? You're giving up on Lexi?" My lungs were closing up on me. Once again I couldn't breathe. "What about the prophecy?" I went on in desperation, hoping something I said would hit a nerve with them. "After all, isn't she the 'Chosen One', destined to defeat Naval?"

"No one is giving up on Lexi," Annak placed his hand on my shoulder, "we all care about her, but we must be realistic and face the facts. Lexi has gone and we still have to complete our mission." He looked up at me, "We can sit back, feel miserable and dwell about it, or find another way to get her back so that we can finish what we set-out to do and help her fulfil her destiny."

I looked around, first at Annak, then Azzurro, and finally at Ari, who was still holding on to Lexi's Doppelganger, making sure It could not get away. "What are you suggesting we do?" he asked

"First we need to confine the Doppelganger," Azzurro said, as he turned to Ari. "I'm sure you can handle that."

"It will be my pleasure." Ari replied, and asked me, "can you take over and hold It tight, Jimmy? Be careful, It is stronger than you think."

I walked towards Ari. My heart was pounding so fast, I could feel the blood being pumped out of it and through my veins, as my eyes locked on the Doppelganger. I got very close, was about to get hold of It, when suddenly Its' eyes changed from their soulless, deep black, into Lexi's blue eyes.

"Jimmy, help me; please don't do it. Don't let them, they will kill me." I heard Lexi's voice pleading with me.

I was now standing so close, face-to-face, that I could feel the cold emptiness radiating from Its' body. "Wow, you are good; with the eyes and the voice, no wonder it took me a bit of time to realise you weren't her. But you see, as much as you can look and sound like her, you are nothing like Lexi! Your eagerness and selfishness, even arrogance at times, making everything all about you. Lexi would never put herself before others, least of all her friends. She is unpretentious and very much grounded; her strength comes from within, it's pure and incorruptible. She will never let power blind her as it does you. So, don't you ever dare take her form again! I swear to you, I will find a way to destroy you without hurting Lexi. I'll use my own two hands if need be. I will destroy you!"

The creature was laughing out loud, a vicious screeching sound that drilled through my ears and resonated in my brain, as It changed its appearance back to its dark self. "Go ahead, believe what you want, but deep inside you know I am right, We are One now. It would have been impossible for me to awake unless her darkness called me," It sneered.

"Never! Not Lexi. I know her since we were little kids, playing together in the sandpit in the park. We were inseparable, there is no way I wouldn't have noticed that darkness you talk about, in all those years. You speak out of desperation, you are afraid of what will happen to you." I felt that once more I was in charge. I took It from Ari's hands and held the thing as tight as I could.

Ari positioned himself in front of Lexi's Doppelganger. He started to turn his hand around in circular motions, as if he was holding an invisible ball between them. Every so often he would stop, and with his right hand pull out a string of invisible rope. Once he was done he kneeled down at the Doppelganger's feet and started twisting the rope around it, beginning with Its' ankles. The Doppelganger tried to break free, wriggling vigorously, like a frightened little worm when picked up from the ground and held in the air. But it didn't matter; as soon as Ari bound an area of the body it was impossible to move it or get free of its hold. When Ari got to the Doppelganger's head, It made a final effort to try and get away from the ropes that were encircling it. All in vain; within minutes Ari had It all tightly bound. I slowly lay Lexi's Doppelganger down on the wooden boards of Azzurro's caravan. Ari kneeled by Its' side and bent forward as close as he could, then started to blow hot air all over the stiff body, spreading it with his hands. By the time he was finished the Doppelganger looked like a mummified waxed version of Lexi.

"It's okay, I didn't kill the Doppelganger, merely put it in hibernation for its own safety." Ari smiled at me, then turned to Azzurro and asked, "Where would you like to keep it?"

"I have just the place for it," Azzurro replied, as he started walking towards the two beautifully decorated closed glass-doors, at the far end of the caravan. He swiftly opened them, revealing his sleeping compartment. It had a double bed that fitted exactly from side to side. It was resting on a solid wood frame which had two carved drawers fitted inside. Azzurro pulled out one of the wooden drawers and said, "I'm sure It will be quite safe in here," and gave us a wink.

We carefully lifted the Doppelganger and placed it inside the big drawer, then quietly went back to sit around the small table.

"How did you know?" Ari broke the silence.

I began to explain: "It's like I told her Doppelganger; Lexi never felt comfortable with the fact that she was the 'Chosen One', she kept questioning it over and over again, and yet the Doppelganger was so eager to find more about how It could gain power, making it all about itself; reminding everyone that It was the saviour of Terah, disregarding the rest of us altogether. This is exactly the opposite of what Lexi would do. She would never put herself before her friends! Another sign was how angry and aggressive the Doppelganger would get. I mean, it practically jumped out of its seat trying to grab the Map, then lunging at Azzurro, trying to attack him. And there were other little things as well, such as the Doppelganger's restlessness and impatience. The first time I noticed something was not right with 'Lexi' was when Azzurro served us Louiza tea last night. The way It reacted to the green liquid. It made a strange hissing sound and its head twisted in a weird way. However, it was very subtle and I guess the excuse It gave, that 'the drink was hot', was plausible enough, so I let it go. But today at breakfast, It didn't remember anything about Annak's arsenal of weapons back at the tavern. And when It asked for coffee my doubts about Lexi surfaced again, as she's never been a coffee person. I started having serious concerns about her well-being, especially as she felt very cold to touch. I could feel the cold radiating from her body just by sitting next to her. But it was something you and the Doppelganger said that made it all click." I paused and looked at Ari.

"Me!?" Ari's voice broke in surprise, "what did I say?"

"It was your reaction to Lexi pouring herself a second cup of coffee," I replied.

Ari looked confused, "But all I said was that Annak's coffee can wake-up the dead."

"Exactly!!" I cried out with excitement, "and Lexi said 'Another cup of hot coffee and I'll have this body ready to go.' Suddenly it all made sense to me. Lexi's strange behaviour, being funny and sensitive, her old self one minute then strange, aggressive and on edge the next. It was in that moment that I knew, for certain, that That was not Lexi!"

Darkness ends

"Over here! I'm over here! Jimmy, Ari, is that you? Just follow my voice. Please hurry, I'm so cold, I don't think I can move.   Jimmy?...

No! Wait! What are you doing? Who are you? Where are my friends? Where are you taking me?!..."

Lexi

"You will feel much better once you are out of those wet garments you are wearing."

"Where am I? Where are my friends? What did you do to them? What do you want from me?"

"You will feel much better once you are out of those wet garments you are wearing."

"Is there anything else you can say, or is that it? What **are** you anyway? You look like a living marble statue, with your pale, white pasty skin and, well, white everything come to think of it. Your hair, your clothes - if it wasn't for your red eyes, you would completely disappear in the background."

"What is this place? It's quite bright in here and yet there are no windows, no visible lights anywhere. No!! Wait! Your hand! It's disappeared inside the wall! What?!... How did you do that? How is it even possible? You only touched the wall and created an opening, a window. What are you?!"

"We are one with her."

"What do you mean 'one with her'? Who is **she**? Did she pull me out of the darkness? Does she have my friends? Can I see my friends? Are they okay? Can I talk to her?"

"You're not talking very much! Quite a fountain of information. Do you mind if I look outside this window you created, you know, maybe I can find out where I am? Since you're not being so helpful."

"This is incredible! It's solid when I touch it but there's no glass. It's as if it's open, yet sealed at the same time. I can feel the fresh air coming through it. How is it possible?"

"Whoa, how high are we? I can hardly see the ground from this window; it's very misty out there. Can you create another window, on the other wall maybe?"

"This is the only external wall in this tower."

"Tower?! Is this some kind of castle?"

"She is the 'White Fortress'."

"The 'White Fortress'?? You mean, I'm in **Navara**?!"

"You will feel much better once you are out of those wet garments you are wearing."

"Oh, we're back to that again? And **'garments'**?! Can't you say clothes?"

"Okay! Give me your 'garments' and I'll put them on, if it helps me to get some more information from you."

"You must be joking!! There's **no way** I'm wearing a dress!! And it's white as well!! Forget it, I'll stay in my clothes, they're almost dry anyway."

"Wait!! Where are you going?! Was it something I said?"

"Please don't do that... Don't step into the wall, STOP!!"

"Where are you going??? This is all so frustrating!!!"

"Hey, you're back! For a moment I thought you forgot about me."

"I'm only teasing you. It's a joke. So, you **can** smile... You freaked me out a bit with your 'vanishing into the wall' act. Where did you go?"

"Rrr-ight..... not much of a talker. So what now?"

"I shall draw you a bath."

"Amazing!! You literally just pulled the tub out of the floor. You raised your hands over that spot and out comes a white bath, full of steaming water and bubbles! Seriously, how **DO** you do that!?"

"Your garments please."

"Funny, for a minute there I thought you wanted me to get undressed."

"Holding out your arm to me doesn't help."

"Your garments please."

"Oh, you're not kidding. Well, do you mind giving me some privacy?"

"Can you maybe turn around?"

"Your garments please."

"Fine!! I'll take them off! But you're not getting my underwear till I'm in the water and covered in bubbles!"

"There you go, you can have those now."

"Hey!! Where are you going with my clothes? You didn't even leave me a towel!!"

"What is going on here!? I DEMAND TO TALK TO SOMEONE IN CHARGE!"

"Great, it's you again!"

"Your garments are hanging on the wall behind the dressing screen. They are all cleaned and pressed for you."

"Where? I can't see them."

"They are behind you."

"Oh yeah, now I see them. Thanks. Do you have a towel for me? I'd like to get out of the bath now."

"I shall hold it up for you."

"No need. Just leave it on the floor next to me, I'll get it myself."

"Very well."

"You still haven't told me how you do all those things. Disappear into the walls, create things from nothing or just pull them out from the walls and floor."

"We are one with Her. We take care of her needs as much as She provides ours. We only think of something and She will create it for us, from us."

"Are you telling me that the 'White Fortress' is ALIVE!"

"We are created from her, to serve her."

"How many are there like you?"

"We are one and many at the same time."

"Are you telling me that every time you came back to see me I was actually talking to a different clone of you?"

"Not clones. We are one, connected in mind and matter. One thought, one purpose, many ways of executing it. All in Her service, all for Her."

"Hold on, so what you are saying is that the 'White Fortress' is a living organism, operating through you? Looking through your eyes, hearing with your ears, creating with your hands and speaking with your voice?!"

"Yes. We are one."

"This is incredible!!!"

"Hmmm, and what about Naval? How does he fit in with all that?"

"He is our Lord. He commands us all."

"Can you take me to him?"

"He awaits your presence."

"Well then, we mustn't keep him waiting!"

Aftermath

Azzurro's caravan was filled with silence. It was as if we were under a spell, the four of us sat there around the small coffee table, not saying a word, frozen in our seats. No sound could penetrate the walls from outside and no sound was made by anyone inside. No-one moved, no-one wanted to be the first to talk. I couldn't stop staring at the drawer under Azzurro's bed, thinking of that thing in there, thinking of Lexi. I felt lost, despaired, just like that time when I was four and wandered off alone, away from my parents, at one of the big department stores back home. I knew that Annak and the rest were here with me, and I knew that they would do all that they could to find Lexi. But what if they didn't find her? What if they eventually gave up on it all? And they might give up on it; after all, their 'saviour' had gone. How long can they look, how much can they go on fighting, before giving up? And then what would I do? What would happen to me?! The longer I stared at the drawer the more convinced I was that I could see through it, and what I saw was my best friend, the only family I have in this world. The more I looked, the clearer it became to me…. I will find Lexi and we will go back home. I took a deep breath and just like that the spell was broken.

"Azzurro? Can I come in?" I heard Soulange' sweet voice calling from outside.

Azzurro got up and opened the caravans door for her, "You most certainly can," he said, with a welcoming smile for her lighting up his face.

Annak quickly folded the map and put it on the small bench next to the coffee table, together with the rest of the books we had looked at earlier in the day. I grabbed Lexi's pendant, put it back in its pouch, and safely placed it in my pocket.

"It is long after lunchtime," Soulange said as she climbed up the stairs and into the caravan, holding a tray with a large covered dish on it. "You have been locked in here quite a long time, you must be starving. Here, I brought you some food." Her cherry-red lips curved into a smile.

"Ah! Lunch! Thank you," said Azzurro, as he took the copper tray from her hands and placed it on the small table in front of us.

I was mesmerised by her; my face must have caught the fire of her hair, it felt warmer and warmer the longer she stood there.

"Care to join us?" I suddenly heard my own voice.

"Thank you," she said, smiling right at me, "but I must finish my chores."

"Ah. Of course, chores… that's ok we're busy here too, maybe we play another day…" I stumbled on my words, "Not play… I mean, catch up another day." The more I spoke the bigger an idiot I sounded. What was wrong with me? Why couldn't I just talk like a normal person?!

Soulange giggled and her eyes sparkled. She started to step out of the caravan but then stopped, turned and looked around the caravan, "Where is Lexi? Have you managed to drive her away with all your silliness?" she teased.

"Lexi had to leave us for a while," Azzurro replied, lowering his voice.

"Oh," she said surprised, "well, I look forward to her return soon."

"Yes. We all do," he said, "and Soulange, I will need your help soon."

She nodded her head gently in reply and left the caravan. We sat down for lunch. The tray on the table was very impressive, and not only by its huge size, but also with the dish it was serving. It reminded me of our cook, Mrs. Rodriguez's special meat and vegetables on yellow rice paella. I was so hungry I couldn't wait for Azzurro to serve us. As soon as he handed me my plate I just filled it up and started eating.

"Easy there," Azzurro said, "you don't want to choke on a piece of bone now, or you won't be able to go and play." He winked at me.

I turned red again and nearly really did choked on my mouthful. Ari and Annak burst into laughter.

"Don't you want to play with us?" Ari was teasing me. "Are we not fun to play with?" he continued.

I shot up from my seat and was ready to throw a punch at his face. Luckily for him, Azzurro pulled me back into my chair. He, too, was laughing now. It was so loud I was sure the whole caravan camp could hear him.

"Here, have some cold water to cool that hot head of yours down," he said. as he poured me a tall glass."

I drank the cold water, but didn't stop staring at Ari the whole time. Does he think that just because Lexi is not here to tell him off he can pick on me and no one will stop him? Well, he's got that wrong!

Azzurro put his hand on my shoulder, "Calm down. My niece has that effect on men, especially hot-headed, hot-blooded young ones like you. You are most certainly not the first who turned into a blabbering fool around her."

"Women! Dangerous creatures!" Annak mumbled under his breath.

"Yes, but we are all stupid enough to willingly take the risk and face that danger." Azzurro laughed.

"Indeed we are!" Annak replied. "For the prize is well worth the risk!"

Ari and I exchanged some confused looks.

"Prize? What prize are you talking about?" I asked.

"The best one of all!!" Azzurro replied.

"Hah?" Ari and I said, almost in unison.

"Love!!" Annak called out, "A women's love!"

"You two sound like a couple of giddy little girls, giggling over some silly nonsense." Ari said.

I think we all needed that bit of laughter and foolishness to wind down after our very intense morning. We had our lunch as Azzurro and Annak kept teasing each other over who was the bigger adolescent of the two, and how love is the best thing you can ever find.

"The two of you are behaving like a couple of love-struck idiots." Ari was teasing them even more, "I wonder what Lexi would have thought if she saw you like that?"

"She would agree with us, of course!" Azzurro replied. "She's a young girl and they always think it is all so dreamy and fluffy and wonderful." He spoke in a soft high-pitched voice, imitating a woman's voice.

"Lexi? Fluffy?? You clearly haven't met the real Lexi," I said, while trying to compose myself from all the laughter. "She is as far from being a 'girly-girl' as any of us. I've known her all my life and I've never seen her acting like a girl. She would probably think that you've added a bit of something into your drink."

"Well, she would be right!" said Azzurro, "a spoonful of that sweet nectar of love!" He looked at me and added "and you, my young friend, are in danger of tasting it too."

"Hah!" I gasped in surprise, going all red again.

I stuffed my mouth with some left-over rice from my plate as the three of them burst into loud laughter.

We all calmed down as Azzurro declared, "It is time to resume our previous engagement."

He got up, picked the big tray with all our plates and cutlery on it, and took it outside the caravan. He climbed back up the three steps leading back into his caravan, but stopped before getting inside. He turned to face the darkening afternoon sky, then put his two left fingers in his mouth and released a high-pitched whistle. I instantly recognised the sound of it, it was the same whistle he had used before, when he called Tercel. And just like then, Azzurro stretched his long arm out, and a minute or so later the magnificent Gyrfalcon landed on it. They both entered the caravan and joined us back at the table. Tercel looked around, his small beady eyes constantly moving, scanning the caravan quickly.

"I see we are short one player," he said, "where is our young saviour?"

"It is complicated!" Azzurro replied.

"Complicated? How so? You do not mean to tell me that you have lost her, do you?" Tercel asked jokingly.

"Sort of," Azzurro paused, then, "That is why I have called you," he continued.

Tercel looked at us, clearly surprised, and dropped his sarcastic tone of voice. "What happened?"

"We discovered something very disturbing. Something we did not anticipate." Azzurro lowered his voice, "Doppelganger!" he whispered.

Tercel's eyes widened into two big circles and his head moved, stretching his neck as far back as it could go.

"Impossible!!" he finally said, as his head shot forward once more.

"I can assure you it is not," Azzurro said.

"But how?"

"The 'Labyrinth of Souls'. We suspect it happened there."

"I see…" Tercel said, as if he was contemplating something, then added "and I assume you know the whereabouts of both counterparts?"

"Only one of them," Azzurro replied.

"You were there," I suddenly cut in, "flying above us, you must have seen something that could help us find Lexi!"

"I am sorry, but once Ari pulled her out from under the water I flew away to get the Nomads."

"But you saw her being pulled towards Black Pool Lake; maybe you saw something that at the time you didn't realise was important, or even possible." I hoped to jog his memory.

"As I recall, it was very hard to look through all the gushing water around you. As it was, I could barely spot Lexi, let alone notice her double."

"What about later, after we were pulled out by the Nomads. Could you have seen something on your way back to your post in Navara? Someone.. a body maybe.. swept to shore there, or floating in the Great River."

"No. I truly am sorry. But, for all our sakes, I will keep a very keen eye open as I fly above. We may still find her yet."

"Thank you." I quietly replied.

"We still have a big task ahead," Azzurro reminded us.

"One which requires Lexi," Annak added. His tone of voice only emphasised the predicament we were in.

"How do you suggest we solve that?" Tercel asked.

Azzurro, still holding Tercel on his arm, got up from his chair. Slowly he started walking toward the door.

"There really is only one way to do it," he said, looking towards Tercel, "we need help and you know where to get it. But you must hurry, we cannot lose any more time." And with that he stepped out of the caravan and lifted his arm as Tercel took to the sky.

"Where did you send him?" Ari asked.

"You will soon find out. But until that time comes, there is plenty for us to do. Let us get back to planning our next move. We do not know if Naval is aware of the existence of the Doppelganger, or if there is any connection between them. But we have shared some vital information in Its' presence and therefore we mustn't delay any longer," he replied.

"What are you thinking of doing?" I asked, all geared up now with enthusiasm and ready to go.

"We start by getting the rest of the Artefacts first," Azzurro began, then went on, "Whilst searching for them, we can slowly find out the number of people ready to resist. The rumours about the arrival of the 'Chosen One' have raised hope amongst the people. We must spread the news that the resistance is growing, and tell everyone to wait for our final word."

Annak pulled the map out from between the books on the bench next to him. He carefully opened it and let the hologram appear, then pointed to an area between the edge of the Labyrinth of Souls and the top of Black Pool Lake.

"We are here," he began, and then with both his index fingers he slightly zoomed in on that area. With one finger he held down that spot as if to pin it down while with his other index finger and thumb he zoomed-in on another section of the map. There were about a dozen houses there, surrounded by what looked like agricultural fields.

"This is 'Katiff,'" he said. "As you can see, it is the closest village in the Kingdom of 'Eashzar' to where we are. Most importantly, we have friends there whom we can trust to help us." He let go of the hologram.

"Is that where the Spectacles of Vision are hidden?" I asked him.

"No. But it is a good place to start our search for them," he replied in his deep husky voice.

"It will take us about three days to get there," said Azzurro, "we shall ready the caravans and leave as soon as Tercel is back."

"Won't it be easier if only the four of us go?" I was a bit confused as to why Azzurro would want the entire camp to join us, "If time is working against us, as you say, then surely it will be a lot quicker and less complicated travelling without excess luggage?"

Ari looked at me and said, "The boy is right; the four of us alone, we will be able to find the Artefacts much faster. And without Lexi, no one will suspect any of us of being the Chosen One. It will be easy."

"Easy!" Annak snapped at him, "Easy is what got us all here!"

"Sometimes you need to take the 'long way' around, make harder choices for the greater good," Azzurro responded calmly. "It is not just about achieving your goals, but how you do it, so that it will stand the test of time."

"But how is taking everyone along with us better for the 'greater good'?" Ari asked.

"Think!" Annak pointed to his head. "How will travelling together with the Nomads help us?"

"COVER!!" I cried out in excitement. "We pretend to be one of them, that way we can travel through the kingdoms without being stopped or questioned about it. Plus, once we find them, we can hide the Artefacts in the caravans."

"Correct." said Annak.

"And there is another reason why we must stay together with my people," Azzurro added.

I looked towards the drawer at the bottom of Azzurro's bed, "The Doppelganger."

"Yes" he said, "we mustn't let it out of our sight!"

By now it was getting very dark outside, and the strong smell of bonfires all across the camp was in the air. Strangely enough I felt good. Although the thought of continuing this journey without my best friend by my side was bothering me, it also filled me with excitement. For the first time in my life it was me looking after Lexi; it was now my turn to keep her safe from harm, and make sure she returned home safely. I knew she was out there, alive, somewhere waiting to be rescued, and I was on my way to do just that!

Angel of Souls

The loud sounds of the Nomads packing away the caravan trailers woke me up. The sun was already high in the sky, but for the first time since we arrived there were dark clouds heading our way. I looked around for Annak and Ari, but they must have woken up much earlier and gone out, as they were nowhere to be seen. I got myself out of my bunk; it was quite cold, so I put on my clothes as quick as I could, threw on one of the sheepskin coats that Ari's aunt had given us, and left the caravan. All over the camp everybody was busy doing something: putting away all the pots and pans which were used to cook for everyone, packing chopped firewood onto one of the carts, getting the caravans tidied up and ready to move. The kids were helping too, folding the bed linen and blankets that had been hung out to air, and putting the Nomads' instruments and artwork away. They covered the paintings and statues with large pieces of canvas to keep them safe. A small open wagon had returned to the camp carrying huge ceramic jugs in its back, all filled with fresh cool water from the Great River, ready to be used for drinking and cooking while on our way. No-one seemed to be bothered by the big, black, cluster of clouds, rapidly getting closer and closer to us, when suddenly a bolt of lightning and a loud clap of thunder drew everyone's attention. Within minutes, anything left outside was quickly packed away and lifted into the wagons. And with not a moment to spare, the rain came pouring down.

"Jimmy! Jimmy! Quick, over here!" I heard Azzurro call.

I ran towards his caravan as fast as I could. But it was no use. In the two minutes it took me to reach his caravan I managed to get completely drenched.

"Can you believe that rain?" I asked, as I stepped into the caravan.

"You better take that dripping sheep that you are wearing off from you, before you drown in it," Azzurro joked as he peeled the coat off me, leaving it on the doorstep, hanging over the bottom-half of the caravan's door.

Surprisingly, apart from my hair being all wet and dripping, my clothes under the sheepskin has stayed completely dry.

"Looks like everyone's ready to go," I said, "why did you let me sleep-in so long?"

"It sounded like you needed it" Ari replied.

"Bad dreams" Annak added.

"Who? Me? No way! I slept like a baby," I protested.

"A very loud baby!" Ari was teasing, "you kept us up for most of the night with your sleep-talking."

"Sleep-threatening more like it!" Annak corrected Ari.

"Me?" I couldn't believe what they were saying.

"Oh yes!" Ari said, then went on to imitate me "'Who do you think you are, taking her away! You have no idea what I'm capable of doing! Let her go or I'll destroy you!'"

I looked at the three of them, full of embarrassment. It was clear that I had been re-living my encounter with the Doppelganger from our previous day, in my dreams.

"Here," Azzurro brought me a cup of Louiza tea, "this will calm you down, ease your thoughts. It was a big day for all of us."

I took a sip of the tea and asked, "So, has Tercel returned yet? Are we ready to move on?" hoping to change the subject.

A long, high-pitched shriek, came from outside and Azzurro

walked towards the caravan door. He stretched his arm out, but instead of Tercel landing on it, Azzurro grabbed hold of a hand. A moment later a strange figure stepped into the caravan. It was hard to make out who it might be, as they were wearing a heavy cloak with a large hood, which covered their entire head and face.

"Can I help with your cloak?" Azzurro asked.

"Thank you," said a woman's voice, as the stranger untied the cloak around her neck and started to lift the hood from her face.

"MOTHER?!" Ari cried in surprise.

Mikaela handed her cloak to Azzurro and walked straight over to Ari. She spread her arms wide and grabbed Ari, hugging him tightly and nearly squeezing him out of breath.

"My darling son! Oh, How I have missed you so much!" Said Mikaela with emotion. "And you too!" a moment later, as she grabbed hold of my arm and pulled me toward her, "I am so glad to see you are well." She hugged me tight, the same motherly hug she gave me when we left the Tavern.

"What are you doing here? Have you any idea how dangerous it is out there? And who is left to mind the tavern?" Ari was clearly shocked at seeing his mother there.

Mikaela gave him another reassuring hug. "I am fine," she said. "It is sweet of you to worry about your 'old' mother like that, but there really is no need. You know very well I can take good care of myself." She let go of me and continued, "Besides, I was not alone. Tercel was with me the whole way, from the moment he told me I was summoned here, until my safe arrival. As for the tavern," she paused, "I left it in good hands, a long time ago."

"A long time ago??" he asked.

"I left the tavern as soon as I received the letter from your aunt, telling me that she had seen the three of you on your way north, and that you were all well. She also wrote about what had happened at 'Shaar' and how your uncle has been taken away. I knew she was too proud to ask for help, so I have turned to our trusted neighbour to mind the tavern while I was gone, and rode on to 'Shaar' to be with her."

"So all this time," Ari paused, "you were that close to us, in 'Shaar'?"

Mikaela smiled at him, her face was calm and full of love. "Yes," she replied, "But now I am here, and I am so glad to see you," and she hugged him again. "All of you," she added, as she gently let go of him. "Annak, my dear friend," she said, and they took hold of each other's arms, locking them in and shaking them once. "Azzurro! It has been far too long," she told him, as they too hugged, like old friends who haven't seen each other for a very long time do.

"Shall we all sit down?" Azzurro suggested, pointing at the chairs around the coffee table.

We walked towards the coffee table, while Azzurro took the brewing teapot off the stove. Then he grabbed a few glass cups as he came over, poured us all some tea, and then sat down.

"Can I see it?" Mikaela said suddenly, staring at the drawer at the bottom of Azzurro's bed.

"So you already know?" I asked, surprised.

"Yes," she replied softly, turning her head to look at me, "Tercel informed me of what had happened, when he told me my help was urgently needed."

"And how did you know where It was kept?" I went on.

"I felt It as soon as I walked into the caravan." Mikaela turned to stare at the drawer again.

"But how??" I didn't understand how she could 'feel' that thing. After all the thing was enclosed inside the cocoon Ari created, tucked in the drawer under the bed, way over the other end of the caravan.

"Well, it is to do with the energy around us. We, all living creatures, influence the energy surrounding us by the way we feel and act. For example, when you are happy you surround yourself with positive energy, which will attract good things to you. And also, being somewhere full of positive energy will make you feel up-lifted, happy. When I walked into Azzurro's caravan, it felt very stuffy in here. As if all the air was sucked out. The energy was so low and heavy that I still find it very hard to breathe here. As I walked towards the table and sat down opposite Azzurro's bed, I could feel the cold emptiness of the Doppelganger radiating out, pulling me towards It."

"It is very strong." Ari said. "I have never felt so drawn to the depth of despair as I did when I was close to It, sealing it in the cocoon."

"Was that the only time you felt it?" Mikaela asked

Ari looked aside, sending a quick glance at the drawer, "No. I also felt it when we were standing on the bank of the Great River, when Lexi changed into that awful thing and I had to tear the pendant from her neck."

I couldn't believe what I heard, "Why didn't you say anything before?"

"But I did." Ari snapped at me, then went on, "The first time I felt it I thought it was the Labyrinth of Souls triggering something in the 'Eye of Truth'. Something which then brought out the dark side in Lexi's soul, just like I told you when the Nomads found us." He stopped and looked at me.

"Go on," I said, trying to keep calm.

"As a Galyan I am trained to sense things I cannot see. We learn how to connect to the Aether of life, feel the energy around us, but not to let it get hold of us."

I stared at Ari, sitting on the edge of my seat, as I felt the anger rushing through my body and up to my head. "You could have SAVED her!!" I shouted at him, "you had all those feelings, sensations about her and you did nothing! You could've been a bit more persistent with your theory about the connection between the 'Labyrinth', Lexi and the 'Eye of Truth'!" I could hardly contain myself. My heart was beating fast and my head was pounding.

"A bit more persistent!" Ari was on his feet now. "I told you the

'Eye of Truth' was trying to warn us against going through the 'Labyrinth'! And I also told you that the 'Eye' was exposing the dark side of Lexi's soul, bringing it out to the surface, so we could see it! But you dismissed it all!"

Mikaela grabbed his hand and gently pulled him back to his seat. We sat there staring at each other, not saying anything else, and yet our silence was very loud.

"Hush, you two." Mikaela quietly scolded us, and we immediately broke off our staring competition. She always had that calming effect. No matter how angry or upset you got, the calmness radiating from her voice was enough to immediately dissolve it all.

"It is about time that the two of you put aside your differences. Maybe Ari should have explained things better, seeing that, as a stranger to our world, Jimmy did not fully understand his words of warning."

"But…" Ari started to say in protest, but Mikaela went on.

"And maybe Jimmy found it hard to believe that his best friend, the one person he knew better than anyone else, had such a dark and evil side to her, a side which he had never encountered before. So he did the logical thing, he dismissed it, choosing to believe only in the goodness of Lexi." She gave us both one of her soft, mothering looks, and said, "There is no good dwelling on what should have been. We must concentrate on what we can do now." Mikaela turned to Azzurro, "And I understand that you have called me here for exactly that reason."

"You are right, as always," he replied, "the problem is that without Lexi fulfilling her destiny, our mission will be much harder to accomplish, if not impossible."

"But we don't have Lexi!" Ari stated the obvious.

A big smile appeared on Azzurro's face, "We might not have Lexi, but we do have…."

And right on cue she was standing at the door of the caravan.

"Ahh!" he said as he stood up, "Soulange, please join us."

Ari and I exchanged puzzled looks. What was Azzurro thinking? How could Soulange possibly help us? She would be more of a distraction than help.

Soulange slowly opened the door and walked towards us. Azzurro pulled another chair from under the coffee table and held it for her, as she joined us around the table. Mikaela's eyes sparkled as she looked at Soulange, who was now sitting right opposite her.

"What do you think?" Azzurro asked Mikaela. Both of them looked as if they had struck gold.

"It is too dangerous!" Annak interjected.

Azzurro shook his head. "No, not dangerous, perhaps a bit risky, but not dangerous."

"Are you willing to take the risks involved? Particularly given what we were told by the Doppelganger, about the possibility that a fusion had occurred between the two of them?" Annak asked.

Mikaela and Azzurro looked at Soulange. Ari and I were completely baffled by what had been said, as we tried to understand what it was that they were all talking about and why Soulange was there. However, it didn't take too long before all was revealed to us.

"I know what it is that you are asking of me," Soulange said, looking at each and every one of us in turn. "I am not afraid! This is who I am! I am the 'Angel of Souls'. That is the sole purpose of my existence!" Her green eyes were sparkling and her hair seemed on fire, you could feel her passion in the way she spoke.

"You truly are a remarkable and brave young lady," Mikaela said. "You bring great honour and pride to your family."

Soulange blushed as she said, "I am glad to be able to help in the fight against Naval. I just never thought I would play such a big role in it. Becoming the vessel which carries the soul of the 'Chosen One' is a great honour. I hope I will not disappoint you." She paused and looked at me, then continued, "All of you."

Lexi again

"Do you have a name?"

"What shall I call you?"
"We have no name for we need not have one."
"But what if I want to call you? Ask you for something?"
"There is no need to for you to call us. We come when we are needed."
"Yes, but how can you know when I need you unless I call you?"
"She knows."
"She? You mean, the 'White Fortress'?"
"Yes, our lady. We are one."
"Well, than I shall call you 'Lady'. How would you like that?"

"I'll take your silence as a yes."

"We must go now."
"Yes, we mustn't keep him waiting. Please lead the way... but, there's no door in here, how do you suggest I follow you? I can't just walk through the walls as you do."

"Impressive! You just hold your hand against the wall, and it melts an arched opening into it. Nice!"

"You know, Lady, it wasn't until you walked through the arch you created, that I've noticed you never actually break your connection with the 'Fortress'. Your white gown, it doesn't have a hem at the bottom. It's just absorbed into the floor. There's no end to it, no gap. It's as if you have no feet!"

"You really are, quite literally, 'one with her'!"

"So where are we going now? I see no other openings, just this one long corridor that we're on."

"Ahhh, of course, the one long corridor we are on, and the new arch you are creating on your left. This is fantastic! We need to move forward on our way, so you are creating it as we go! It seems that every arch opening you create is automatically connected to a new corridor, the further we walk down each corridor, the longer it becomes. It's actually adjusting itself to our navigating needs, while closing up behind us any of the previous corridors and arches no longer needed."

"You know what else, Lady? It's very bright in here. However, I can't see any windows, or any lights anywhere. It's as if we're walking through a glasshouse, with big thick opaque glass panels to it. I wonder... what does it feel like? "

"Brrr... It's cold! Icy cold and damp too! But it's not cold in here. In fact, it's quite warm. And the walls... despite them being damp, the walls are not even dripping any water, in fact it's dry all around us. Tell me Lady, am I right to assume that the 'White Fortress' is made out of ice?

"We are ice and snow. We are her and she is Navara."

"Are you telling me that somehow you are all connected to each other!? You're connected to the 'White Fortress' and she's connected to Navara? To the vast land of the north? But how is it possible?"

"We are created from her, and she is created from Navara. We are all one."

"You mean, you are an organic living organism?"

"We are one."

"Fantastic!"

"This is as far as I can take you. He is beyond this door."

"Lady, I'm nervous. Can you hear my heart beating? It's going so fast, I can actually feel the blood being pumped in and out of it. Tell me, what is Naval like? Is he alone in there? Will you come, if I need you?"

"He awaits you."

"Right. I guess I should go through then. Thank you Lady."

"It is open now."

Opposites

'Come on Lexi, you can do it, just walk through the door...' Lexi told herself as she stood in front of the door that Lady had created, building up the courage to open it and face Naval. She closed her eyes, took a deep breath, and then reached her hand forward, gently pushing the door open.

"DAD?! What are you doing here? How did you get here? I thought I'd never see you again!"

The figure facing Lexi seemed so well-known to her at first glance. He had the same eyes, the same strong face, and, given the colour of his eyebrows and neatly trimmed short beard, would certainly have had the same black hair, although his had been replaced by a shiny bald head. Nevertheless, the impression he made was of a great man. Something about his calm look, his posture, full of confidence and grace, drew you to him, allowed you to drop down your guard and be swept away by him. He stood there, not moving a muscle, just staring at her, looking like a Greek statue, perfect in every way.

"Well, well," he finally said, "what a surprise!"

"But how is it possible?" she cried at him, "you look just like my father!"

"So it **is** true!" he replied calmly.

"What is true? **Tell me!!!**" she demanded.

"My dear brother..." Naval replied, "... is the father of the **'Chosen One'!**"

"**Brother?!** What are you talking about?"

"I, my dear Lexi, am talking about how your father, my TWIN brother Lavan, has managed to keep the existence of you and I well hidden from each of us."

"Twins?! You and my Dad? Twin brothers?! No way!!"

"I am afraid it **is** true." Naval said. "Lavan and I are twins, born from the same mother on the same day, only a few minutes apart."

"You're lying! My Dad could never be related to someone like **you**!"

"I may be many things, but liar is not one of them. Let me prove it to you."

"And how do you plan to do that? Show me your birth certificate?"

"Better than that. Let me show you something else, which I am sure will convince you that Lavan is my twin brother."

Naval pulled up the white sleeve of his shirt and walked close enough towards Lexi so that she could clearly see his wrist.

"Dad's birthmark! The one he has on his right wrist." Lexi took a step back, gently touching her lower back.

"Yes! It is called the 'Navarian Snowflake', with the Northern..."

"Star in the middle of it," she burst in. "But yours is on the left wrist, and much darker than my father's."

"So he did tell you something about this place," Naval started to say.

"No," Lexi corrected him, "he used to joke that because he was born on a cold, dark winter's night in a small town in the far north, he got this birthmark. A snowflake to represent the season he was born in, and the Northern Star, to remind him how to find his way home."

Naval gave her a cynical look, and then said, "It's a very sweet little story my brother came up with, and most of it is true. But you see, the truth is that he was born here, in Navara, in this fortress, the second heir to the throne of Navara!"

Lexi couldn't believe what she just heard. Her father and Naval, brothers? Twins? That was the last thing she expected to hear. "If you truly are identical twins, as you claim, then how come your birthmark is different in colour to my father's? His is so pale it almost blends with his skin tone, while yours..." Lexi looked at Naval's birthmark again, "it's so dark, it's almost black."

"We are not ordinary twins, you see," Naval started to explain as he slowly pulled down his sleeve to cover his birthmark. "We might look the same on the outside, but we are very different on the inside. In fact we are quite the opposite of each other."

Lexi didn't quite understand what Naval meant by 'opposite'. "Are you telling me that you are two halves of the same person? How can that be?"

Naval raised his arms and a white throne rose from the floor. As he sat down the throne began to glisten and take on a cover of hoarfrost. Naval started to recount the story of his birth to Lexi. "When it became clear that my dear mother could not have children of her own, my father would not accept the reality of his family's line ending with him. He called upon a great sorcerer and asked him to cast a spell over my mother, one that would allow her to create life inside of her. Of course the sorcerer refused, warning my father that meddling with the powers is dangerous and forbidden. But, father insisted and obviously persuaded, the sorcerer to relent." Naval stopped and looked at Lexi. "But before casting the spell," he continued, "the sorcerer also told my father that if he went ahead he would be condemning the future of his bloodline."

"What do you mean by 'condemning the future of his bloodline?" Lexi asked.

"Patience, my dear niece," Naval said. "Soon my mother was with child and everyone in the kingdom rejoiced at the news that an heir would be born when winter returns to Navara. All seemed to progress well and my parents forgot the old sorcerer's warning - that is, until my mother was in labour." Naval looked penetratingly at Lexi, then continued, "They say that her screams could be heard all across the kingdom. She lay there from the very early hours of the morning till long after the sun had set, screaming for help, begging for it all to end. But no one could help her. She began to shake as her pregnant belly was twisting and twitching, stretching bigger and bigger as the child inside her began to split in two, creating another in his image. Finally, it was I who forced myself out of her, leaving behind devastation and a second screaming baby, your father, Lavan."

With tears running down her face Lexi looked at Naval and said, "You killed her? You murdered you own mother!"

"By casting a spell on my mother the balance of life was altered. The only way to restore that balance was to create two halves from the same soul, one representing all that is pure good and one that is...."

"An abomination. Pure evil!!" Lexi burst in, looking up at Naval with disgust. He smiled back at her. "Why such harsh words? I was about to say, one that is stronger, better. In fact, much superior to his kin and therefore a lot more suitable to rule."

Not falling for Naval's smoothness, Lexi wiped the tears off her face and demanded, "What did you do to my father? How did he end up in my world?"

"Lavan and I were raised together as two regular brothers and despite showing clear qualities for... shall we say greatness, on my part ...your father never stopped trying to turn me into another clone of himself. The more he tried, the more I was drawn to the opposite side and, as a visual confirmation of that, my birthmark got darker and darker as the years went on. I offered to rule the kingdom together with him, as equals, but he saw right through me. There was no way I would share my power with him! Realising there was nothing he could do to change me, Lavan left, knowing it would be better, as I would surely have to rid myself of him and his threat to my throne." Naval stood up, "It is my right to rule! I am the first born!"

"Yes, and by being the first born you have condemned your bloodline! You have no heirs! No one to love you and care for you! You have killed the only one person who could have helped, in exchange for her power! You are nothing but a pathetic old man!" Lexi spoke sharply, lashing out at him.

Naval burst into loud laughter, barely able to contain himself. "Zarah?! You are talking about Zarah? She was merely a pawn, a means to an end."

"And what about me?! Am I just a pawn too?" Lexi asked, staring straight into his eyes.

Naval started walking slowly towards her, never breaking Lexi's eye contact with him. He stopped in front of her and Lexi could feel his breath blowing down on her face.

Then he spoke softly, as he bent forward so that his face was opposite Lexi's, and said, "You were nothing to me, a prey to be hunted down. From the moment you returned to **MY** world, I was playing a game of 'hide and seek' with you."

Lexi was clearly taken by surprise.

"How did I know you returned, you wish to ask?" Naval said, "your pendant, it triggered the tracking signal I planted in it the night I killed Zarah." He stepped back and turned away from her, "Did you really think I was stupid enough to leave it behind? I knew how great its power was. Yet, it was no good to me, I could not find a way to possess it because of its blood link to the 'Chosen One'. Knowing that a new, so-called saviour, will be born to take the place of the one I killed, I let a drop of my blood fall onto the crystal in the middle of the pendant, where it was absorbed, linking it to the crystal in the middle of my ring." Naval swiftly turned back and showed Lexi his hand.

On Naval's middle finger was a big insignia ring. There was some writing and strange symbols on each of its sides, which Lexi could not make out. The top of the ring was shaped like the palm of a hand, holding a round aquamarine crystal, an identical crystal to the one in the 'Eye of Truth'.

"It is called, 'The Hand of Fate'," he said, "because it allows the one wearing it to control their destiny, to steer them towards that which they so desire. The crystal in the middle was created from the same rock of which the one in the 'Eye of Truth' was taken, linking them together. So you see, once my drop of blood was absorbed in the crystal on the pendant, it linked them, and when your blood was added to it, the crystal on my ring began to glow, alerting me to your arrival."

Lexi stood there, not knowing what to say or how to react to this revelation.

"I thought it would be fun, hunting you down," he smirked at her, "another 'One' to kill for my amusement. But you are no ordinary 'One' are you?!" Naval started walking back towards Lexi, circling her as if she was his captured prey. Then he continued, "You are my niece! What a wonderful turn of events! Fate has once more played her hand and brought you to me." Naval came very close to Lexi, put his lips beside her ear and whispered, "Your blood is **my** blood! And that birthmark on your back makes you the rightful heir to **my** throne!"

Shocked by the news she looked around, trying to find something she could grab hold to, as her head started spinning and her legs gave up under her own weight. Naval reached forward and held her before she fell. A bed rose up from the floor, and he gently laid Lexi onto it. Then he placed his hands on opposite sides of her head and closed his eyes. The palms of his hands started to warm up, radiating the heat into Lexi's head. Slowly, slowly, the warmth began to flow through her body, filling it up with rejuvenated energy. Naval took his hands from Lexi's head and she started to open her eyes.

"Is there anything else you should tell me?" she asked.

"Much more," Naval replied. He held out his hand to take hold of hers, helping her to sit up on the bed. "But there is time enough for you to hear it."

Omen

"NO!!" I cried out as I pushed my chair back and stood up, still looking at Soulange. "No, you cannot do that! You'll kill her! Look, no one here would like to get Lexi back more t han me, but what you are planning on doing…" I stopped and turned to look at the drawer under Azzurro's bed, then continued, "you'll kill her, you'll kill both of them and then it is really over, for all of us." It was hard to catch my breath.

"It is fine," Soulange said softly, the sweetness of her voice calming me down. "Truly, there is no need to worry so much. I was born with the ability to contain another soul in my body. So you see, it is all going to be just fine."

I looked at her, completely mesmerised by her voice, then asked, "How can you be so sure it will work? Have you done it before?"

"No," Soulange replied, "but I trust Mikaela to know what she is doing and I trust my body to accept the new soul."

The softness of her voice as she spoke, together with her self-confidence, and belief in what she could do, was very convincing. I turned to Mikaela and asked, "Are you sure it can be done without harming either of them?"

"Nothing is for certain in what we are about to do," Mikaela replied. "As Annak pointed out, it is, a very dangerous thing we are attempting to achieve and we mustn't take it lightly, any of us. But it isn't impossible." It was the first time I heard Mikaela speak with such a serious tone.

All eyes were now on Soulange as we sat quietly around the small coffee table, reflecting on what had been said.

"When do we start?" Soulange broke the silence.

"We need to wait for the sun to set, and for the moon to beam in its full light so that we can harness its power." Mikaela replied.

"What do we do until then?" I asked. "There are still a few hours to go."

"We shall continue on our way to Eashzar." Azzurro replied.

Annak got up, "I shall go to my caravan and ready the horses." He walked to the door, " 'til dusk then" he added, as he stepped outside and disappeared down the stairs.

"I better be on my way too," said Soulange, "I will see you all later." With a smile left the four of us behind.

"Well then," said Azzurro, "I suppose I should get behind the reins of this caravan and start everyone going." He got up. "Oh, and Mikaela," Azzurro looked at her, "please make yourself at home. It will take a few hours before we shall stop for the night."

Mikaela waved her hand in the air, as if to dismiss Azzurro's politeness, and said with a laugh, "Really Azzurro, we have known each other for a very long time, there is no need to be polite with me; we are like family."

"Wait!" I suddenly called out to him, just as he reached the caravan's door. "Do you mind if I join you at the front? It'll be nice to breathe some fresh air and get to see the view on our way. Besides, I'm sure Ari and Mikaela have lots of catching up to do."

Azzurro stopped and turned, "Why not, I would like some company."

We made our way around to the front of the caravan. The rain had moved on, the big black clouds had moved on, taking the rain away with them, leaving a clear blue sky above, but lots of muddy puddles all over the heavily saturated ground. The air was fresh, but so cold that it hurt to take in big deep breaths. Azzurro's caravan was at the head of the Nomads, leading everyone on our way to Katiff. Holding onto the side, I turned my head to look back and see if I could spot Soulange driving her caravan. The colourful convoy that had formed behind us was a beautiful sight.

"She's not there," Azzurro said suddenly, startling me.

"Who? What?" I stuttered, turning around to face him.

"Soulange, she's not riding at the front of her caravan. She will be sitting inside, preparing herself for tonight."

"Soulange?! No, I was trying to spot Annak back there." My face was burning up with embarrassment.

"Ah! Annak. Of course," Azzurro teased me.

"Honestly," I protested, "I wasn't…"

Azzurro gave me a nudge and winked, then gently whipped the horses with the reins to quicken their pace.

"Azzurro," I asked, "that ceremony that Mikaela will perform tonight, what will it do to Soulange? I mean, will it physically transform her into Lexi? Or… how does it actually work?"

"The truth is," he turned and looked at me, "I do not know. This will be the first time it will be performed."

My heart sank again, "Are you telling me that Soulange will be the first EVER 'soul-angel' to go through a merging?!"

"Yes."

"How can you remain so calm about it? This is even more risky than what I thought before. I mean, I was under the impression it would be Soulange's first time undergoing a merging ceremony, not that this will be the first time ever that its been performed!" The fresh crisp air was closing in on me, my heart was beating faster and faster, and a cold sweat was covering my entire body. I was having a panic attack.

Azzurro quickly twisted the reins around his right hand and held them tight, so he wouldn't lose them. With his left hand, he pulled out a small silver flask from under his big coat, removed the cork cap with his teeth, and with a sharp movement thrust the neck of the flask into my throat. The strong, sweet-sharp liquid pouring from it was quickly absorbed in my body as it flowed through my veins, bringing me back out of my panic.

"What was that?" I asked, as I felt warm waves rushing through my body.

"We call it 'Bole's Elixir'; it's made from the trunks of the ancient tall trees in the Great Forest of Galya. You obviously needed a shot of something strong to calm you down." He winked at me again as he loosened the twisted reins from around his hand and took hold of them again in both hands.

"Yes… thank you," I said. "This is all still very strange for me. It's so different from how things are where I come from. Even after experiencing all the strange and amazing things that can happen on this world, I still find it hard to have the same confidence in the 'mystifying unknown' as all of you do. I just want to help my best friend get back here, so we can finish what we started and go home."

"I can understand your feelings, but I must say, you have adapted to my world much better than you might think. As for the 'mystifying unknown'… well, all you need is to accept that there are things at work which are beyond your reach, or understanding. Believe in what you cannot see, cannot touch, and you will come to learn how to feel it inside you. Trust it to guide your way even if, sometimes, it leads you away from it. Remember, nothing is as it seems, and you are never alone."

"I guess you're right." I said, staring into the distance at the road ahead. "I never thought I'd be doing it without Lexi though. I so wish she could be here now…"

Azzurro placed his hand on my shoulder. I turned to look at him as he said in his confident voice, "And tonight, Mikaela will bring her back to us. In spirit at least." His pale-blue eyes sparkled.

We kept on moving, now riding in silence. The sun was right

above us now, its rays were so pleasant and warm that I took off my heavy sheepskin coat and let the warmth from the sun wash over me. I closed my eyes and thought of Lexi. She looked beautiful, wearing a long white dress. She was sitting on a white throne, a clear crystal crown resting on her long black hair. Suddenly she turned and looked at me with her piercing blue eyes.

"Lexi!" I called out loud, as I opened my eyes.

"Easy there." Azzurro grabbed hold of my arm. "Are you okay? You nearly fell off the waggon."

I looked around me. Was I daydreaming, or did I actually see Lexi with my mind? Either way it felt real.

"I must've dozed off a bit," I replied, saying nothing of what I had just seen – or imagined.

"Well, it is a good thing you woke up anyway, we are about to stop…" I could hear Azzurro's tummy was rumbling.

"Is it time for lunch already?"

"I guess it is." He patted his stomach, and we both burst into laughter.

We moved off the main road and travelled towards the Great River. I could hear the gushing water getting closer and closer, until we finally stopped close to the banks of the river.

Azzurro tied the reins to the side-bar of his seat and called out, "Lunch!"

I swiftly jumped off my seat and landed firmly on the ground. Like a well-oiled machine, the Nomads busily began getting lunch underway. The young ones got some logs out from the back of the firewood waggon, as the older women unloaded pots and pans and started organising a field-kitchen. Some of the older men tended to the horses, as the young girls set off towards the river to get fresh water.

I decided to go and check on Annak, see if he needed any help. I was making my way over to him when, suddenly, I felt drawn to turn towards another caravan. The outside of it was beautifully decorated with drawings of fields of wild lavender bushes, with their pale purple flowers blooming. Half-hidden behind the bushes, different phases of the moon were set, against a big backdrop of stars that seemed to be moving in a huge circle. As I got closer to the caravan the stars indeed appeared to be really spinning around. The moon changed from one phase to the next, and the long lavender stems were gently swaying, spreading their perfumed scent around. I was completely intoxicated by the calming smell of lavender that began surrounding me. I could not stop walking, as if an invisible force was pulling me closer and closer towards the caravan. I found myself standing at the foot of its wooden steps. One step, two steps, three… and I was standing at the arched entrance. The door was wide open and a sweet smell of burning oils, mixed with that of melted candle-wax, greeted me.

"Soulange?" I called out quietly, as I made my way into the caravan, not waiting to be invited in.

The curtains were drawn tightly together, not allowing any sunbeams to shine through. While a myriad of tiny candle lights were flickering all around. It took my eyes some time to get used to the deeper darkness inside the caravan. I was about to turn around and leave when suddenly I saw her bright red locks shimmer against the candlelight's flames. I could barely make out her slim silhouette as she lay down, on a very low single bed, in the middle of the caravan.

I took a step forward. "Soulange?" I whispered her name. But she didn't answer. I took a couple more steps and found myself standing directly above her. She looked so peaceful, lying there, in a long white lacy dress. Her hands were folded over her chest. The long sleeves covered them, only the tips of her fingers showing. Her curly red hair rested on a small silk cushion. She looked like an angel. I couldn't stop staring at her, memorising her gentle features, drawn nearer and nearer towards her, until my face was so close to hers that I could feel her warm breath against my cheeks. Another deep breath, and my lips softly brushed against hers. Completely surren-

dering to the moment, I closed my eyes and kissed her.
 Soulange opened her eyes.
 "I'm sorry. I didn't mean to do that." My face was burning up.
 She looked at me.
 "I mean, I did, but…." I straightened up. "I should go," I added, and quickly ran out of the caravan, bumping into the corner of the bed, hitting my shin on the way out.

Proposal

Lexi slowly looked around the empty chamber, still shocked by what she had just discovered about herself, trying to make sense of what she had been told by Naval, her uncle.

'How could it be?' she thought. 'Is it possible that someone else also knew about her connection to Naval? What about Madam Giselle, was she in on the secret? Did my parents tell her who they really were? Who I was?'

"You said you had more to tell me. Go on then, I'm listening." Lexi finally said, staring into Naval's cold blue eyes.

"I admire your feistiness," he replied calmly, "but patience is a virtue, and so you must wait."

"Don't play games with me. You obviously have plans for me, so spit it out!"

"Hmm," Naval played with the ring on his finger, turning it one way then the other. "No, it is your turn now to tell me a few things. And Lexi," he bent forward towards her, then whispered in her ear, "make it interesting!"

Naval turned away and started walking, almost gliding, back to his icy white throne. Lexi got up on her feet and took a couple of steps forward, away from the bed. Just as it had risen up from the floor earlier, the bed disappeared into the floor once more, leaving nothing but a smooth white surface where it had stood.

"I'm not quite sure I understand what it is that you wish me to tell you? Didn't you say you already knew of my arrival to Terah? So you must have also known what I've been up to," Lexi replied, hoping to buy herself some time, to learn how much Naval actually knew.

"And who is it now that is playing games, my dear niece?" Naval said.

Lexi didn't reply, she just stood in her place, focusing her look on Naval, hoping he would reveal more of what he already knew. It was a long and intense moment, which felt forever as neither of them spoke.

"Very well then," Naval finally said. "I shall go first and lay down the track for you to follow in your story." He raised his eyebrow and smiled at her. "The day my brother Lavan, your dear father, fled my Kingdom and indeed this world, he did not only leave his heritage behind." Naval sat down on his throne. "No, in fact, he abandoned Terah and all of those who live here. You see, nature always finds a way to balance itself, otherwise we are thrown into chaos. But it seems my brother never knew that he was my balance, the one who, supposedly, had the ability to control me, since we complete each other, two halves of the same soul."

Lexi was listening intently to every word coming out of Naval's mouth. "Are you saying that my dad could have stopped you? He could have saved Terah? Saved Zarah?"

"NOTHING CAN STOP ME!" Naval screamed at her.

"Maybe nothing can't, but someone..." she stopped in the middle of her sentence, thinking to herself, 'I can, I have the ability to do it and that's a different story.' Her heart was racing but she tried to maintain a calm composure as Naval went on.

"Nature tricked me, not once, but twice! You see, by leaving Terah my beloved brother managed not only to save his life, but he also created **YOU**, the perfect reincarnation of the **One** who could bring my demise." Naval laughed out loud at the irony of it all. "The 'Chosen One', created with **my** own blood! Now there's a dilemma." He paused and bent forward slightly, holding the arms of his throne to keep himself balanced, saying with a sneer to Lexi, "Shall I kill you now, just as I did with your predecessor, and save us both the agony of dragging out this 'loving' family reunion any longer, or..." as he sat up straight again, "let fate play her hand?"

"You need me!" said Lexi slowly, walking forward as she stared at Naval, "you need me alive, otherwise I'd be dead already." She came to a stop only a few steps away from his icy throne.

"When I found out that Lavan left, I sent my 'Elite Guard' to track him down and bring him back." Naval smiled at Lexi, "so I could kill him myself. But he was gone, nowhere to be found in all of the five kingdoms. Impossible! I thought no one could disappear without a trace, just as they cannot appear into existence from out of nowhere."

'He's talking about a bridge between our worlds', Lexi thought, 'the one that Jimmy and I must have crossed.'

"I learned a long time ago not to be quick to dismiss that which cannot be explained logically, no matter how ridiculous it might seem at the time. So when rumours started to come my way, about Lavan crossing over to another world, I kept an open mind. But it was the arrival of you and your friend to Terah that confirmed the existence of 'The Rift' to me," Naval concluded.

Lexi's heart was beating fast; she realised now what it was that Naval wanted from her. "I don't have it!" she burst out at him.

"I know you don't, but you **will** help me get it back!" Naval declared.

"Even if I was willing to help you, which I'm **not**, there is nothing I can do." Staring at the floor, Lexi lowered her voice and whispered, as if to herself, "I lost it in the Labyrinth of Souls."

Naval got up on his feet and started walking towards Lexi. He stood facing her. "But you didn't" he whispered back.

Surprised, Lexi looked up at him then said, "No, it is lost. I know it is, see." She revealed her bare neck and throat, around which the 'Eye of Truth' was no longer hanging.

Naval took a step back. "Rest assured, my girl, the pendant is not lost!"

"But how do you know that?" Lexi was trying to understand how it could have survived the strong currents of the Great River.

"As I told you before, the aquamarine crystal in the centre of your pendant, like this on my ring, are carved from the same source. If the 'Eye of Truth' was truly gone, the crystal placed in the palm of the 'Hand of Faith' would have lost its glow, and the fingers of the hand would close in on it, crushing the crystal and turning it into nothing but pale blue dust."

Lexi slowly let out a breath of relief. 'All is not lost', she thought, 'I just need to get back to Jimmy and the others, they will know what to do. How we can find the 'Eye of Truth' again.'

As if Naval had read her mind he continued, in a haughty tone, "I am your only hope of **ever** finding the 'Eye of Truth' again."

Astounded by Naval's declaration Lexi stumbled backward, almost falling down on the ground.

"I have the ring, it will locate the pendant for me," Naval declared.

"Well, if your ring can do that, what do you need me for?" Lexi responded, trying to find out what he was planning to do with her.

Naval stretched his hand forward towards her. "Join me," he said quietly. "Join me as heir to my throne. Together we will be unstoppable!"

Lexi backed away from Naval, 'He's mad!' she thought.

Panic was taking over from her. "You will never let anyone stand beside you and rule, you said so yourself. You'd kill anyone who tries!"

"Yes, you are right," Naval said, slowly gliding towards her. "But **you**, Lexi, are different from all the others. **You**, my dear niece, are the **key** to everything." Naval placed his hand on her shoulder. "Join me and I will show you how great your destiny could truly be."

Lexi tried to calm herself down. "And what if I refuse? I'm sure you could compel me to join you. Just as you forced all those poor men to 'join' your elite guard."

Naval released his hold of her shoulder, his face turned serious, "I have never compelled anyone to join me. All are agents of their free will. Without it being their own free choice, I would not be able to absorb their minds into my consciousness, become one with them."

"So, if I agree to join you of my own free will, I'll be turned into one of them? A shadow of myself, a puppet you can control, to do your bidding for you, anytime and anywhere as you please?" Lexi felt trapped, frozen in her spot.

"No," Naval said, "you will keep your free will, you are created from my own blood; I cannot control you. You will join me as equals. But know this," Naval paused and looked straight into Lexi's eyes, seeing his own reflection in them and said, "there is always a price to pay for the choices you make, no matter how noble or justified you think they might be."

He made his way back toward his throne, allowing Lexi to ponder upon his proposal.

Preparations

In pain, and bruised both in my ego as well as my leg, I limped towards Annak's caravan. I really needed something to get Soulange off my mind and Annak was the right person for that.

"Annak! Are you there?" I called out loudly as I reached his caravan. "I thought maybe we could practise some more with your weapons?"

There was no answer. Still in pain I started to climb up the wooden steps leading to the caravan's door.

"Annak?" I called again. Suddenly I felt a smack behind my knees. I immediately lost my balance on the ladder and fell flat on my back.

"Are you crazy?!" I shouted at him, "you trying to kill me?"

Annak stood right above me, wearing armour on his upper body, holding a long wooden staff, with one short stubby arm stretched out towards me. His height was barely enough to block the sun out of my eyes.

"Are you resting or fighting?" he grunted.

I grabbed hold of his outstretched arm. With one strong tug, he swiftly lifted me up from the ground and landed me firmly on my feet.

"Ow!" I yelled, grabbing hold of my right shin while trying to balance myself on my left foot. "Have mercy on a wounded man..." I begged.

"Mercy?" Annak looked at me, then bent my left knee again with a jab from the long fighting staff he was holding.

Once again I found myself lying on the ground.

"Are you kidding me? Seriously, can't you see I'm limping?"

"You wanted to practise, no?" He pulled me up again.

"Yes, well, I thought maybe you could show me some new moves, since I can't do much because my leg hurts."

He looked down at my leg then back at me and asked, "Does it hurt very much?"

"Yes." I replied, glad to get some compassion from him at last.

"Good!" He laughed, "That means it is still there!"

"Funny! You're a funny guy..."

"Now stop whining and get ready. Concentrate and try to avoid the staff. Don't let the pain dictate your defeat. Fight through it. Use the pain to channel your moves."

He lifted the staff flat over his head, then started to turn it around and around between his hands. My eyes were fixated on it, following the circular motion of the staff as it turned faster and faster in the air.

Whack!! The tip of the staff slammed the ground hard where I had just been. I managed to leap back and avoid another hit.

"Good!" Annak called out to me.

"Wow! What a rush!!" I said, "Let's try again."

Annak nodded his head. Once again he lifted the staff above his head, only this time he was twisting and turning it all over and around his body. It was much harder trying to focus on the staff, as it kept changing its position very quickly.

Slam!

"Two out of two!" I teased Annak.

"Let's see if you can do it three times in a row?"

"How about I try and knock you off your feet?" I challenged him.

"As you wish." He handed me the long staff.

I lifted the staff up and held it in front of me, then started turning it between my hands.

Whack! The staff hit the ground so hard my whole body was vibrating.

"Try again." Annak said, as he stood about a meter away from where the tip of my staff hit the ground.

I lifted the staff up again, this time above my head, hoping that a high shot would be more effective.

Smack!

Once again Annak was nowhere near my blow.

"Not as easy as it looks," Annak was saying, as he walked back towards me. "Look into your opponent's eyes, then without breaking your gaze, mentally measure his size, memorise his features. Is he wearing armour? Does he have a shield? Where are his 'vulnerable' spots? Where will you make the most damage when you strike him? Then charge."

I took a step back and looked into Annak's eyes. Without breaking my gaze I lifted the staff above my head. I slowly swung it from side to side while trying to decide on the most vulnerable spot on Annak's body. I started to increase the pace in which I was moving the staff around until I gained enough momentum.

Slam! Annak bent forward holding the right side of his stomach, then he fell on his knees all crunched up.

"I'm sorry!" I quickly got to him and helped him to get up on his feet. "Are you okay? I'm really sorry. I didn't think I'd actually hit you. I feel so bad."

Annak slowly straightened up, grabbing my arm as he tried to balance himself on his feet. "You have done well," he said, "very well. I have underestimated you; you have shown me you are a fast learner. But most of all, you are learning to trust your instincts, your feelings, and that is good." He patted me on my shoulder. "Very good!" he added.

"Thanks, Annak." I smiled at him, "I guess I looked for an opening and went for it."

"And a good choice it was." He smiled back at me.

"I figured that due to your height I wouldn't do much damage trying to hit your knees, so the next best thing would be aiming at your stomach. But you are wearing armour, so I had to find a way to penetrate it. And there it was, the gap between the front and back panels of the armour, between the laces binding them together. So I went for it!"

"Excellent, Jimmy!" He nodded his head in agreement, adding "and how does your leg feel now?"

"Hah," I said, "You know what? I completely forgot about it."

"Well in that case, let us go have some lunch. I think we have earned it."

Annak tossed the long staff into his caravan and off we went to the improvised dining area, set up by the bank of the Great River. It was a busy scene with Nomads everywhere, some sitting on the ground with their plates resting on their knees, others sitting up on short wooden stools around improvised field tables. The children ran around between the grownups, causing mischief as they played a sort of 'tag', bumping into some of the diners as they scurried around.

"Jimmy, Annak. Over here!" I thought I heard Ari's voice calling us.

But it was so busy and noisy I couldn't make out where the voice was coming from. I kept looking around trying to locate him, when suddenly I heard a loud whistle and saw two long hands waving at us. We hurried up, trying to avoid stepping over anyone on our way. When we got there we found Ari and Mikaela had already organized some food for us all.

"Nice spot," said Annak, trying to sit himself down without looking too awkward, as he still had his armour on.

"Yes, it was nice to find somewhere cool and shady," Mikaela replied.

"Where is Azzurro?" I asked, looking around.

"He is checking on Soulange," Mikaela said. "She has been in deep meditation since we started on our way this morning. And since it is only a few hours until we perform the ceremony, Azzurro wanted to make sure she is not disturbed."

"Annak and I were practising Long Staff fighting." I tried to change the subject, as I didn't think it would be a good idea mentioning what had happened when I went to visit Soulange.

"Did it hurt much, hitting the ground over and over?" Ari teased me

"He is quite the natural." Annak declared, before sinking his teeth in a fresh bread roll.

"Really?!" Ari looked at me.

"Well don't look to disappointed," I teased back. "I bet I can take you down anytime."

"I'd like to see you try."

"Honestly, you two," Mikaela said. "Will you ever put away your differences and, at least, try and be more civilised towards each other?"

"No!" we both answered.

"Hmmm." She gave us a scolding look.

We left it at that and began enjoying our lunch. After that, feeling quite full and a bit drowsy from the large meal I had just finished, and with the warm sunbeams that slipped through the big branches of the tree, I decided to lie down, close my eyes and relax.

But it wasn't too long before I heard Azzurro's loud voice calling, "Lunch is over!"

I lifted my head and found him standing right next to us.

"Sorry to spoil your afternoon interlude," he said, "but it is time we got moving. We still have a few hours to go, before reaching our destination for the night."

I decided to make the rest of the journey with Ari and Mikaela, travelling with them inside Azzurro's caravan. On the small coffee table stood a large black granite mortar and pestle, with bunches of dried leaves tied together inside it. Three glass bottles full of some sort of liquid stood beside the pestle. A long thin dagger with colourful crystals decorating its hilt was carefully laid on the table, beside five silver candles. It was then that I felt the very strong scent in the air. It smelt like some sort of sweet disinfecting substance. I looked around and discovered its source. A small cauldron, with thick white smoke rising from it, stood on Azzurro's stove, spreading this strong smell around.

"What is that smell?" I asked, waving my hands in the air, trying to clear it.

"Camphor and Lavender oil" Mikaela answered. "We need to burn it in order to purify and cleanse the caravan for the Merging ceremony tonight."

"It looks as if you're trying to smoke something out of here. The smoke is so thick, if it starts spreading around the caravan I don't think we'll be able to see anything." I started coughing.

"The thicker the smoke, the longer the camphor needs to burn and cleanse everything," Mikaela explained.

"Well, by the looks of it, it's going to be a long time before it's finished."

"Yes, it will. We must make sure the caravan is fully cleansed and ready."

"How do you know when it's done?"

"When all that is left is a thin trail of white smoke rising to the air then, and only then, we can start the ceremony," she said, adding another chunk of camphor to the cauldron, followed by eighteen drops of lavender oil from one of the three small bottles on the table.

"And what's with the rest of those things on the table?"

"Come," Mikaela said, gesturing with her hand for me to come and stand beside her. "I'll show you."

It was only then that I saw Ari, half-sitting, half-resting on the low wooden bench alongside the coffee table, his long legs stretched out so that his feet rested on a chair nearby.

"Why don't you hold the mortar," he said, straightening up then adding with a disapproving tone in his voice, "might as well help out, if you're already here."

"Don't mind if I do," I responded cheerfully, pulling out a small chair from under the table and sitting down beside Mikaela.

She placed the entire content of the mortar on the table, then pulled out a bunch of small dried leaves, asking "What can you smell?" She held them close to my nose.

"Mint?" I asked.

"We call it 'Na'ana,'" she explained. "Now smell this," handing me what looked like a small piece of tree bark rolled in on itself.

"I recognise this smell," I said. "It's cinnamon."

"Right, only we call it 'Kinnamon,'" she said placing them both back inside the mortar. "They are used to evoke the spirits. The power of burnt, dried Na'ana leaves, will also protect against the evil eye," she explained. "Now carefully take the pestle and start crushing them together in a circular motion, until they mix into a fine powder."

I picked up the heavy pestle and followed her instructions.

"I shall add some of these leaves and dried flowers. Can you tell by the smell what they are?" she asked.

"Ah, it's lavender. My grandmother used to dry them and hang them in the kitchen in summer."

"Very good." Mikaela smiled at me. "We use lavender to purify and cleanse a place or someone's aura."

"You mean Soulange's aura?"

"Yes. But also we must make sure that Lexi's soul will be in its purest state when merging with Soulange's body."

"What next?" I asked, and then added, "I never thought plants and herbs could have such a powerful use, besides adding flavour and colour to food."

"Well, nothing is ever as it may seem. A beautiful flower can turn deadly if used the wrong way, while a plain and simple garden weed can turn into an antidote when needed," she explained.

"So now you wish to become a herbalist?" Ari mocked me.

"He is certainly showing more interest in the art than you." Mikaela looked up at Ari, who was still half-sitting up on the bench behind the table. "Just because you are blessed with a natural gift for our ways, doesn't mean you are exempted from practising them. One day you will take my place as the high priest and then what will you do?" She raised her right eyebrow at him.

"Let me show you then." He straightened up and picked up one of the small bottles from the table. "Olibanum oil," he said, pulling the cork top off and allowing five drops to drip into the mortar. "You need to add the oil to the rest of the herbs, then let them slowly burn while performing the ceremony, in order to increase the purification and protection of both Soulange' and Lexi's souls as we perform a sort of exorcism on Lexi's Doppelganger." He then grabbed a few dried leaves from the last bunch on the table. "Last but not least, a sprinkle of Rosemary, to accelerate the spiritual growth of all of those taking part in the Merging ceremony." Ari added them to the mortar then said, "Now mix them all well and let them set till the sun goes down."

"Then what?" I asked.

"Then you place them in five burners and light a candle under each burner. The fumes evaporating from the mixture of herbs and oil will play their part in the ceremony," Ari said, pleased with himself.

"No need to be arrogant about it," Mikaela scolded him, "a bit of modesty will go a long way. But never the less, you have done well." She looked at both of us then added, "I see some great potential in you as well, Jimmy."

I felt my face turning red. "What is in the third little bottle?"

"That is Olive oil, we use it to anoint the Soul Angel," Mikaela explained.

I looked around. "What comes next?" I asked.

"We need to prepare the caravan for the ceremony, the sun will be setting before long," said Mikaela.

I placed the mortar on the stove, next to the still-smoking cauldron. Mikaela cleared off the coffee table, placing the small bottles together with the candles and dagger on the bench by the table, while Ari and I folded the chairs, putting them back under the table, then together we lifted the table and moved it further aside to leave the middle of the caravan clear and as empty as possible in such a small space.

"Ari can you help me place the circle in the centre of the floor, please?" Mikaela asked.

Ari pulled out a large piece of heavy white velvety cloth from a leather rucksack, which had been leaning against the bench he previously sat on. As they held it open, raising it up in the air, I noticed it was indeed round in shape. They carefully placed it on the floor and stretched it out so it lay flat and smooth all over.

"Now, we need to stand the five candles on the floor around it so they will create a pentagram. Each candle symbolises one of the five elements of life, Air, Fire, Water, Earth and Aether." Mikaela continued explaining to me as she and Ari placed the candles on the floor by the velvet cloth. "The circle of life is nearly complete, all that is missing is a living body," she added.

"You mean Soulange," I said.

Mikaela nodded her head.

"And what about the dagger?" I asked, pointing at the silver dagger lying on the bench.

"That is for later," Ari said quickly, without giving any other explanation.

Mikaela looked at the smoking cauldron on the stove. "Good, the smoke is thinning down now. It is a good sign. We are but a short while away from having everything ready for the Merging ceremony." She gave me an encouraging smile.

The caravan came to a stop. I walked towards the door to see what was going on and heard Azzurro's voice calling out, "All right everybody, let's set up camp for the night."

Once again everyone was busy organising themselves for the

long-awaited night rest. Within no time at all, the bonfires were blazing, making sure there was plenty of light to keep any 'Night Snatchers' away from our camp.

Standing at the door of the caravan, I could see Azzurro making his way towards us. "How are you getting on with the preparations?" he asked me, as soon as he reached the stairs of the caravan.

"Mikaela says we'll be ready on time, and as soon as the moon is up we can begin."

"Good, not too long then," he said. "I shall go and check on Soulange." Azzurro went off to see her.

I turned back to face Mikaela and Ari again. "So, what do we need to do now?"

"Now, it is time for me to get myself ready," Mikaela said. "If you will both excuse me, I shall leave you and go to meditate." And with that she walked towards Azzurro's sleeping compartment and closed the stained glass doors behind her.

"We should leave her to it," Ari said.

Quietly we walked towards the caravan's door and down its wooden steps. Once outside I looked up at the sky; its colour was a strange blend of dusky pale blue with blood-red streaks running across. Although everybody was busy with doing or preparing something, there was a strange and eerie feeling in the air, as if Ari and I were moving in a completely different place, isolated from the rest of the camp, and that moment in time.

Choices

Naval sat quietly, leaning back on his throne, waiting patiently for Lexi's reply to his proposal. He didn't try to pressure her; it has to be her own decision, her own choice to make if everything was to succeed. But Lexi didn't say a word, didn't move, still frozen in her place, her heart racing, only able to breathe shallowly in and out.

'Can I do it?' she thought; 'can I actually stop him from within? After all, if it is my destiny to do so, as everyone here keeps telling me, could this be the path needed to end it all? To get back home?' Taking a deep breath, Lexi began to feel the blood flowing through her limbs again. Her heartbeat slowed down and a sense of clarity filled her mind. 'Annak was right', she told herself, 'hope is a powerful thing'.

She looked straight at Naval. "You win," Lexi said, as tears started running down her cheeks, "I'll join you."

Merging

It wasn't before long that the sun began to disappear behind the horizon as a full moon took its place, glowing up above us in all its glory. Ari and I sat on the ground beside Azzurro's caravan, not really saying anything. I guess we were both too anxious about what would soon take place to be bothered about having any food, or even being in each other's company.

"You look a bit stressed." I finally broke the silence.

"I guess I am, a bit," Ari answered, his eyes lost, gazing towards the distance.

"Telling the truth," I paused, "…so am I."

"You?!" he suddenly came out of his meditation and looked at me.

"Yes, well, this is a very risky thing, I mean. After all it's never been done before. I can lose everything if it doesn't work."

"You can lose everything?" Ari's face turned all red. "I can lose my MOTHER!" he shouted at me.

"Nobody is losing anyone." Mikaela stood at the top of the stairs.

"No," I quickly replied, "of course not. We were just getting a bit jittery. You know…" I gave her a false smile.

"Why don't you come back inside and relax for a little while before we start. It will help ease your concerns."

I got up on my feet, "Is it that obvious?" I asked her as I climbed the stairs towards the caravan door, with Ari behind me.

Mikaela moved aside so that we could step into the caravan. Everything was ready and waiting for the others to join us. The round white velvet cloth was as we left it, spread in the middle of the caravan's floor. The five silver candles still standing around the circle. Five ceramic burners, each filled with some of the herbal mixture I had prepared earlier, were placed around the caravan. The first burner was standing on the stove, next to the still-smoking cauldron. The second one was standing on the small coffee table, with the dagger resting next to it. Another burner was placed on the floor, by Azzurro's bed, and the fourth one was carefully placed near the caravan door, but far enough so no one could knock it over or accidently bump into it. The fifth and last burner was standing right behind the top silver candle, placed on the floor, next to the white velvet circle. None of them were lit yet, but the scent of the mixed herbs together with the spices and Olibanum oil already filled the caravan. Scattered around the caravan were dozens of tiny candles, all lit up, just like in Soulange's caravan. Their yellow-orange flames softly illuminating the interior of Azzurro's caravan.

"Where do you need us to be?" Ari asked.

Mikaela looked around carefully and then said, "Ari sit yourself behind the silver candle at the top of the circle, facing Azzurro's bedroom." Then turning to me, "Jimmy dear," she said, "I will need you to sit opposite Ari, but close by Azzurro's bed."

"What about us?" I turned to see Annak stepping into the caravan, followed by Azzurro. Soulange, still in a deep trance, was gently held in his arms. Her long white dress trailing behind almost touched the ground.

"Ah," Mikaela said, "you have arrived, wonderful. Azzurro, can you please place Soulange in the middle of the circle, with her head in front of the silver candle at the top of the pentagram, so that Ari will be sitting right behind it."

Carefully, so as not to disturb her trance, Azzurro laid Soulange softly on the white velvet cloth. Mikaela straightened her dress so it covered her legs. Then she spread the hems of it, placing each of its folded corners next to one of the silver candles on the floor, so that they lay to the bottom right and left of the pentagram. Covering the tips of her fingers with the long sleeves, Mikaela placed Soulange's arms close to the edge of the circle and next to each of the silver candles standing at the top right and left of the pentagram.

Mikaela then lit each of the silver candles, before turning to ask, "Can each of you please light the burner closest to you? The ones containing the herbal mixture." She walked towards the stove, carefully picked-up the smoking cauldron and walked back towards the centre of the caravan, where she came to a stop standing at the top of the pentagram, beside the silver candle.

Mikaela raised her hand, holding the cauldron up in the air. Then she began waving it back and forth three times. When she finished she walked clockwise to the next silver candle, then the next one, repeating the ritual above each candle until completing a full circle and returning to the first silver candle. Barefoot, Mikaela very carefully stepped onto the white velvet circle. Holding the cauldron directly above Soulange's head, she let the white smoke rising from it to stream above Soulange's body; first the head, then each of Soulange's stretched arms, and finally down the length of her body to end at the hems of her dress.

That done, Mikaela stepped out of the circle and turned to face me. Lowering the smoking cauldron to the floor she said, "Jimmy, can you please take out the cocoon from under Azzurro's bed and carefully slide it towards me, until it is lying parallel to Soulange."

I looked at her, "Do you mean, Lexi's Doppelganger?"

"Yes." Mikaela replied, "we need it if we are to save Lexi's soul."

I pulled out the big wooden drawer from under the bed. There it was again, the paralysed body of Lexi's Doppelganger, encapsulated in this wax-like cocoon. I stared at it, reminding myself it was not Lexi in there.

Soon you will get what you deserve, I thought, You will be gone and Lexi will finally return to us! I could not help it, but a smile was spreading on my face.

"Do you need a hand?" Azzurro's voice brought me back from my thought.

"Please." I replied.

We lifted the cocoon out of the drawer and carefully laid it on the wooden floor. Azzurro closed the drawer and sat back next to Annak. Carefully, I started to slide the cocoon towards Mikaela.

"That will do. Thank you," she said, and walked towards the coffee table to pick up the third small bottle, which was still full to its top.

"Pure virgin olive oil," she said as she pulled the top out and let some of the light-green liquid drip down her index and middle fingers. She sat down beside the Doppelganger and stated drawing, reciting the names of the five elements of life with every symbol she drew on the outer shell of the cocoon. Once the last symbol was drawn, Mikaela rose to her feet, picked up the still smoky cauldron, and held it above the cocoon.

The white smoke coming from the cauldron became thicker and thicker as she walked around the cocoon. Five times she circled the Doppelganger, each time calling out the name of another one of the elements. "Air, Fire, Water, Earth, Ether."

When she finally finished the last encirclement, she bent forward and placed the cauldron at the top end of the cocoon.

"Please take off the pendant around your neck and hold it inside the white camphor smoke," she asked, looking straight at me.

I was amazed. "How did you know I am wearing the 'Eye of Truth'?"

"I can feel its energy," Mikaela replied.

I did as she asked and let it soak in the white smoke. "What shall I do with it now?"

"Now, I need you to place it around Soulange's neck."

With trembling hands I gently placed the 'Eye of Truth' around her neck, making sure the pendant was resting straight on top of her dress.

"Annak, the dagger, if you may," Mikaela commanded.

Annak picked up the dagger from the coffee table and handed it to her.

"Ari, hold Soulange' right hand for me," she ordered him.

Mikaela went down on her knees, sitting next to Soulange's open hand opposite the pendant. Slowly she pulled the dagger from its sheath, before placing the sheath on the floor next to her. Raising the dagger above her head, with both her hands, Mikaela looked up at its sharp point.

"I call upon the five element of life; Air, Fire, Water, Earth and Ether, to bless the soul of the 'Chosen One' and help it find its way safely into this pure vessel which we present before you." She closed her eyes and said again, "I call upon the five element of life; Air, Fire, Water, Earth and Ether, to bless the soul of the 'Chosen One' and help it find its way safely into this pure vessel which we present before you!"

Then she opened her eyes; they had turned murky white and were without pupils. She looked as if she had gone blind. Without saying a word, letting her other senses guide her, she lowered the dagger and, just as she had done with Lexi the first time we met, pricked Soulange's index finger.

As soon as it began to bleed, Mikaela picked up Soulange's hand, holding the bleeding finger above the aquamarine crystal of the 'Eye'. The blood dripped directly onto the crystal. Once again the drops fell, but instead of running all over the pendant, they were immediately absorbed into the crystal, turning it red, before the colour disappeared, leaving the crystal a clear aquamarine blue once again.

"It is done!" said Mikaela.

At that exact moment the flames from all the candles in the caravan flared up. The shutters and windows of the caravan slammed open, as a gush of frosty wind came rushing from outside, to extinguish the hovering flames.

Two yellow dots glowed in the dark. The eyes in Lexi's Doppelganger opened in its cocoon.

Mikaela screamed as she collapsed to the floor.

"MOTHER!!!" Ari yelled, leaping forward to catch her before she hit the wooden beams.

"NO!!!" cried Annak, as he slammed the small wooden coffee table with his fist, toppling over the burner standing on it, and scattering the herbal mixture inside everywhere.

"I'm sorry," I whispered, "I'm so sorry." Repeating myself over and over again as tears flooded my face.

Soulange sat up. Her eyes were fixated on Mikaela's lifeless body, now resting in the arms of her son, Ari.

"She is awake!" Azzurro announced.

Backlash

Naval stood up, never breaking eye contact with Lexi. Slowly he made his way towards her, until they were standing facing each other in silence.

"You have chosen wisely, niece," he said, and with a swish of his fingers he evaporated the tears off her face.

Lexi said nothing, as she stared into his eyes.

"This inferior existence that has been yours until now will soon come to an end, and we shall ignite the birth of your true destiny." Naval held her right hand up as he spoke, and with his index finger cut into the flesh of her palm, allowing the blood to rush out and slide down her outstretched arm to drop onto the icy white floor. Using the same index finger, he then made a small cut in his silky white shirt, right above his heart. Almost immediately a growing red stain appeared on the shirt; it was Naval's own blood, running out from where he had made the cut. His eyes turned deep dark red. Black, vain-like lines, started to appear over his perfect olive-coloured skin, covering his entire body. His gaze was fixated on Lexi, never breaking his eye contact with her blue eyes.

Naval placed Lexi's bleeding hand over his heart and called out, "Your blood is my blood, my blood is yours!" He then placed his hand over her heart and continued, "Two hearts beating together as one. Me inside you, you inside me; two halves, one soul! One soul united forever!"

Lexi took a deep breath as she felt her heart beating simultaneously with

Naval's. It felt as if they were dancing to the rhythm of the same drum. She could feel his blood running through her veins as if his blood cells where merging with hers and hers merging with his. They were becoming one being, one soul.

And then it was over.

Lexi looked at her right hand, the blood was gone, leaving no trace of a cut anywhere. She turned and looked at Naval's chest, but it too showed no signs of any blood or wound. His eyes were once again blue, and the black veins had disappeared, revealing once more a smooth, unblemished olive skin.

Naval turned away to walk back to his empty white throne. It was at that moment that the crystal in his ring started flashing. He turned quickly and looked at Lexi. She was hovering lifeless in mid-air. Her head was thrown back, hands and legs flapping downwards towards the ground, as if pulled there by force of gravity.

In one quick movement Naval lunged forward towards her, but he was too late. He could not touch her. An invisible bubble surrounded Lexi, keeping her isolated from everyone and everything around her. He tried to push through this invisible force-field, but was thrown backwards and away from it.

Naval got up back on his feet, raised his arms in the air and commanded out loudly, "I call upon the northern winds, give me lightning to break my way in!" A harsh rumble was heard as a bolt of lightning shot out of Naval's hands in the direction of Lexi. It hit the invisible force field surrounding her, then bounced back shooting sparks in all directions.

Naval did not move. Focusing on the invisible barrier he started rubbing the palms of his hands together, calling out "Southern winds hear my call, give me heat to melt this wall!" His hands turned bright red, as he held them open towards the barrier. Streaks of red lines started to appear around the force field, glowing like the hot elements of an electric heater. Thin smoke rose from the direction of the barrier, but it did not melt. Naval lowered his hand and took a step back. Using his right index finger, just as he had done before, he made a cut where his heart was. Naval covered the palm of his right hand in his own blood, as it run out from the fresh cut he had made.

He walked back to the barrier and placed his bloody palm on it calling out,

"Her blood is my blood, my blood is hers, one united soul, never apart!"

Lexi dropped onto the ground. The barrier was down.

She opened her eyes and turned to look at Naval. Two black eyes stared at him, her face pale white, with dark blue veins all over: "I am free again!" Lexi's Doppelganger said, smiling at Naval.

The Balance of Life

Ari held Mikaela's lifeless body, gently stroking her golden locks. His tears were running down his face and falling on to her dress, leaving an ever-growing wet patch on it. Annak stood behind him, his right hand grasping Ari's shoulder, seeking to comfort him, as his own tears disappeared into his short trimmed beard. Azzurro made his way to Soulange as she sat there, still in the middle of the white circle, looking disorientated as she stared down at Mikaela, lying lifeless in Ari's arms.

"Soulange, is it you?" Azzurro asked, as he got down on one knee beside her, not sure if it was Soulange or Lexi that had woken up.

She turned her head and looked at him. "What happened?" she asked, as her green eyes filled with tears.

"My dear Soulange," Azzurro pulled out a small handkerchief from his waistcoat and handed it to her, "I am sorry you had to wake-up to such bad news, but as you can see, the outcome of the Merging ceremony has come at a very high price." He turned his head and looked at Ari and Mikaela, then turned back and stared closely into Soulange's face. "How are you feeling? Is Lexi there with you?"

She wiped her tears with his handkerchief; "I am fine," she said, with a quick smile, "we are both fine."

"So…" Azzurro started to say hesitantly.

"Yes. It worked," Soulange replied, then went on to explain, "Lexi is here with me, but as long as I am conscious and alert Lexi remains dormant, in a state of suspension at the back of my mind, so she cannot hear you." Azzurro looked at Soulange, somewhat bewildered. "Shall I bring her forward?" she asked him.

Azzurro nodded his head.

Soulange stood up, closed her eyes, and took a deep breath. When she opened them again a pair of piercing blue eyes were staring back at Azzurro.

"Lexi!" Azzurro let out a sigh of relief. "This is incredible!" he called in disbelief, "It's Lexi's eyes I see, for sure, but the voice and the body are Soulange."

Shocked and confused by Azzurro's words, Lexi scanned the caravan from behind her new face as if seeking to get her bearing.

"Jimmy!" she called out at me, with a big smile on her face.

Not realising my legs were completely numb from sitting on the floor for such a long time, I jumped to my feet, only to fall back down onto the floor. Excitedly I called back at her from across the caravan. "Lexi! I can't believe you are here. This is so weird!" It was hard for me to contain my excitement. 'Lexi is finally back with us, even if only in spirit, for now'. I kept wiggling my legs trying to get the blood to flow faster through them, so that I'd be able to get up again and go to her.

Lexi's expression turned serious as she looked down at Mikaela, finally realising that Mikaela wasn't moving. Lexi looked at me again, then at Annak, and then at Ari. "Mikaela…, is she…?"

"Dead!" Ari burst out at her, "Yes, my mother is dead! There, I've said it out loud; my mother is dea…" he couldn't finish the sentence again, his voice was breaking up.

Lexi reached out her hand and gently placed it on his. "Oh Ari," she said, "I am so sorry."

I finally got the sensation back in my legs, got up and hurried to Lexi's side. She grabbed hold of me and gave me a big hug. It was strange, and very awkward, having Lexi hug me with Soulange's body. I slowly let go of her embrace, trying to concentrate on Lexi's blue eyes rather than Soulange's body.

"Jimmy, I don't understand, what happened?" she asked. "How did I get back here? I mean, one minute I was standing opposite Naval and the next…"

"Naval?" I cut her short, "did you say you were with Naval?" I turned and looked at Azzurro and Annak.

"Yes," she said, "he held me at the White Fortress. Why?" She paused, then with a questioning look on her face asked the three of us," Where did you think I was?" Before we could answer that, "And what happened to my body?" she said, examining her hands and body.

"We thought you were lost in the Great River." I replied. "Maybe even dead, although I always believed it couldn't really be true, that you had to have made it somehow!" I looked at the others, happy they had been proved wrong. "However, after discovering your Doppelganger harbouring amongst us and it telling us that you were gone, well…"

"My what…?" she asked.

"Your Doppelganger, you know, your evil self." I said. "That's how you ended up in Soulange's body. In order to bring you back from the dead, we needed a host for your soul to live in and Soulange…" I paused, "well, she is the Angel of Souls."

Azzurro cut in, "There is quite a lot of catching up and much more explaining to do, but enough for now." He looked at Ari as he continued, "We need to prepare to say our goodbyes to our dear friend."

Lexi looked at Azzurro suspiciously. "And who might you be?" she asked.

"Oh, wow," I said, "Of course, you wouldn't know who he is because it wasn't you we pulled out of the Great River." It felt very awkward. "Lexi, this Azzurro, leader of the Nomads and leader of the resistance against Naval."

Azzurro starched his arm towards Lexi's and said, "I am glad to finally meet the 'real' Lexi. Jimmy has told us much about you." He gave her one of his cheeky winks.

"Excuse my initial suspicions, glad to have you on our team," she grabbed his hand and shook it firmly. "Now, who is this Soulange you mentioned before?" she turned and asked me.

"Soulange is Azzurro's niece and your gracious host, for the time being," I replied. "But as you can imagine there is a much longer explanation to it all. We can do all that at a later time. We really need you to send Soulange back now," I said, disappointed we couldn't go on talking.

"Well then, I better send Soulange back to you," Lexi concluded.

"Do you even know how to do it?" I asked.

"Yes," she replied with no hesitation, "I don't know how I know, but I do."

"It's good to have you back Lexi." I smiled at her.

"It's really good to be back, even though I'm still not clear as to what or how it happened. And Jimmy," she added, "thanks for believing in me." Lexi closed her eyes and took a deep breath. When she opened them again a pair of green eyes were staring back at me.

"Soulange..." my face turned red again.

"Jimmy," she smiled, "hello; how was Lexi?"

"Confused." I replied, trying to calm myself. "I guess it's strange for all of us, this soul-merging thing."

"Good! It is you again." Azzurro said, "We shall need your help in the preparations."

"Of course," she replied, "what would you like me to do?"

Azzurro looked at Ari then turned back to Soulange and said, "I would like you to help Ari in getting Mikaela ready. I am sure there are things better left for a woman to do. But as he is High Priest now and leader of the people of Galya you will need to follow his instructions."

"Azzurro, how can I help?" I asked.

"For our own safety, we need to clear my caravan from all evidence that the Merging ceremony ever happened, starting with putting the Doppelganger back in the drawer under my bed."

Azzurro and I dealt with the Doppelganger, while Soulange went over to Ari and Annak who was still comforting him. She sat down by Mikaela's head. Pulling out from under her sleeve the handkerchief Azzurro had given her earlier to wipe her tears, Soulange used it to tenderly wipe away Ari's tears that were still falling onto Mikaela's face.

"Ari," Soulange said in a quiet, but firm, voice, "it is time to get her ready for her last farewell. I will take good care of her, I promise." She held his hand and looked at his face.

As we closed the drawer below Azzurro's bed, with the Doppelganger once more safely lying there, Azzurro made his way back to Soulange. He bent slightly forward beside her, and got down on one knee again.

"You can let go of her now," he said to Ari, "I am only taking her to Soulange's caravan." Azzurro started to slide his arms under Mikaela's body.

"No!" Ari said sharply, "I will do it. It is my duty."

Together with Azzurro and myself, Annak helped Ari get on his feet. We held him up straight, keeping him balanced until he could move his numb legs again. Then Soulange gathered the long train of Mikaela's dress in her hands, Ari straightened his posture, and with his head held high and Mikaela firmly grasped in his arms, he made his way towards the door. Making sure Mikaela's train was out of the way, Soulange followed silently as Ari carried his mother back to her caravan.

Using his sleeve to wipe the tears off his face and beard, Annak turned to Azzurro and asked, "How could this happen? What was it that went so wrong, for Mikaela to pay with her life?" He wiped his face again, as new tears came sliding down. "All this time we were worried about what might happen to Soulange, only to find that it was Mikaela's well-being we should have concentrated on."

I felt guilty. "As glad as I am to have Lexi back with us, I never wanted anyone to pay with their life for it, least of all Mikaela."

"You mustn't blame yourself, Jimmy," Azzurro said, grabbing my shoulder, "we all knew the risks involved."

"Yes, but we based them on the wrong assumptions," Annak added.

I looked at him puzzled and asked, "How do you mean?"

"Well, the only reason we considered the merging of Lexi's soul with Soulange's body was because we assumed Lexi was dead." He paused, then continued "But you were right all along Jimmy, Lexi was still alive." He shook his head and took a deep breath, "Lexi was alive" he repeated, as if to himself.

"But the merging worked so…?" I didn't understand what Annak was trying to say.

"You see," Azzurro started to explain, "Lexi was alive when the ceremony took place and you are not allowed to merge a living soul with the body of a Soul Angel. Someone must pay the ultimate price for intervening with the delicate fabric of life itself."

"So why Mikaela? Why not any of us?" I asked. "We were all present when the ceremony took place."

"Because Mikaela performed the ceremony. She was the one who worked the bonding of Lexi and Soulange together," Azzurro replied.

"Life must balance itself," Annak added.

"Shame it couldn't use the Doppelganger to balance itself." Azzurro said, half-jokingly.

"The Doppelganger," I exclaimed as I suddenly remembered, "Its eyes were glowing just as Mikaela finished the merging."

"Are you sure?" Azzurro's voice turned serious.

"Yes, I'm sure," I replied, "but they were only glowing for a second."

Annak gave Azzurro a fearful look. "Do you think…?" he stopped in mid-sentence, shaking his head in disbelief.

"It must be," Azzurro said, "life must balance itself." He too sounded very worried.

"What are you talking about?" I shouted at them in frustration, feeling as if both of them were having a private conversation without me.

"Sorry, Jimmy, we didn't mean to keep you out, but if what you say is true, then things have taken a turn for the worst," Azzurro told me.

"Worst? How?" I asked, looking at them both.

"It is very simple," Azzurro started explaining to me, "Mikaela, unknowingly, pulled Lexi's soul out of her still living body. By doing that Mikaela accidently created a void in the balance of life which needed filling. So, the only way for Lexi's living body to remain 'alive', was by hosting Lexi's own Doppelganger's dark soul in it. Meanwhile Lexi's soul merged with Soulange's body, as we planned." He stopped for a second, then delivered the final blow. "But unfortunately for us, if Lexi was indeed with Naval at the time of the merging, then that means the Doppelganger is now with him."

"It knows all our plans," I said, "everything we talked about while It was pretending to be 'our' Lexi. So now Naval knows everything." At last I had realised the severity of our situation.

Annak and Azzurro shook their heads in agreement. There was no need for them to say anything more.

"So what now?" I asked, horrified.

"Now we need to finish clearing my caravan, then we need to prepare for Mikaela's final farewell." Azzurro replied calmly.

Gaps

It was very late at night, way past any of our 'bed times'. The endless shimmering stars lit up the dark sky, as the moon beamed bright in its full glory. It should have been a night of celebration, but instead it turned out to be a night of heartache and grief.

Having Lexi back was great, but was the price really worth it, I kept wondering. Mikaela's loss was devastating indeed, especially to Ari, who had now lost both his parents in the fight against evil. But now, the fact that Naval had been united with the Doppelganger, and It knows our plans, was no less a heavy blow. It felt as though time was running out while we were fighting a lost battle.

"Jimmy, what's on your mind?" Azzurro asked me, as he moved the small coffee table back to its place under the caravan's window.

"I'm just thinking what a rotten situation we are in now," I replied.

"Yes, well, it is not quite what we planned, but…" Azzurro gave me a mischievous look, and continued, "we have Lexi back and she has valuable information that can help us," and then he winked at me.

"How can you remain so calm about it all? I wish I could share some of your optimism," I said crossly.

Annak, who was standing beside me, said in a quiet voice, "Hope."

"Excuse me?" I asked him.

"Hope," he said again.

"What's hope got to do with it?" I was getting frustrated.

"As long as you have hope in there," Annak placed his hand on my heart, "you will find a way to overcome anything. Nothing is over until you have taken your very last breath." He patted me on my shoulder.

"I suppose you're right," I muttered. "It's just really annoying. Every time we seem to get a break, things only end up getting worse then when we started. When will it be our time to have the upper hand?"

"Soon," Annak replied.

I turned and looked at Azzurro, who was nodding his head in agreement.

Trying to be a bit more optimistic, I helped Annak fold the large white velvet cloth that was spread on the caravan's floor. We collected the five silver candles that were still standing in their place and placed them inside the velvet cloth, then returned everything inside the leather backpack where they had originally been. Azzurro cleared the content of the burners into the black cauldron and set them alight. Almost immediately the caravan was filled with the scent of the burning herbs. It was quite pleasant and relaxing. I picked up the silver dagger from the floor and held it in my hands.

Still examining it, I turned to Azzurro and asked, "Where does this go?"

"It needs to be returned to Ari, it belongs to him now," he replied.

"Ari, the High Priest," I smiled to myself, "now that's something I never thought of before…"

"He might just surprise you," Azzurro said to me in a serious tone.

"Hah," I grunted and tucked the dagger into my belt, behind my back.

Azzurro looked around the caravan as he picked up the last empty burners, placing them on the stove, next to the smoky cauldron.

The caravan was once again back to the way it had been before the 'Merging' ceremony took place. By now the first beams of the rising sun came shining through the caravan door.

"Coffee anyone?" Azzurro asked, as he lit a small flame under the kettle.

"Sure," Annak and I replied together.

"A new day is dawning upon us," Annak said, staring outside.

"A new day, a new beginning," Azzurro added, pouring the thick dark liquid into the glass cups.

"So what is to happen today?" I asked them, as I sat down on the bench by the table.

Azzurro and Annak pulled out a small chair each, from beneath the coffee table. Then Azzurro brought the cups of coffee over and they sat down.

"Well," Azzurro said, "Soulange will have to finish preparing Mikaela's body for the farewell, which will take place tonight, while the moon is still in its fullest form." He paused, then went on, "Ari will need his time to prepare for the ceremony, and we need to talk to Lexi." Azzurro looked directly at me.

"I'm guessing you want me to fill her in on the 'good news' about where things stand?" I asked him, knowing what his reply would be.

"It is certainly better if Lexi hears it from you," he said.

We sat there quietly, slowly sipping our coffee, looking outside as the new day began to unravel itself, listening to the busy noises of the Nomads as they bustled about with their morning preparations.

It wasn't much later that Soulange's voice came calling from outside the caravan. "Azzurro? Can I come in?"

"Morning my dear, do please come in and join us," he replied.

I could hear her slowly climbing up the three wooden stairs leading to the caravan's door. I don't know what excited me more, the thought of seeing Soulange or being able to talk again to Lexi. Either way, my heart had started racing. On one hand, I still wasn't sure if Soulange remembered what had happened in her caravan, and on the other, I really wasn't looking forward to being the bearer of more bad news to Lexi.

"Good morning," Soulange said as she walked through the door, "I didn't realise you were all here already." My heart beat faster as she smiled at me.

"We never left," Annak replied, his husky voice sounding a bit grumpy.

"We had to clear up the caravan," Azzurro explained. "It was an eventful night for all of us, but for you in particular. How are you feeling today my dear? And how is Ari doing?"

Soulange helped herself to a cup of coffee from the remainder that was left on the stove. "Ari is really amazing," she began, "he is so brave. The way he took over his responsibilities as 'High Priest', explaining to me what I need to do with Mikaela, how I should prepare her. He is a true leader. I could tell he was hurting inside, my heart went out for him." She took a sip from her coffee and continued, "He waited outside while I washed her and put her in a white dress. Then, as Ari had instructed me, I brushed her hair and braided it into one long golden braid. Once I finished, Ari joined me in the caravan. He placed Mikaela's hands over her chest and gently kissed her on the forehead. Then the two of us together wrapped her in a silver silk shroud that Ari brought from Annak's caravan. Now she is all ready for tonight's ceremony and Ari is preparing her pyre." Soulange took another sip from her cup, then continued, "so, after what was a very long night I am quite exhausted, both emotionally and physically, but fine otherwise."

"Good," Azzurro murmured, then went on to ask, "and how is Lexi doing? Can you tell?"

"I cannot 'feel' Lexi inside me, but I am aware of her presence and all seems well. It is a very strange sensation," Soulange replied. She walked over to me and sat herself down by my side. "Jimmy," she placed her hand on mine, staring into my eyes, "and how are you feeling now that you have your Lexi back? You must be very happy."

My face turned red, my whole body turned red as I began to sweat. "Ah..., yes..." was all that I managed to say.

"What did she tell you?" Soulange let go of my hand, still looking at me.

I took a deep breath and tried to calm my nerves, "She was quite confused at first, but then she said..."

"Of course she was, the poor thing, who knows what she has been through." Soulange burst in, sounding concerned.

"Actually, she's been with Naval," I went on.

"Naval?!" she looked at the three of us, her green eyes wide-open in horror.

Azzurro reassured her, "Lexi is a strong young girl, she is fine. But, as you can imagine, we have a lot of catching up to do... so."

Soulange nodded her head, "Of course you do. I shall bring her forward."

She closed her eyes and took a deep breath, just as she had done the night before. When she opened them again, it was Lexi's piercing blue eyes staring back at us.

Annak was the first to talk. "Lexi," he called her in his husky voice, "I didn't have a chance to welcome you back last night, it was very..." he paused and look down for a second, trying to compose himself, "It is good to have you back, 'Chosen One.'"

Lexi smiled back at him, "Thanks Annak, It's good to see you too."

It was Azzurro's turn then to spoke, "Lexi, last night you said you were with Naval this whole time. We need to know everything that happened, what was said, no matter how insignificant you think it might be."

"Alright," she said, "where should I begin?"

Azzurro thought for a second then replied, "You better start a bit before you ended up with Naval. Why don't you start at the last point we believed you were still with us, when the three of you arrived at the Labyrinth of Souls."

Lexi bit her lower lip. "Wow, that was so long ago now, I don't remember much, to be honest. It is all a big blur." She tried to concentrate. "All I remember is walking along the Great River together with Jimmy and Ari. Ah, yes, and we had that white falcon with us," she looked at me, "you know, Naval's spy."

"Actually, he wasn't Naval's spy," I interrupted, to correct her, "he's really on our side, helping Azzurro and the resistance."

The surprise on Lexi's face only emphasized how much she had missed, all the time she had been away from us, and just how much knowledge her Doppelganger possessed about us.

"That poor falcon," she eventually said, "what have we done to it?"

"Don't worry," I said with a smile, "he's fine, we have apologised and we are all friends now."

Lexi settled down in her seat, "So we were walking along the river and…" she stopped again as she tried to remember what happened next, "I'm sorry, I can't remember, it's as if my memory is blank and all that is left is a big, black empty hole instead."

"That makes sense," Azzurro said, "it is the first time your Doppelganger was trying to take over your consciousness, before creating a clone of your body for it to exist in."

"You've mentioned that Doppelganger thing before, how did it get here? And why is it that, apparently, only I have one?"

"Well, in short, Doppelgangers are exact duplicates of any living creature, only they possess the essence of one's evil and darkness." I repeated what Azzurro had told us. "But it's a long and complicated story and I promise you I will tell you all about it another time," I said.

Lexi appeared shocked with what she had heard, "The essence of my darkness…" she paused for a second, "why should I be surprised, really, I mean after all evil is in my blood, being Naval's niece and all."

"You are **what**?!" I nearly jumped up off my seat.

"Yes," Lexi confirmed, "apparently Naval is my father's twin. Can you imagine that?" She spoke casually, but with a hint of irony in her voice.

Azzurro, Annak and I exchanged very surprised looks between

us. This was something we definitely had not expected to hear.

"That means you are the rightful heir of the Navaran throne," Azzurro said.

"Yes," Lexi replied, "that is what Naval told me too."

"And he still let you live? Knowing you pose a threat to his throne?" Annak looked puzzled, "Why didn't he kill you?"

"He needs me. He's planning to cross through The Rift and he can't do it without me. Apparently killing me and absorbing my powers, as he did before with Zarah, won't work this time. Naval needs me alive in order to cross between the worlds. He even offered me to join him, as his equal."

"And you said no, of course." I continued her sentence.

"Actually, I agreed to his proposal."

"You WHAT?!" I shouted at her, "have you completely lost your mind?" I looked at Azzurro and Annak and said, "Naval must have done something to her, there is no way Lexi would have agreed to join him otherwise." I quickly pulled out the dagger from behind my back, and pointed it at Lexi.

"Trust me, Jimmy," Lexi said quietly, moving my hand that was holding the dagger away from her. "I know what I am doing, what I planned on doing, anyway, before you brought me back here." She looked at me and went on to explain. "Being Naval's niece, having his blood running in my veins, that gives me some leverage over him. For him, I am more than just his niece, or just another Chosen One. I am a powerful combination of both, a power he cannot control or possess himself. That is why, I think, he offered me the chance to join him. Naval's obsession with gaining power is stronger than him, he cannot allow himself to lose such a rare opportunity with me, especially if he is planning to expand his realm beyond this world. And that is why, I believe, he did not kill me. My importance is blinding his better judgment." Lexi looked carefully at each of us, as if to emphasise what she has just said.

"She has a point there," it was Annak who broke the silence.

"A good one," Azzurro agreed, "especially now that we know for sure Naval is looking for The Rift."

"So what now?" I looked at the three of them as I put my dagger away.

"We need a plan," Lexi replied.

"Yes," I said, "but before we get to that, there are some things I need to fill you in on." I paused and gazed quickly at Azzurro, "Important things that you missed while you were gone and that you must hear about."

Lexi nodded her head and stood up on her feet. "Perhaps it's better if you and I talk about them outside in the fresh air. Shall we go for a walk then?"

"Good idea," I replied, as Annak and Azzurro nodded their heads in agreement. Outside, all around us the Nomads were busy with their painting, practicing with their musical instruments, or working hard on some artwork or other, as their children scampered around the campsite. Lexi was completely mesmerised by what she saw, and the Nomads themselves kept waving and wishing us "Good Morning," as we passed by, not realising it wasn't Soulange I was walking with.

After a while we found a quiet spot under some trees, close by the caravan camp, and there we sat down to talk. I told Lexi what had happened to her when we got close to the location of the Labyrinth of Souls and what she had done there. How Annak and the Nomads found and rescued us from the stormy water of the Great River. I explained about the Map and its connection to the 'Eye of Truth', about the Extraordinary Artefacts of Terah, and how we came to realize that she was no longer with us when I revealed the existence of her Doppelganger amongst us, and finally I explained to her how we came up with the plan of saving her soul by using Soulange's special ability as the Angel of Souls.

"Oh Jimmy, how awful!" Lexi exclaimed and hugged me, as she said "I can't imagine what you must have gone through all this time."

"It hasn't been easy, thinking I would be stranded here forever, without you," I replied. "But the others were great, they wouldn't let me lose hope or feel that I was on my own. They have truly welcomed me into their fold."

Lexi gave me a warm smile. "I'm glad you were okay and well looked after," she said. "When I was held in the darkness, all cold and damp, I was sure I had lost you." Tears started to flood her blue eyes, as she hugged me tight again, "I never thought I'd see you again."

"What do you mean, in darkness? Lexi ,what exactly happened to you?"

She let go of me and wiped her tears with her sleeve. Then it was her turn to tell me. "As I said before, I don't remember much from when we got close to the Labyrinth until I woke up in that dark place." She described her encounter with 'Lady' and the White Fortress, and how they are all connected together; her meeting with Naval and the true story of her father, prince of Navara, and his family.

"Listen, Lexi…" I started to say, trying my best to sound as serious as I could. "There is one more thing you need to know," but before I could tell her about our suspicions that the Doppelganger took her place with Naval, and all that means, a loud shriek shattered the peaceful morning break.

Farewell

I looked around, and then up at the clear blue sky above us, trying to locate the source of that shriek. All I could see was a small white dot in the far distance, which kept getting closer and closer. It moved so fast that soon enough I was able to make out its shape. I straightened up, not breaking eye contact with it.

"We have a visitor," I said, pointing at it.

A moment later the falcon landed on one of the lower branches of the tree next to us.

"Tercel," Annak called out, as both he and Azzurro ran fast towards where Lexi and I were sitting. "What is it?"

"I have some dire news for you," the falcon said. His head turned towards me as he continued, "Lexi is alive! She is held in the White Fortress, and said to be under the close supervision of Naval himself."

I looked at Tercel, "We know."

"You know?!" Tercel's head was bobbing around, looking at us from one to the other.

Azzurro stretched out his arm, "It is better if you come closer."

Tercel flew down and landed on Azzurro's arm, "So you have called off your plans for the Merging? Good! I shudder to think what would have happened if you had gone through with it."

The four of us exchanged looks, wondering which one of us

should tell him he was too late.

"What is it?" Tercel asked. "What am I missing here?"

I answered him, "Well, the reason we know Lexi was with Naval is because…" I stopped and looked at Lexi, then continued, "she told us herself."

Clearly shocked by my revelation, Tercel opened his little beady eyes as much as he could, followed my lead and turned to look at Soulange. "Lexi?!" he called out in surprise, as her blue eyes gazed back at him.

"Hello Tercel," she quietly said.

"But… when did this happen?" Tercel was clearly confused by now.

"Last night," Azzurro replied. "We held the ceremony last night."

"So it worked," Tercel said happily, "you returned Lexi alive to us." His relief showed as he went on, "And no ramifications as a result."

"I'm sorry my friend, but it is not all good news, I am afraid," Azzurro told him. "the ceremony returned Lexi to us, but it took the life of Mikaela."

Tercel bowed his head down. "No…" he whispered, "then I was too late…" a single teardrop fell from his eye.

Azzurro stroked the falcon's head. "But you are here now, and still have a chance to say your goodbyes."

"Mikaela's 'Farewell' ceremony will take place tonight," Lexi added, hoping it would help to comfort Tercel a bit.

Tercel straightened his head and looked at Azzurro. "But she is the High Priestess, her send-off must take place at the Gwir."

"You are right." Ari's voice came from behind us. "According to Galyan tradition, as High Priestess and leader of our people, my mother's final 'Farewell' should be held at the Gwir, our most sacred place. However, we are quite a long way from there, and time will not allow us to return. We shall hold the ceremony here, tonight. Once we have accomplished our mission, I will take her ashes back to the Gwir and scatter them around her Tree of Life, the same tree that sprang out from beneath the ground on the day she was born."

Tercel turned on Azzurro's arm to face Ari. "My dear boy," he started to say, "where shall I begin…?" He stretched out his right wing towards Ari and with the soft feathers at its edge gently stroked him.

"Thank you, Tercel," Ari told him, then turned to face Lexi and said, "contrary to what you might think, I am truly happy to see you are well and back where you belong. I apologise if my reaction last night made you feel less than welcome." He stretched his arm out towards her, seeking a handshake.

Lexi's blue eyes were sparkling as she grabbed hold of Ari and gave him a warm embrace. "I never, even for a minute, thought anything bad about your reaction to my return last night. I am awfully sorry for your loss, but am very glad we are still friends."

"And I give you my word," Ari began, looking intensely into Lexi's eyes, "as High Priest of Galya, that I will do everything in my power to reunite your body and soul again. I will never stop until it is done and you will become stronger than ever, able to stand against Naval and defeat him."

"I know you will," Lexi replied, smiling back at him.

"Hey, your 'holiness,'" I teased Ari, "how about some lunch in the meantime?"

"You do realise that with my new abilities I can, quite easily, silence that annoying voice of yours?" Ari turned and looked at me.

"Well, I am glad to see you two have not lost your fondness towards each other," Azzurro intervened. "Only Ari, you will not gain your mother's abilities until after the Farewell," he added, in a half-serious but half-jesting tone.

Ari shrugged his shoulders and replied, "I know, but it was worth it, only to see that shocked look on Jimmy's face."

As I looked into Ari's eyes, I could see his pain reflecting back from them, his whole facial expression had changed into a serious and more mature one, well beyond his seventeen years. Having already suffered the loss of his father didn't make it any easier for Ari, when his mother was taken from him too. So it was good to see him joking and in good spirit, after all that had happened last night.

Azzurro came closer to Lexi and suggested, "I think it would be wiser if, before we join the others for lunch, Soulange would join us again. We don't want to raise any suspicions if people talk to you, thinking you are Soulange, expecting to see her green eyes and instead have your blue ones staring back at them."

Lexi nodded her head in agreement. "I guess I'll see you all later then." And with that she closed her eyes, took a deep breath, and sent Soulange back to us.

"Hello every one," said Soulange, "I hope you had a productive morning." Then she saw Tercel, "And hello to you too," she added.

"A most productive morning indeed," Azzurro answered her, adding, "but now it is lunchtime," as he rubbed his rumbling tummy.

Tercel flew off Azzurro's arm and up onto one of the higher branches of the tree, where he would wait for our return, while we made our way towards the kitchen for some lunch. The smells coming from the huge trays of food already placed outside were so tempting, and the long line that had formed in front of them was moving so slowly, that I didn't think I would be able to survive another minute without putting something in my stomach to calm my hunger down.

"Here, have some bread, you can nibble on it till we get to the main dishes." Soulange handed me a piece of fresh bread that she had torn off from the loaf in front of her.

Embarrassed by the loud sounds coming from my stomach, I quickly took it from her hand and stuffed it in my mouth. "'Ank you," I said with a full mouth.

She smiled at me and said, through a giggle, "You are welcome, but try not to choke on it, we are almost at the meat tray."

Holding our plates, now piled high with delicious food, in one hand, and cups of some sweet nectar in the other, we went back to where Tercel had perched, and sat down under his tree, to enjoy our lunch at last.

"So Jimmy, tell us all you have learned from Lexi," Azzurro said, as we finally put our plates aside with contented looks and full stomachs.

I took a last sip of nectar, "From what she has said, it appears she was held at the White Fortress in Navara the entire time she was missing. However she cannot remember how she got there."

Tercel came flying down and landed on the grass beside us. "Well, then," he said, "that confirms what I have told you."

"Hmm, but was there anything else?" Azzurro asked.

"Perhaps some valuable information we didn't already know," Annak anxiously added.

"Yes, Lexi said she got the impression that the White Fortress is some sort of a living being. Together with anything or anyone else that might be inside, everything is connected to Naval, and somehow he controls it all."

"How do you mean?" Azzurro asked, puzzled.

"Well," I went on, "Lexi said that the fortress was like a big block of ice, and that the chambers, the corridors leading to them, and the windows in the rooms, were all created when and as needed by this 'white being' she called Lady. Lexi also said that when she was with Naval, in his chamber, he created the furniture from out of the floor, lifting things up at will and then dissolving them back into it when they were no longer needed."

Azzurro looked at Tercel, "Were you aware of that? Is it the same with the quarters of the 'Falconry Guard'?"

"No!" Tercel shook his feathery head, "I was certainly not aware of that! The falconry is indeed a part of the 'White Fortress', but we have lived in the same complex we were given ever since Naval captured us and forced us to work for him."

"How do you communicate with him then? Whom do you report to?" Annak interjected, leaning slightly forward towards

Tercel as he spoke.

Tercel leaped back a bit, apparently feeling threatened by Annak's line of questioning, maintaining a safe distance from him. "We inform the Chief Sentinel then he, and only he, reports back to Naval. That is how we learned about Lexi being held there. Upon his return, the Chief Sentinel told us that while flying on his way to deliver his latest report to Naval, he caught a quick glimpse of a young woman behind the opening of a porthole in one of the very top and isolated towers."

"How could your Chief Sentinel know it was Lexi?" Annak inquired further.

"He certainly did not know!" Tercel replied. "However, with his extremely sharp eyesight he could clearly see the face of the young lady, and was able to describe her to us in detail. I, of course, immediately recognised her as Lexi, but said nothing to the others. As soon as it was safe to do so, I took off in search of you, to warn you of Lexi's whereabouts, hoping that I would be able to stop you from going ahead with your plans for the Merging."

Feeling the tension building between Tercel and Annak, Azzurro quietly intervened. "You have done well, my friend," he said, as he stretched out his arm so that Tercel could fly over and sit with him.

"Yet, I was too late," Tercel said again.

Sitting next to Azzurro, Soulange leaned towards Tercel, "Yes," she said, "but you tried to get here on time, putting your own safety at risk, despite the dangers involved in doing so." Then, looking at Annak before continuing, "I am sure Mikaela would have appreciated your efforts had she been here with us."

Realising he may have appeared too aggressive towards Tercel, Annak agreed with Soulange as he muttered, "Yes..." in his husky voice.

Annak and Tercel having made peace with each other again, I continued with the rest of what Lexi had told me.

"And he killed his own mother?!" Soulange said, finding it hard to believe how Naval could tear his way out of his mothers' pregnant belly, "a baby and such pure evil…"

"Yes, that's what Lexi said too," I replied.

Soulange looked at Azzurro, "How are we ever going to defeat such evil?" she asked him.

Azzurro stretched out his hand to stroke her hair, trying to comfort her, then replied, "We are not. It is not our destiny to do that, it is the Chosen One's. Lexi must face him on her own, for it is she who is the one destined to do that. We are only here to help and guide her, and to protect her on her quest."

"But he is her uncle, surely you do not expect her to kill him now that she knows of her kinship to him?" Soulange asked.

I took hold of her hand, saying confidently, "Don't worry, Lexi will come through! She knows what she needs to do and she will do it."

"How can you be so sure?" Soulange asked, looking directly at me.

"I know Lexi better than anyone else, and I know she will always do the right thing."

"But that was somewhere else, you were different people then. Here she is the Chosen On, and also the rightful heir to the Navaran throne." Soulange argued her point.

I turned and looked at the rest of the group to say, "Well, she has never failed me before!"

Annak nodded his head at me, then turning to face the others, he said in a most definitive tone of voice, "One thing is for sure, if we are to defeat Naval it is imperative for us to find the rest of the Artefacts."

Everyone agreed with that.

"Friends," Azzurro then said, "as the day is coming to an end, and it won't be too long before the sun sets and the full moon rises, I would suggest that we all have a bit of a rest before tonight's Farewell ceremony." And with that he shook Tercel of his arm and got back on his feet.

We all followed his lead and got up from the ground, collecting our empty cups and plates as we did so.

"Ari," Soulange called, "will you need me at the ceremony, or would you like me to send Lexi?"

Ari looked at her as he paused to think for a moment, "It is very kind of you to offer to send Lexi to the ceremony, I think she would like to be there. I am confident I will be able to handle the ceremony on my own, since your help earlier in preparing everything for me was most important. Thank you for that, Soulange," he said, giving her a warm smile.

"Well then, if you gentleman will excuse me, I shall rest for a while before sending Lexi to you." And with saying that, Soulange made her way to her caravan.

"I need to go and prepare myself too," Ari added, as he set off walking back towards Annak's caravan.

"Wait!" I called out to him, "I've got something here of yours."

Ari stopped and turned, waiting for me to catch up to him. "What is it?" he asked when I got there.

I put my hand to my back and pulled out the silver dagger stuffed in my belt. "I believe this is yours," I said, as I handed it to him.

Ari's eyes opened wide, "Where did you find it?"

"In Azzurro's caravan," I replied, "you left it there last night."

"Thank you, Jimmy," he said, as he took the dagger from me.

"Sure," I said, and we both walked silently together towards the caravan camp.

I was absolutely exhausted after not catching any sleep the night before, and I assumed Ari would want to be alone before the ceremony started. So I said good night to him as we reached Annak's caravan and made my way over to Azzurro's. I climbed inside and tried to make myself comfortable on the small bench behind the coffee table, using a couple of chairs to add to the length of the bench.

"Do you honestly think you will be comfortable like that?" I heard Azzurro's voice coming from the caravan's door. "Why don't you get up and I'll bring you something a bit more comfortable to stretch out on."

I did as he said, and Azzurro handed me the thick quilted cover from his bed together with a woollen blanket. I folded the quilt in two and placed it on the floor, then lay down on it and covered myself with the blanket. Before I knew it, I was asleep.

"Jimmy, Jiiiiiimmy…" I could make out Azzurro's voice calling my name.

I awakened slowly and opened my eyes, "Is it already time?" I asked him.

"Very nearly," he replied, "I brought you some fresh cool water and left it outside, if you wish to wash your face and freshen up a bit."

"Thanks Azzurro, that's a good idea," I got up and folded the quilt and blanket and laid them carefully on the small bench before stepping outside to freshen up.

It was already dark outside, and the only two sources of light brightening up the camp came either from the bonfires around, or from the big full moon above us. I found the wooden bucket of water Azzurro left for me, took off my shirt and placed it on the stairs leading to Azzurro's caravan. Plunging my hands into the bucket, I gathered some cold water in my palms, quickly splashing them over my face, then ran my wet fingers through my hair, trying to make it look a bit tidier than it felt. Then I washed my arms and the rest of my upper body.

"Here, take this, you look like you need it." It was Soulange's voice, coming from behind me.

"Sssoulange…" I stuttered in embarrassment, trying to cover myself with my arms and hands as turned around to face her. "Oh, Lexi!" I said, relieved to see her blue eyes smiling at me.

"Here, I brought you a towel and a clean shirt from Annak."

I stretched my arm to take the towel from her hand when she suddenly pulled it away from me, "Wow! Jimmy, I don't remember you ever having a six-pack body before".

I quickly took a couple of steps forward and grabbed the towel, covering myself up, "I guess it was all that training with Annak," I said, putting on the clean white shirt she handed me.

"Are you two ready to go?" Azzurro was standing at the door of his caravan.

"Is it time then?" I looked up at him.

"It is," he replied, as started to come down the stairs and walk towards us.

Tercel flew over us as Azzurro led the way, and we followed towards the far end of the Nomads' camp. The entire Nomad clan was there, old and young, men and women, all quietly standing to form one big circle. Inside the circle, forming a smaller circle of their own, were five flaming torches, and in the middle of them stood four wooden poles with a low bed nearby. Annak was already positioned beside one of the poles and Azzurro, Lexi and I joined him to take up places beside each of the other three poles. A few minutes later the Nomads' circle opened to reveal Ari standing there, dressed in a long silver cloak. In his arms he carried Mikaela's body, which was wrapped in a silver silk shroud. Very slowly he made his way towards us, an intense look on his face. His gaze was focussed directly at the low bed near to us. When he finally passed through us into the inner circle he got down on one knee and gently placed Mikaela onto the bed. Then Ari reached inside his cloak and brought out the silver dagger I had handed back to him earlier. He held it in his right hand, using the exposed blade to cut the palm of his other hand. As his blood quickly began to drip from it and cover all over his hand, he placed the bloody palm over Mikaela's chest, at the exact spot where her heart had once beaten strongly before.

Ari looked up at the moon and called out in a loud voice, filled with emotion, "Your blood is my blood, my blood is yours! From mother to son, from the High Priestess to her next in line, through endless generations of Galyans, the fountain of knowledge and the source of life now runs through my veins as it once did in yours."

Then Ari took his hand away from Mikaela's chest, transferred the dagger to be held in his bloody palm and raised the blade above his head. With one smooth movement, as his blood was still running over it, he struck down and plunged the blade into Mikaela's heart, calling out at the same time, "I summon you, elements of life; Air, Fire, Water, Earth, Aether, come take this holy and pure soul and let it merge with you. Bathe it in light, guide it through eternity, as it is now yours, and let me take its place amongst my people."

At that point the bed on which Mikaela's body was lying burst into flames and began to rise up in the air, bearing Mikaela with it, until it was hovering above the four poles beside which we were standing. Slowly it came down to rest on all four poles. As soon as Mikaela and the bed were safely in place, Ari's body began glowing with an intense white light.

The light was so blinding we had to close our eyes. A moment later, it was gone and Ari was on his knees on the ground, beside the burning bed, holding the back of his neck.

Annak and Azzurro stepped forward and helped him to get back up on his feet, as Lexi and I tried to see what it was that Ari kept rubbing at the back of his neck.

"It is done!" Azzurro declared, "you are now High Priest of Galya, leader of your people." He paused for a second before lowering his voice and adding, so that only the four of us could hear, "and that mark of the 'Eye of Truth' on the back of your neck also makes you head of the Council of Truth."

Continuity

The Nomads were long gone, leaving only the five tall torches, still burning where they stood during the ceremony. The wooden poles, along with the bed and Mikaela's body which had laird on them, had been totally consumed in the fire and everything was now a pile of smouldering ash still surrounded by the five tall torches. Tercel was hovering above as the rest of us sat quietly on the ground, waiting patiently with Ari for Mikaela's ashes to cool down so that he could collect them for safe keeping and take them to the Gwir, where he would scatter them around her Tree of Life.

Almost on cue, the sun began rising as the flame of the last torch died. As we sat around, Ari rose to his feet and walked towards the pile of grey ash on the ground in front of us.

"I swear to you, Mother, that I will fulfil my duties as your son and bring your ashes to the Gwir." Ari got down on both knees and gently rubbed the palm of his hands together. Then, holding them above the pile of ashes, he started to move his fingers slowly, as if he was playing an invisible keyboard.

Within seconds the ashes rustled as they separated into two piles. The lighter, more white-coloured ashes, rose to the air, leaving the darker grey pile from the burned wooden bed that Mikaela's body had rested on, lying on the ground. As soon as the separation was complete, with the white ashes still hovering in the air, Ari pulled out a leather pouch from under his cloak. In one swift movement he swooped Mikaela's white ashes straight into the pouch, which he was holding firmly with both hands.

When he was sure that all of his mother's ashes were safely inside, he pulled together the drawstrings of the pouch and tightly wrapped them around the top, tying them together over and over again to make sure the pouch was securely fastened.

Then he turned to face us. "Thank you all for taking part in the ceremony last night, and for staying with me till morning. It is a right usually done by members of the family and I would like you to know that my mother and I have always considered you to be nothing else but family."

Annak got up on his feet and walked towards Ari. "You are turning into everything Mikaela was hoping you would. She would have been very proud of you," he said, and nodded his head approvingly as he looked up at Ari.

Lexi, still in Soulange's body, together with Azzurro and myself, then stood to join Ari and Annak and, in an act of almost synchronised spontaneity, we all stretched our arms forward and placed our hands one on top of each other. "Family!" we called out at the same time.

It was Tercel's shriek that brought us back to reality. We immediately raised our heads and looked at him as he swooped down fast towards Azzurro's out-stretched arm.

"Naval's 'Elite Guard'. They are making their way towards the Nomad's camp," he said as he landed.

"But I thought we lost them by choosing a route in the opposite direction to the one that had brought them to the tavern." I was confused. "Is it possible that they can move so fast that they have managed to catch up to us?" I looked at the others.

Ari was the first to come up with an answer. "It is possible that they have caught up to us because it is not the same platoon of

Guards," he began, "how is it, do you think, that Naval can spread so much terror amongst the people of the five kingdoms? Every time he 'recruits' new members to his Elite Guards he assembles a new platoon, charged with enforcing his rule."

"Tercel," Azzurro barged in, "how long do we have before they arrive?"

"No more than an hour or so," Tercel replied. "They are advancing with some speed."

Lexi turned to look at Azzurro, "It's me they are looking for. Naval must have realised I was gone. I've put you all directly in the path of danger!"

"It's okay, Lexi," I said, "they can't find you if you're not here…"

"Jimmy is right," Azzurro added, "we need Soulange back."

Lexi nodded her head, she knew what to do. "Please be careful!" we heard her say as a moment later Soulange was back with us.

"Hello," she said looking around, "what is going on? Why do you all look very worried? What has happened?

"Naval's 'Elite Guard' is on their way," Azzurro replied, "and we haven't much time before they reach us."

"Why is it that every time I return, I find that something has gone horribly wrong?" Soulange asked, not really expecting an answer.

Azzurro turned to Tercel, concern in his voice "You must fly up and keep a watch, let us know how close they are," he said, as he released Tercel from his arm.

"We should get rid of the torches and scatter the remaining ashes around, so they won't find anything," Ari declared.

"Right," Azzurro said. "The three of you take care of clearing up the place, then make your way back to the camp as quickly as you can.

"Ari, you will need to change your clothes into something more casual, and hide anything to do with your new rank.

"Soulange and I will return to the camp and warn the Nomads. Then we must all start acting as if we are rehearsing for a new show we are producing for the people of Eashzar." As soon as he had finished explaining his plan, Azzurro and Soulange headed back to the Nomads' camp.

It didn't take too long for Ari, Annak and I to finish clearing the area where Mikaela's Farewell ceremony had taken place the night before. The last thing left for us to do was to take the torches away. We collected what remained of all five of them and quickly set off back to the camp.

Upon our arrival we found the Nomads already busy putting on a show; it felt as if we had walked into a fairground, with performers everywhere, all showing off their special talents.

"This is fan-tastic!" I stopped in my place and looked around. "Look at that…" I pointed at the man standing a few paces away from us, "he's blowing horses out from the torch in his hand. See how they're jumping out of the flame and galloping away? Wow! They're evaporating into thin air, merging into nothing in the far distance! How does he do that?" I was completely mesmerised by the magic. We were about to leave when the Fire-Breather blew into the flame again. "Wait!" I called at Annak and Ari, "I want to see what's coming out next." A second later a beautiful swan came floating out of the flame, leaving small ripples of orange and gold as it swam away and, just like the pack of horses, disappeared in the far distance.

A few steps away from the Fire-Breather stood another Nomad. In front of him was a large easel with white canvas stretched across it. A young lady sat in front of him, keeping very still as he began to paint her portrait. Curious to see what marvels this artist would conjure with his brushstrokes, I took a step forward.

"But it's empty!" I called out in surprise, "there's nothing there!" I kept shifting my look from the empty canvas to the young lady, who kept very still, then to the artist's hand holding a colourless brush against the blank canvas.

"Look closer." Annak's voice came from behind me.

I bent forward some more, squinting my eyes as I concentrated as much as I could. "Nothing, there's still nothing there! In fact, now

I'm looking closer... there isn't any paint anywhere either." I straightened back up, "What kind of artist is he if he doesn't use any paint for his work?"

Annak took a step forward and stood beside me; "he doesn't need any for the kind of paintings he creates," he whispered at me. "Keep looking and you will soon see." So I did.

"How much longer do I need to concentrate? My head's pounding so bad, and my vision is becoming so blurry, that I think I'm imagining things appearing on the canvas."

"You are most definitely not imagining things. It is nearly finished," Annak said.

I shook my head, trying to focus on the canvas as a painting did begin to appear, "It's very beautiful... but strange. I thought that as she was sitting so still he was drawing her portrait; instead it's a painting of her laughing, dancing in a field of wild flowers. She's not even wearing the same clothes, but, instead she is in this flowing, summer dress, very bright and colourful, so that she almost blends in with the background."

"He's a Mood-Artist," Annak began to explain, "he captures the mood you are in when you sit in front of him, your innermost desires reveal themselves to him."

"I guess you wouldn't want him to paint you if you had something to hide..." I half-joked, thinking of all the secrets we were harbouring.

"C'mon, we better get going, we haven't much time to organise everything before the Guards arrive," Ari interrupted, bringing me back to reality.

We were walking towards Annak's caravan when suddenly I heard that angelic voice echoing around us. I looked around, hoping to get a glimpse of her as she sang, but Soulange was hidden from my sight, only her tender voice caressing me. The more time I spent talking with Lexi, the more relaxed and comfortable I felt being around Soulange. But it was her voice, as she sang, that held me completely under her spell.

"Jimmy! Snap out of it!!" Ari slapped the back of my head, "we have no time for this now."

"Sorry," I said as we turned towards where Annak's caravan stood.

A few moments later we had reached the caravan and climbed into it.

"We better hurry up now," Ari said. "You can put these away while I change into my regular clothes." He handed us the torches.

Ari took off his ceremonial attire and carefully folded it all, before placing everything at the bottom of Mikaela's old rucksack, making sure his own clothes were resting on top of them, so that if anyone was to look inside they would have to turn everything out before they could see them. "Where shall I hide my dagger?" he asked, as he pulled it out from his belt.

"Here, give it to me. I shall place it on the wall between all the other weapons I have on display. No one will notice it there," Annak suggested.

"What now?" I asked, "I mean, what do you propose we do when the Elite Guards arrive?"

"We fight," Annak replied immediately.

"We what?! Isn't that exactly the opposite of what we should do?" I asked.

"I meant, we put on a show." He walked back towards the door, grabbing a long wooden staff from beside it, and throwing it to me. "As you showed some promise when we practiced with this before, I thought the three of us could show our skills as part of the Nomads' artistic production. This way, we will also be armed in case things do not go according to plan." Annak tossed another long staff towards Ari.

"Good idea," Ari and I replied together.

"Shall we begin then?" Annak asked, as he stepped out of the caravan.

We followed him outside. Finding a clear area nearby, we positioned ourselves so that we were facing each other.

"Close your eyes and breathe deeply," Annak instructed us. "Concentrate on your heartbeat and as you exhale try and listen for the other two heartbeats within this circle. When you find them, allow yourselves to connect with them, as if they all came from the same beating heart."

I closed my eyes and did as Annak said. With every deep breath I took I felt my own heartbeat pounding throughout my whole body. Then as I exhaled I could hear the other two heartbeats beside me. Annak's heartbeat sounded heavier and much lower, almost as deep as his voice, while Ari's heartbeat was fast and steady. They sounded out of sync, as if someone was beating two different kinds of drums at different paces. But the more I concentrated on their sounds, the more I felt my own heartbeat tuning into the rhythm of the other two, until finally all three rhythms merged into one strong beat. We opened our eyes together.

Annak was the first to lift his staff above his head, and started to turn it between his hands. Ari was next to follow, leaving me the last to join in. One by one we lowered our staffs, and each of us started twisting our own around our bodies. Then, without saying a word, we clashed our staffs, holding them diagonally towards the middle of our circle. Once again Annak was the first to break away from the rest, as he pulled his staff back and turned it in his hand, then lowered it in a striking move towards Ari's legs. Ari instinctively jumped up as he pulled his own staff back, imitating Annak's move on me. As if we had previously planned it, I too followed Ari's lead, and managed to avoid his staff by copying his moves, this time aiming at Annak's legs.

To anyone watching us from the side, it must have looked like a very well-choreographed and rehearsed fight-dance, as we continued exchanging strokes while allowing our bodies to avert themselves from getting hit.

I am not sure how long we were practicing our moves, and if it wasn't for Tercel's high-pitched cry, which broke our concentration, we would have still been engulfed in our 'fight dance' when he arrived.

Azzurro was running towards us as Tercel landed on top of Annak's staff, carefully balancing himself on it.

"The Guards are but a few miles away now. It will not take them much longer to reach the campsite," Tercel said.

"Thank you my friend. You better fly off before they see you," Azzurro suggested.

"I shall stay hidden close by," Tercel replied, before taking off towards the top branches of the trees at the edge of the river, overlooking the Nomads' campsite.

Azzurro turned to us, "Are you all ready?" He asked the question with a clear note of concern in his voice.

"As ready as we could ever be," Ari replied, with a touch of defiance.

"They know what to do," Annak added, looking at Ari and me.

"Good! Then let us join the rest and get ourselves ready for the show," Azzurro ordered.

We quickly made our way back to the fairground, to join the Nomads performing there.

"Shouldn't we stay close to Soulange? You know, just in case…" I asked the others.

"Yes, but we mustn't stay too close in order not to draw particular attention towards her," Azzurro said.

I nodded my head in agreement, "Fair enough, so where shall we position ourselves?"

"Soulange will be performing close to the Fire-Breather, as he will create the characters she sings about, with his fire," Azzurro explained. "Therefore it will be best for you to stand between both of them, but slightly in front and towards the middle of the performing arena," he pointed at a clearing close to where the Fire-Breather stood.

"But won't it look strange if we are blocking her performance from view?" I asked. "I thought the idea was not to draw any unnecessary attention towards her."

"No, she will be standing on a small podium, so that everyone will be able to see as well as hear her singing," Azzurro said, "and with the three of you positioned at the front, you will create a sort of barrier if it comes to protecting Soulange."

We walked quickly towards the spot Azzurro had pointed out to us. With staffs in our hands we positioned ourselves in place. Ari and I stood opposite each other, while Annak took his place in front, all of us facing outwards and slightly at an angle.

A few moments later I saw Soulange making her way towards the small, wooden-carved podium behind us. She wore a beautiful deep-green silk dress, embroidered in gold all over it. It hugged her body perfectly, complementing her sparkling emerald eyes and highlighting her fiery red curls. She stepped onto the podium full of confidence, and quietly waited for her turn to perform. It was then that I noticed that the thin golden scarf, softly wrapped around her neck and draped gently over her shoulders, was hiding beneath it the pendant which connected her soul to Lexi's. The 'Eye of Truth' much like Lexi, was now hidden in plain sight.

"Come forth, come forth, and explore your perception of fantasy and reality. This is the show that will dazzle your eyes, expose your hidden secrets, delight your very senses, one by one and all at once!" Azzurro's voice boomed out from the centre of the performing circle.

And come they did…

Deception

As if on cue, they appeared from behind the trees along the river, Naval's Elite Guard. They just stood there, not moving, maybe not even breathing, staring at the Nomad's theatre, assessing us all from afar.

It was my second encounter with them, and yet, once again it surprised me how that small group of heavily armed, cloned and soulless men, in their dark crimson leather armour and masked faces, moved together in such synchronicity that it really did feel and look as if they were one big living organism.

Azzurro bowed, signalling to the Nomads to start the show. They truly were masters of their crafts. Not only did they perform effortlessly, but they also managed to do so despite their fear, knowing for whom it really was that they were performing. Everyone could sense his presence; after all, Naval was always connected to his Elite Guard. He felt what they felt, heard what they heard, saw what they saw, and spoke the words coming out of their synchronised lips as they talked.

Yes, there was no doubt the Nomads knew whom it was they were performing to, but they didn't know why. They may have encountered Naval's Elite Guard whilst performing in a town or a village in one of the other Kingdoms, but they never had the Guard appear near them when travelling on the roads. Yet, there they were, unmoving beneath the trees, staring and obviously waiting for something.

One by one, each in their own turn, the Nomads carried out their acts. Then the watching Guards slowly began making their way towards the performing arena.

"Are they walking or gliding towards us? Because I can hardly see any leg movement there," I whispered to Annak and Ari.

"It wouldn't surprise me if Naval was actually pushing them along a playing board in front of him, with 'Elite Guard' dummies placed on it. After all, he controls them as if they were puppets," Ari whispered back.

The closer they got, the more anxious I became. My hands were becoming sweatier and my breathing heavier with every movement they made.

"Focus!" Annak said, through grinding teeth. "Take deep breaths and focus your mind, calm it down," he whispered as he turned slightly toward me.

I could tell he was as tense as I, because the scar running all the way down the left side of his face was visibly pounding.

Doing as he said, I gained my composure again. "Look, they have stopped again," I whispered to the others.

"Why?" Ari asked, "What are they doing?"

"It seems they are interested in the juggling performance at the front of the circle," Annak replied.

"It's the ice-balls they are juggling," I whispered to them, "see how the ice changes its form into something new every time the balls are thrown into the air? I guess they like that."

"No, not them, Naval" Ari said. "After all, the jugglers are performing with ice and snow, two things he has plenty of in Navara."

The Guards kept moving from one act to the next. Sometimes they stood, staring at a performance for a few minutes, other times just moving on and giving no more than a twist of their collective heads as they passed by another performer. Azzurro was walking a few paces behind them, accompanying them as if they were his esteemed guests, although they paid not the slightest attention to him. Azzurro was clearly making sure everything was going according to plan, while keeping a close eye on them, just in case.

The Guards were getting closer to us and had almost reaching the Mood-Artist'. After that it would be the Fire-Breather and Soulange's performance. I started to panic again.

"Stand ready!" Annak ordered quietly, his lips hardly moving. "Concentrate!"

Slowly I turned my head a little, to see how Soulange was reacting. From the corner of my eye I could see her, standing on her wooden podium. "Something's wrong!" I turned back, and said to the others, "Soulange, she looks all pale, almost blue."

The three of us turned and moved slightly closer towards her, trying not to draw too much attention to ourselves.

"Soulange, are you ill? What is wrong with you?" Annak asked, almost in a whisper.

She did not move, her eyes fixated on the Elite Guard.

"Soulange…." Ari quietly called to her.

"It must be the pendant!" I said, the answer coming to me suddenly. "She is reacting exactly the same way as Lexi did, the first time we encountered the Guards back at the tavern. Remember?"

"Jimmy is right," Ari said, "the pendant must be warning her about 'evil' being close by."

"This is not good!" I warned. "We must get the pendant away from her somehow, or it's all over."

Annak took command of the situation. "Ari, see if you can signal Azzurro to slow down a bit, so that Jimmy and I can get to Soulange before it is her time to perform."

"And now," Azzurro's voice called out as he turned in his place while sending a quick glance towards us. Luckily it was long enough for Ari to tip his long staff slightly towards Soulange. A subtle gesture, but well observed by Azzurro. "Please, turn and face the centre of our circle as it is my great pleasure to introduce, the Flying Acrobats!" he announced, and swiftly moved away from the Mood-Artist, the Fire- Breather and Soulange, followed by the Guards.

Out of nowhere, two beautiful shimmering huge butterflies came flying down towards the centre of the performing circle. They stopped halfway between the ground and the sky, fluttering around, looping in the air, leaving a long sparkling trail behind them. Another blink of the eye and three more butterflies appeared. It wasn't until I got a better look that I realised these gorgeous creatures were actually Nomads, all dressed up in amazing costumes, and performing a fantastic dance in mid-air, without anything visible to hold them up there. It was beautiful and mesmerising. Like me the Guards were watching as the performers hovered above, weaving a glittering and colourful pattern which covered the entire caravan like a big dome. Every time they moved, the pattern changed its shape and colour scheme, and I was seeing it as if I was peering through the hole of a magical kaleidoscope.

"Jimmy, we must hurry and get to Soulange," Annak called to me.

"I will keep watch," Ari said. "If the Guards turn in your direction you will hear my staff hitting the ground, as if I accidently dropped it."

"Let's do it," I said, and we quickly made our way towards Soulange.

As we draw closer to her, it was clear the scarf around her neck was not properly hiding the pendant beneath it. The crystal in the middle of the 'Eye of Truth' could be seen flashing vigorously.

"Jimmy," Annak called me from behind her, as he climbed on to the podium, "you will have to do it, I just cannot reach the lock at the back of her neck."

"It's okay, everything will be fine," I whispered to Soulange, as I joined Annak behind her.

Annak moved aside and glanced towards Azzurro and the guards, as he took Soulange's hand in his. "You must hurry up," he told me, "she is almost completely frozen. You need to get the pendant from her now!"

Standing directly behind Soulange, I could feel the cold emanating from her body. Trying not to create any disturbance in her pose, I slowly put my hands under her long red curls, trying to find the pendant's lock, which was tucked beneath the silk scarf around her throat.

It took precious time to find it. "Damn!" I called out, "my fingers are freezing up, the lock keeps slipping out of them."

"Try harder," Annak commanded, "we haven't much time and we are starting to draw attention."

"Hold on, I have an idea." I took my hands out and placed them close to my mouth, blowing hot air on them. Then I moved Soulange's hair slightly to the side and bent forward. I started blowing hot air at the place where I knew the lock should be, then once again put my hands under her scarf, keeping my fingers warm by constantly blowing hot air on them.

"Got it!" I quickly slid the pendant from Soulange's neck and placed it against my back, hiding it beneath the wide leather belt around my waist.

Almost immediately, the colour came back to Soulange's cheeks as she drew a deep breath.

"Thank you," she said, "another minute and I was sure it would be the end of me." She turned to face me, then closed her eyes and kissed my lips.

My heart skipped a bit; hell, it was racing all over the place.

"We should go back now," Annak said, pulling me down from the podium, not allowing me to savour the moment.

We quickly returned back to Ari, taking up our previous positions.

"You've done well," Ari whispered at me.

Not sure if he was applauding our actions or teasing me over the kiss, I decided to ignore him.

The butterfly Nomads had just finished weaving their final

pattern, and were spiralling up towards the stars appearing in the sky. Then, all at once, they disappeared, leaving a display of fantastic fireworks above us. It was clear that the Flying-Acrobats act would have been the closing performance of the Nomads' show, but due to our unexpected turn of events, Azzurro had to create a spectacular diversion… and what an amazing one it was.

"Our esteemed guests, please turn your attention to the unique works of our next artist." Azzurro made his way back towards the Mood-Artist', with the Guards following behind him. "If you would now stand still for the next few moments," Azzurro told them.

Given the fact that it was Naval who was controlling the Elite Guard, I was sure that all that could possibly appear on the canvas of the Mood-Artist was the dark of Naval's soul. Intrigued to see what might appear, I took a couple of small steps forward and stared intently at the blank canvas, waiting for it to turn black.

"Impossible!"

As soon as the artist placed his brush on the centre of the canvas, a small light- blue dot appeared. Slowly, slowly, with each stroke, the dot grew into shape. A few strokes later it began to resemble something too familiar.

"The Eye of Truth!" I muttered, turning to look at Annak and Ari, whose faces reflected the same shocked look showing on mine.

Within seconds of the painting revealing Naval's secret desire, the canvas burst into flames and disintegrated into nothing. Hoping to control what had now turned into a very dangerous and potentially volatile situation, Azzurro smiled at the Guards and waved towards the podium where Soulange was standing.

"It is my honour and pleasure to introduce before you my niece, Soulange, who together with our Fire-Breather will present our next mystifying performance to delight and enchant you," he said.

Immediately Soulange took a deep breath and started to sing while the Fire- Breather turned her words into beautiful images. Her voice was so soft and caressing that it wrapped itself around all of us, leaving us completely intoxicated, willing to do her bidding without question. I tried to keep focussed and stay alert, but it was harder than I thought, as her voice took me over and conjured images of her red hair, her bright green eyes, and her sweet, full lips, kissing mine.

"Jimmy!" Annak called to me, bringing me back to reality.

I turned to look at him, shaking my head, trying to regain my composure.

"What are they doing?" I heard Ari's voice.

"Who?" I asked.

"The Guard, what are they doing?" he repeated. "Notice how their heads are slightly turned to the left, as if something has caught their attention?"

"Are they moving towards us?" I queried, keeping a close eye on the Guard.

At that moment they came to a sudden stop. Their collective heads twisted and returned to their upright position.

"Something is wrong," Annak said. "Stand Ready!"

Without warning, one of the Guards in the group broke formation as he took a couple of steps forward.

"This must be the Guard's Captain," Ari whispered to us.

"I didn't realise they had 'captains', I thought they were one collective," I whispered back to him.

"They are," Ari said, "but Naval chooses one, who becomes a Captain and is able to act as Naval's mouthpiece, when he wants to talk through him."

"He's walking towards Soulange," I said, worried. "Look at the way he is drawn to her, it's as if he is enchanted by her voice…"

"I guess Naval, too, has his weaknesses," Ari said, half-jokingly.

The Captain moved very slowly towards Soulange, ignoring everyone and everything else around him. He came to a stop close to where the three of us stood, as the rest of the Guards began to follow him. The Guard's Captain just stood, not moving a muscle, focussed on Soulange's voice, waiting for the rest of the Guards to come up behind him.

Suddenly the Captain spoke: "Such marvels, hidden within such a delicate creature."

Ari turned abruptly and stared at him. "Uncle Josh?!" he said in a shocked tone, as if he recognised the Captain's voice.

But the Guard ignored Ari, of course. What had happened, it appeared, was that after his uncle was taken away when other Guards had ransacked his village, Uncle Josh had become a 'volunteer' in the Guards. And by doing that, he lost all that he ever was, all of his memories, and had merged with Naval.

"Uncle Josh!" Ari called out loudly at him again, then once more, but to no avail.

Followed by the rest of his men, the Guard's Captain walked directly to Soulange. He paused for a second in front of her, then pulled out one of the blades embedded in his armour, and with one quick movement he slashed open Soulange's chest before pressing the palm of his left hand hard against the cut, as gushing blood began running down her dress.

Then the Captain and all the Guards started reciting together, as if with one eerie voice, "Your blood is my blood, my blood is yours! Two hearts beating together as one. Me inside you, you inside me; two halves, one soul! One soul united forever!"

Soulange's head dropped backwards, stretching her neck as far back as it would go. Her mouth opened slightly, and a look of excruciating pain was reflected in her open eyes, which had now turned back to blue.

I tried to move towards Lexi - we all did - but Naval somehow held us frozen in our places, so that we could only watch the horror unfolding in front of us, unable to do anything to stop it.

Suddenly the Guards eerie chant went silent, and the Guard's Captain began to speak. "Did you really think you could deceive me?!" It was Naval's voice, talking directly to Lexi. Then the tone changed, "Deceive ME!!" he screamed at her. "We had an agreement. You gave me your word!"

The Guard's Captain moved his head closer to Soulange's ear. Naval's voice spoke softly again, "There is someone here most eager to re-unite with you." Then the Captain straightened up, raised his right hand, and placed his palm over Soulange's face. Her body twitched. She clutched her fists so tightly that her knuckles turned white. With one quick movement the captain pulled his hand back, as if he was pulling her soul out of her mouth and then directing it into his own. Quickly the place where they stood was engulfed by a thick white mist, hiding Soulange and the Elite Guard from our sight. But a moment later the Guards had gone, leaving a long train of mist behind them, and Soulange's body lying lifeless on the ground.

"No….!!!" I cried, and finding myself free to move again, I rushed swiftly to her side.

Azzurro, Annak, and Ari were not far behind me.

Azzurro fell on his knees, slightly leaning above Soulange's body, pressing his hands hard against the open cut, where a little blood was still trickling out. Then he bent forward and placed his ear on her bloody chest. "We must hurry!" he called out, "she is still alive!"

Hope

Ari got down onto the ground opposite Azzurro. As Azzurro pressed down to hold the cut, with tears in his eyes, Ari looked down on Soulange, then began to trace some symbols in the air, right above the cut in her chest. He placed the palm of his hands on top of Azzurro's hands, "It is safe for you to remove your hands," he said calmly, "I have her now."

Azzurro slowly took his hands away and collapsed back on his folded legs. "You must save her," he told Ari, speaking almost in a whisper, as if all his strength was washed out of him, and with his bloody hands he wiped some of the tears from his cheeks.

But Ari didn't hear him. His eyes were closed as he began to draw big deep breaths, holding them in for a second or two then exhaling them out. It was clear that he had gone into some sort of healing trance. Once again it felt as if we were hidden in a time bubble of our own, isolated from the rest of the Nomads and with no concern for anything outside us.

I couldn't speak. The knot in the pit of my stomach kept twisting more and more as once again I found myself alone, without my best friend, and still stranded on this world.

It was a long time before Ari finally opened his eyes. "I have stopped the bleeding and closed her cut," he said to Azzurro, before turning to Annak and me. "We must get her inside her caravan so that I can continue my healing."

I helped Ari pick Soulange up, then gathered the train of her dress in my hands and carefully walked beside him. Meanwhile Annak took hold of Azzurro's arm and helped him get up from the ground. His legs must have been numb from sitting back on them, as it was hard for him to walk, and Annak needed to help him balance himself as he tried to keep pace with us.

Once we reached Soulange's caravan, Azzurro let go of Annak and went up the wooden stairs ahead of us, to open the door. He stepped inside and stood by her bed, waiting for us to bring her in. Very gently, Ari laid Soulange on the bed as I placed the train of her dress on the floor next to her.

"Shall I go and get some Nomad women from the camp to come and help undress and clean her, put her in some fresh clothes?" Annak suggested, once we were all inside the caravan.

"Thank you, yes, that is a good idea," Azzurro quietly replied.

"How is she?" I asked Ari.

"Her wound was very bad, but it is healed now. She will need plenty of rest to regain her strength," Ari replied.

"At least there is good news," I said with a sigh of relief. However the strained look on Ari's face gave away more than he was saying. "What is it?" I asked him, "I can tell there is more else!"

"Go ahead, let us know what it is," Azzurro told Ari, "there is no need for you to bear it alone." He looked directly into Ari's eyes and added, "Whatever it is, we will face it together."

Ari nodded his head, then looked straight at the two of us; "Her body will heal, but her soul…" he paused and looked down at Soulange, "I cannot feel it inside her, and unless it returns to her body, she will remain asleep, trapped between two existences forever."

"But you are a healer, you have the power to fix this!" I burst out.

"I can only fix the physical, but the soul, it has its own will, it is bound to no one but itself," Ari explained.

"But she is the Angel of Souls, how can she lose her own soul?" I asked with some confusion.

"Because her soul is free, it chose Soulange the moment she was created. But it could also leave her whenever it chooses," Ari explained.

"So is that it? Are we to lose both Soulange and Lexi? Is there no hope for us at all?" I was saying my thoughts and desperation out loud; "I guess now I am really stuck here for good. There is no going back home."

"I didn't say that!" Ari replied.

"Yes you did! You just said that Soulange's soul is gone, and without her we will never be able to get Lexi back. Especially not now that she is reunited with Naval again!"

Ari smiled at me, "I said that her soul has left her body, I didn't say it will not return,"

"Okay, now I'm confused. What is it that you are telling me then?"

"There might be many reasons for the soul to leave Soulange's body. I have a theory about it…" Ari looked first at Azzurro, then back to me, "I believe that when Naval pulled Lexi's soul out from Soulange's body her own soul followed that of Lexi's back to him…"

"Which means, we have one of our own hidden close to Naval," Azzurro ended Ari's words.

"Does that mean we can get Lexi back then?" I asked, hope rising in me.

"I am not sure about that," Ari replied, "but what I am sure of is that the stronger Soulange's body becomes, the more the chances are that her soul will return to it, and together with it we will have invaluable knowledge of Naval's plan."

"In that case," I asked, "How good are our chances of reaching Lexi and overcoming that tyrant?"

Ari smiled, "I think we have a very good chance."

"Then Soulange might need this back, to help guide her soul safely to her," I said, and pulled the 'Eye of Truth" from inside my belt and placed it around Soulange's neck.

Once again this amazing and wondrous world had shown me how much our lives are intertwined with each other, and how our bonds, strange and unexplainable though they may be, have more to them than meets the eye; that above all, nothing is ever as it seems, and we are never really alone. Not as long as we have hope.

Epilogue

The bright red and yellow colours, reflecting from the flushing neon lights outside her bedroom window, looked like flames that were rising ever higher and higher. She was lying in bed - it wasn't the first restless night she had spent since she had sent the two youngsters over there. But tonight, for some reason, her restlessness was much more intense than ever before. She kept turning and tossing from one side to another, unable to fall asleep, only drowsing in and out of it.

Suddenly she sat up in her bed, cold sweat covering her old body. Her eyes wide open, she realised she was staring at a younger version of herself.

The young woman was hovering at the end of her bed. The red and yellow lights shimmering off the wall behind her made her seemingly translucent body appear as if she herself was on fire.

Staring directly into the old woman's eyes, her visitor said, "They are coming!"

Glossary

Almah   Young lady
Language: Hebrew

Kind, nourishing
Language: Spanish

Annak   Giant
Language: Hebrew

Azzurro   Light blue
Language: Spanish and Italian

Gwir   The pure fluid, the Eather, the principle of life, truth, true, right, just
Language: Welsh

Katiff   Picking season
Language: Hebrew

Kattan   Small, little
Language: Hebrew

Kinnamon   Cinnamon
Language: Hebrew

Lavan   White, 'pure white'
Language: Hebrew

Louiza   Lemon verbena (herb)
Language: Hebrew

Na'ana   Mint (herb)
Language: Hebrew, Arabic

Naval	Villain, scoundrel, vile person Language: Hebrew
	Wonder Language: Hindu
	*Naval is an anagram of Lavan
Nir	Ploughed field (literary), furrow Language: Hebrew
Orra	Light or her light Language: Hebrew
Regev	Clod of earth Language: Hebrew
Sha'ar	Gate Language: Hebrew
Tercel	The male of a hawk, especially of a gyrfalcon Language: English
T'mirah	Tall woman Language: Hebrew
Zarah	Sarah, the wife of Abraham and the first of the four Jewish mothers in the Bible Language: Derived from the Hebrew name Sarah, also can be found in Arabic, English, French and German

Acknowledgements

This book was a long time coming and would not have been possible without my amazing parents, family, friends and mentors, both in flesh and in spirit.

Let me start by thanking my dearest friends, Catherine and Brad Pianta-McGill, for being the first to see the author in me, pushing me to write and twisting my arm to join all those creative writing courses, all those years ago.

I'm eternally grateful to my parents, Alan and Yael Ben-Ami, for always being there, supporting, encouraging and loving me. They have been with me from reading the very first early drafts down to the last word written on the last page. Dad, my literary editor and role model. Thank you for passing on to me your love for the written word. For the endless hours of going over and over my text, correcting, suggesting and mostly, for being brutally honest about my writing, always pushing me further to think and write better. You made me a better author. Mam, thank you for passing on to me your own amazing writing talent. For always being there with your wise words and guidance. For teaching me to never give up.

Special thanks to my sister Michal and brother Aviad, my fantastic daughters, Eleanor and Carmel, and my beloved aunt Rucha for the non-stop encouragement they have given me throughout.

To my creative writing teacher and mentor, Jan Moran-Neil, thank you for sharing your literary knowledge. For teaching me how to 'show and not tell' the story in vivid colours. For believing in my talent and ability to paint such wondrous worlds and characters.

A very special word of thanks to Spike Poyton for the incredible work he has done illustrating the map of Terah.

And last but not least, thank you to Benny Carmi and the team at eBookPro, who have been the final and important link in bringing this book to life.

Printed in Great Britain
by Amazon